"Chase? What are we doing? Don't we despise each other?"

Nevada was floating in a sea of confusion. And burned by a sun called desire.

Chase went very still in her arms, but his gaze didn't waver. "No. It's just strong, that's all. Too strong. Neither of us likes that. We both like to be…on top. So we never got along."

"Until tonight."

He smiled at her then, slowly. "Until tonight."

"What will happen in the morning?"

He considered the question. "Worry about the morning when it gets here."

"But I don't—" Nevada's sentence stopped on a sharp hitch of breath as Chase shifted his body until he lay full-length upon her, his hard legs between her soft ones, and that hungry part of him pressed at the chaste juncture of her thighs. She gasped again.

"Yeah." Chase sighed. "Let's worry about tomorrow…tomorrow."

Dear Reader,

What better cure for a hectic holiday season than settling in with romantic stories from Special Edition? And this month, we've got just what you've been searching for.

THE JONES GANG is back, with bestselling author Christine Rimmer's latest title, *Honeymoon Hotline*. Nevada Jones is November's THAT SPECIAL WOMAN!, and this adviser to the lovelorn is about to discover love firsthand!

Andrea Edwards's latest miniseries, GREAT EXPECTATIONS, continues this month with *One Big Happy Family*. If Big Sky Country is your kind of place, you won't want to miss *Montana Lovers*, the next book in Jackie Merritt's newest series, MADE IN MONTANA.

And the passion doesn't end there—for her first title in Special Edition, Helen R. Myers has a tantalizing tale of reunited lovers in *After That Night*.... Rounding out the month are a spellbinding amnesia story from Ann Howard White, *Making Memories*, and a second chance for two lovers in Kayla Daniels's heartwarming *Marriage Minded*.

I hope you enjoy all that we have in store for you this November. Happy Thanksgiving Day—all of us at Silhouette would like to wish you a happy holiday season!

Sincerely,

Tara Gavin
Senior Editor

Please address questions and book requests to:
Silhouette Reader Service
U.S.: 3010 Walden Ave., P.O. Box 1325, Buffalo, NY 14269
Canadian: P.O. Box 609, Fort Erie, Ont. L2A 5X3

CHRISTINE RIMMER

HONEYMOON HOTLINE

SPECIAL EDITION®

Published by Silhouette Books
America's Publisher of Contemporary Romance

In memory of my Granny,
Sidney Francis Naisby Neall Strand, the most
independent woman I've ever known.

And thanks to Jim Kerr of KNCO Radio, as well as the staff at Oregon State Hospital, for answering all my questions. As always, if I didn't get it right, it's my own fault.

 SILHOUETTE BOOKS

ISBN 0-373-24063-5

HONEYMOON HOTLINE

Copyright © 1996 by Christine Rimmer

Printed in U.S.A.

Books by Christine Rimmer

CHRISTINE RIMMER

is a third-generation Californian who came to her profession the long way around. Before settling down to write about the magic of romance, she'd been an actress, a salesclerk, a janitor, a model, a phone-sales representative, a teacher, a waitress, a playwright and an office manager. Now that she's finally found work that suits her perfectly, she insists she never had a problem keeping a job—she was merely gaining "life experience" for her future as a novelist. Those who know her best withhold comment when she makes such claims; they are grateful that she's at last found steady work. Christine is grateful, too—not only for the joy she finds in writing, but for what waits when the day's work is through: a man she loves who loves her right back and the privilege of watching their children grow and change day to day.

THE JONES GANG

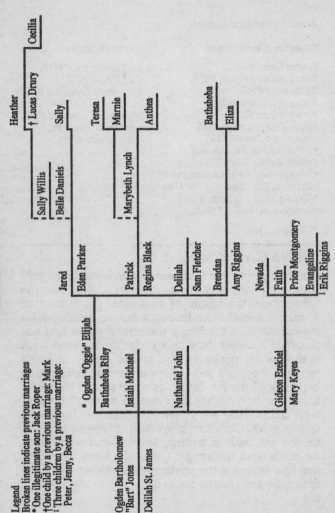

Legend
Broken lines indicate previous marriages
* One illegitimate son: Jack Roper
† One child by a previous marriage: Mark
! Three children by a previous marriage:
  Peter, Jenny, Becca

Chapter One

"**D**arling." Chase McQuaid's fiancée, Virginia Frasier, looked up at him through shining, china-blue eyes. "I had no idea that you knew Nevada Jones."

"I don't, not really," Chase baldly lied, glancing around, hoping that Virginia would be talking about something else by the time he looked at her again.

They stood a few hundred feet from the ranch house where Chase had grown up. People milled all around them. Most of the men were dressed in fancy Western shirts, new jeans and shiny boots. The women wore everything from calico to satin and spangles. Over near the corral, a mariachi band played. The air smelled of mesquite smoke from the barbecue out back.

There was a sharp tug on his arm. "But Chase, you just said that she's your sister's best friend."

So much for hoping Virginia would talk about something else. "That's right," he admitted. "She is."

"So you *do* know her?"

"She's an acquaintance, that's all." Which was true. More or less.

Virginia sighed. "Oh, Chase. Did you know that it's a fantasy of mine . . . to meet her?"

He didn't like this. Not one bit. "No."

"Well, it is. I simply cannot tell you what meeting her would mean to me." Virginia squeezed his arm and looked toward the ranch house. There, on the long gallery that ran the width of the house, Nevada Jones leaned against one of the thick, square pillars that held up the roof, and sipped what looked like a margarita.

"Chase, you don't know what she means, what she *stands* for—to the women of Phoenix." Nevada was the host of a call-in, advice-to-the-lovelorn radio show known as "Honeymoon Hotline." In Chase's opinion it was the purest form of irony that anyone would want advice on romance from Nevada Jones. But then again, most people didn't know what *he* knew.

Virginia gushed on. "She changes people's *lives,* Chase. She *matters,* in the truest sense of the word." Virginia was gazing up at him again, stars in her eyes. "Introduce me to her. Please?"

He cleared his throat, which for some reason felt like it had a log in it. "Virginia . . ."

"Come on." Virginia started pulling on him. The crown of her blond head didn't even reach his shoulder and the hand that gripped his sleeve was slim and delicate. But she was also damned determined about this—which totally baffled him.

Because Virginia Frasier was rarely determined about anything. Her father, a business associate of Chase's, had introduced them. Chase had known from the moment he met her that she was just what he wanted: a gentle, well-behaved woman who had the good sense to let the men in her life make the major decisions. And up until now, Virginia hadn't disappointed him.

So why in hell, he wondered grimly, after six months of catering to his every whim, did she suddenly have to get decisive over meeting Nevada Jones?

Virginia's little hand slid down and locked on his much larger one. She headed for the gallery. Chase went along where she pulled him.

Beneath the canopy near the corral, the mariachi band swung into "Cielito Lindo." Leading Chase like a stallion on a tether, Virginia plowed through the chattering groups of partygoers.

"Excuse us. Thank you. Pardon me." Virginia sent sparkling smiles in all directions. People murmured and nodded and moved out of the way.

Not far from the house stood a row of canopied tables laden with bowls of chips and salsa, quesadillas and a hundred other finger foods. As Chase and Virginia reached those tables, Nevada glanced their way and saw them coming. She straightened and pushed away from the pillar. And then Virginia was towing him up the broad steps and into the cool shade beneath the gallery roof, bringing him to stand before Nevada.

Whiskey-colored eyes cool and wary, Nevada looked from Chase to Virginia and back to Chase again.

Chase knew what Nevada wanted: out of there. Now. But she stayed. They shared the same dilemma here. They supposedly meant nothing to each other. So if one of them were to snub the other, it would cause suspicion.

And neither of them wanted that.

"Chase..." Virginia squeezed his hand and cast him a pleading look.

He picked up his cue and asked inanely, "How are you, Nevada?"

Nevada granted him a smile, one that was about as authentic as a three-dollar bill. But Virginia didn't seem to notice the falseness of Nevada's smile. She gazed at the other woman with the big, soulful eyes of an adoring fan.

Nevada doled out the appropriate banalities. "I'm fine, Chase. How about you?"

"Great."

"Well, good." Nevada sipped her margarita and gave a bright look around. "Your mother really knows how to throw a party." It was his mother, Molly's, sixtieth birthday. The festivities were in her honor.

"I'm glad you're enjoying yourself," Chase said.

Nevada gave him a look of great patience. He knew what she was thinking: *I'd enjoy myself a lot more, Chase McQuaid, if you'd finish up with the polite noises and move on along....*

He felt the same way, so he got on with it. "Nevada, this is Virginia Frasier, my fiancée."

The fake smile got wider as Nevada turned it on Virginia. "Hello."

"Hello." Eyes wide, expression rapt, Virginia stared at Nevada. And then, like a bottle of champagne that had been shaken before the cork was popped, she started bubbling over. "Oh, this is wonderful. To meet you. I can't tell you. I'm such a fan. Your show is... I listen every afternoon. Five days a week. I never miss if I can help it. Sometimes, if I'm in my car, I pull over to the side of the road, so I can give the show one hundred percent of my attention. You have such... insight. Into relationships. I'm with you completely. A woman has to take responsibility in this world. For her life and for loving. She has to stand up and say, 'This is what I want and this is what I'm willing to do to get it.' Society may have cast her in the role of victim. But she can't be content to stay there. She has to stand tall, accept her own power, and learn how to make the best use of it...."

There was more. Chase let it come. Short of dragging Virginia out of there, he didn't know what else to do. He was seeing a totally new side of her, one he didn't particularly like. But maybe, if he let her get it all off her chest now, she would go back to being the gracious, reserved woman he intended to marry.

"Taking responsibility is often difficult, though, don't you think?" Virginia asked.

Nevada, whose eyes looked a little glazed, nodded.

"We're so *indoctrinated*, aren't we?" Virginia demanded.

Nevada made a small sound that could have been agreement—or possibly embarrassment. She finished off her drink.

Virginia still wasn't through. "Linda Lacklove is a perfect case in point, don't you think?"

"Yes, she certainly is."

Virginia glanced at Chase. "Linda Lacklove has trouble with commitment."

Chase had no idea what Virginia was chattering about. "Linda *Lacklove?*"

"Well, that's not her real name, of course. Everyone who calls in uses an alias. Linda Lacklove calls in a lot. She can't seem to form a lasting relationship." Virginia looked at Nevada for confirmation. "Can she?"

Nevada shook her head. Her rusty mane of hair brushed her bare shoulders; the gold hoops in her ears glinted as they swung gently against her slim throat. Today she was rigged out in one of those off-the-shoulder gauze shirts in an eye-flaying fire-engine red that matched her prairie skirt and her shiny red boots.

Chase thought that she should have looked flashy and overdone. But she didn't. She looked terrific—sexy and sassy and ready to take on the damn world.

Virginia continued to babble away about the woman who called herself Linda Lacklove. "With her, it's a new man every night. A merry-go-round of romance. They come and they go. Like a revolving door. And you see, Linda Lacklove thought it was the *men* who were using *her*. Nevada helped her to admit that there was something else entirely going on."

Chase knew he shouldn't, but he asked anyway, "And what was that?"

Virginia turned to Nevada, waiting for her to explain. But Nevada Jones was no fool. She only waved a hand, as if to say, *Go on, you tell him*.

And Virginia did. "Linda Lacklove is afraid of real intimacy. With so many men around, it's been easy not to let any one of them get too close—at least not in the ways that really matter."

Chase got the point. Virginia drove it home. "You see, for Linda Lacklove, sex doesn't count as getting close. It's just a casual act to her. Like brushing her teeth. Or shaking hands."

That did it. Chase refused to stand here with Nevada Jones and his fiancée, discussing some strange woman's sex life. He considered himself a reasonably sophisticated man. But not that damn sophisticated.

He wrapped his fingers around Virginia's arm. "We haven't wished Molly a happy birthday yet. Let's do that right now."

"But, Chase—"

"This way. You take care of yourself, Nevada."

"Thanks, Chase. I will. Nice to meet you, Virginia."

Chase had Virginia pointed toward the front door of the house. But she couldn't resist one last over-the-shoulder request of her idol. "The wedding's next month. June fourteenth. Will you come? Please?"

"I'll . . . do my best."

"Ask Maud. She can give you the details."

"All right. I'll, uh, try."

"Oh, that's great. Really— Ouch!" Virginia glowered at Chase. "You're pinching me. . . ."

"*Inside,* Virginia. Come on."

Nevada watched as Chase dragged his fiancée through the front door and kicked it shut behind them. Then, once they were safely gone, she slumped back against the pillar and told herself that meeting Chase McQuaid's fiancée hadn't been that awful, after all.

And it was good to have it over with. Because it had been bound to happen eventually. Since Chase's sister, Maud, was her best friend, Nevada could hardly expect to get through the rest of her life without running into Chase and his bride every now and then.

Nevada peered down into her empty glass and thought how nice a refill would taste. But then she shook her head. If anything, right now, she should grab a plate and get some food in her stomach.

But it was comfortable in the shade. And for a few minutes more, she just leaned against the pillar and watched the people go by.

A man she didn't know brushed against her, smiled, and excused himself. Absently, she smiled back. Then she turned to look out past the brightly covered tables and canopies, and the groups of guests milling around, laughing and chattering.

Beyond the iron arch that read Bar-M, srub brush dotted the dry, rolling land. Here and there, a juniper or a gnarled mesquite tree stood stark against the endless sky. Far in the distance, Nevada could see the gray humps of the Bradshaw Mountains.

About seventy miles north of Phoenix and twenty miles out of Prescott, the Bar-M had once covered thousands of acres. But that had been in the heyday of Big Buck McQuaid, Chase's father. Buck had been dead for over a decade now. According to Maud, the man had died as he'd lived, gored by a mean bull that he'd just ridden the full eight seconds.

Chase belonged to the next generation of Western men. He took on contractors and city planners instead of bulls.

Maud, Buck's only other child, was the tax partner in a
Phoenix accounting firm. Slowly, over the past twenty
years, the family had sold off most of the Bar-M land.
Now Molly, Buck's widow, kept fifty acres and a few
horses for pleasure riding, as well as the low, cool, stone-
and-stucco ranch house where she still lived.

A waiter approached, costumed for the occasion in se-
rape and sombrero. Nevada set her empty glass on his tray
as he went by.

She heard a man's laugh, deep and rich, somewhere
behind her on the gallery. It sounded like Chase. But of
course, it couldn't be. Chase had gone into the house,
with his fiancée, who was young and pretty and had
seemed quite nice. "Think Grace Kelly, only short," was
how Maud had described her.

Remembering the gleam of adoration in Virginia Frasier's eyes, Nevada sighed. She could have done without
Chase's fiancée's being a fan.

Nevada leaned her head back against the pillar and tried
not to even think about Chase—or the way he had looked
at her, with such guarded speculation. A distant look that
had nonetheless sent little prickles of awareness moving
just beneath the surface of her skin.

She also tried not to ponder the fact that something was
missing between Chase and Virginia. There hadn't been
that glow around them that couples in love always seem
to have. They lacked that bubble of hope and brightness,
so beautiful it hurt a little to look at it.

Nevada closed her eyes. The relationship between
Chase and Virginia didn't concern her. It didn't concern
her at all. In less than a month, they would be married.
And she wished them well.

She pushed herself away from the pillar and stepped out
into the sun. She would find Maud. They would wander
around behind the house and check out how Rafael,

Molly's cook, was doing with the barbecue. And then maybe, after she'd appeased her empty stomach with ribs and spicy chili, she would treat herself to another of those luscious salty margaritas.

Chapter Two

"But I do. I really *do* want love. And marriage. A home and a family," Linda Lacklove insisted. Then she sighed. "I know, I know. If I *really* wanted those things, I'd find a man who wanted them, too."

Nevada chuckled. "You know the answers, Linda," she said into the remote microphone, which was suspended from her earphones on a set of featherlight wires. "All you really have to do is *act* on them. Or *refuse* to act on them. It's a choice. *Your* choice." Music faded in: a Bonnie Raitt song, "Something to Talk About." From the booth on the other side of the soundproof glass wall, Tully, the engineer, was giving Nevada the countdown to commercial.

"Linda, we have to take a break."

"Okay."

"Get back to me. But *do the work* first."

Do the work was Nevada's trademark phrase. Every weekday afternoon, between four and seven, she counseled, exhorted and prodded her listeners. And after they themselves figured out what needed to be done, she always invited them to check back. After they'd "done the work"—which meant, after they'd taken the next step toward building better, more meaningful relationships.

"This is 'Honeymoon Hotline,' on KLIV Talk Radio, 850 AM, your station in the sun. Don't go away. Because we'll be right back."

While the commercials played, Nevada scanned the list of calls that Tully had posted on the call monitor for her to choose from. One looked especially intriguing.

Line 2: Ginger. She's getting married. A big wedding in three weeks, and she doesn't love the guy.

When the break ended, Nevada launched into the station ID. "You're listening to KLIV Talk Radio, 850 on your AM dial. I'm Nevada Jones, and this is your own 'Honeymoon Hotline.' You know the number—555-2940. I'm here to talk. About men and women. About love. Whatever your problem is with that special someone in your life, dial the number. We'll work on it. And now, let's get right on to the next call." She punched up line two. "Hello, this is Nevada. You're on the air."

Nevada sensed a presence, but no one spoke. She prompted, "Are you with us?"

That did it. "Uh, yes. Yes, I'm here."

"Great. You want to be called Ginger, right?"

"Yes. Ginger. That's right."

The voice was controlled. Well-bred. Very nervous. And vaguely familiar.

"Refresh my memory, Ginger. Have we talked before?"

"Er... you and me? On the radio?"

"Yes. You and me. On the radio."

"No. No, I've never called in before."

Nevada heard panic in the other voice. She soothed, "Hey. It's all right. You're doing fine." She paused, then asked gently, "Nervous?"

"Oh, yes. Very."

"Well, it's natural. Don't worry about it. You only say what *you* want to say. I'm here to listen, and maybe to help. Okay?"

"Yes. All right."

Another pause. Once again, Nevada scanned the information that Tully had given her. "You're planning a big wedding soon, is that right?"

"Yes. Very big. And very soon."

"In three weeks, right?"

"Right. In three weeks. And my fiancé, uh..."

"Give him a name, all right? Any name will do."

"Fred?"

"Fred, it is. Now, what's going on with you and... Fred?"

"The past week, it's really started to hit me— Oh, how can I say this?"

"What's hit you, Ginger?"

"Oh, God..."

"Come on, tell me. Let it out."

And Ginger did. "I...I don't think I love him. And I don't think he loves me."

Nevada allowed a little dead air, so that Ginger's admission would have time to sink in. She was silent long enough that she didn't have to say anything.

Ginger picked up the ball herself. "Oh, I can't believe I'm saying this, right here, on the radio, with everyone listening in. But it's true. He doesn't love me. I don't love him. And we're getting married in three weeks."

Ginger sounded so disconsolate, Nevada wanted to reach out and put her arms around her. "Oh, honey..."

"We're...the perfect couple. He's in his late thirties and very successful. I'm in my mid-twenties, I look good in a cocktail dress... And I can get along with anybody. Help me, Nevada.''

Nevada stood from her chair and paced the small studio, rolling her shoulders a little and rubbing a hand in her mop of unruly hair. This was why she liked the remote mike. It gave her room to move. "Maybe we should back up a little here. Tell me about Fred. Tell me *why* you're marrying him—if *you* don't love him and *he* doesn't love you.''

Ginger let out a small, birdlike sound of distress. "He's a very... forceful man. And very successful, as I said. He's, well, quite a catch, actually. All my girlfriends are green with envy that he's mine.''

"But you don't love him.''

Ginger moaned. "It seems like I *should* love him. And my father likes him.''

"Oh, sweetheart. I hear you." Nevada paused at the soundproof glass that divided the studio from the engineer's booth. Tully, who felt her eyes on him, looked up from monitoring sound levels and setting up for the next commercial break. He wrinkled his flat nose and crossed his eyes at her. Nevada stuck out her tongue at him. Then she turned away before Tully could make her laugh. She leaned on the wall. "So. Your father likes Fred. But what about you, Ginger? Do *you* like Fred?''

Ginger made a sort of bleating, lost-lamb sound. "Me?''

"Yes, you. Ginger. The powerful, self-determined person to whom I am speaking. Ginger—who controls her own destiny, no matter what her daddy—or Fred—would like her to believe.''

"I...uh...I don't...''

"Do you like him?''

"Yes. I like him. Or I think I could, if he didn't intimidate me so.''

"And do you *love* him?''

"I told you. No."

"All right. So we have the background now. And we've returned to the basic question—if you don't love Fred, then why are you going to marry him?"

"I . . . It's all set up."

"That's a reason to marry someone?"

"I can't back out now."

"Oh, but you can. You can do anything. You make the choices. And whatever course you take, it *will be* a choice. Even if you do nothing. Doing nothing's as much of a choice as anything else."

"Oh, Nevada. I'm so scared."

"That's all right. Scared is all right."

"I feel . . . so trapped. I'll upset everyone if I back out, and yet I feel that I can't get married. That I have to find out who *I* am before I can be someone's wife. And, uh... What did I call him, now?"

"Fred."

"That's right. Fred. Fred is so . . . far ahead of me. He thinks faster than I do. And he has a wonderful sense of humor. But a lot of the time, I can't keep up when he tells a joke. I really think he needs a woman with more . . . life experience than I have."

"We're talking about *you* here, Ginger. What do *you* need?"

"Someone I can relax with. Someone I'm *equal* with."

"I see."

"But if I back out of this now— Oh, it's impossible. I don't want to embarrass...Fred. I really don't. It's not his fault that he's so totally *alpha*, it would never occur to him to ask me how I'm feeling about the two of us."

"For those of you new to the show," Nevada interrupted to explain, "we use the word *alpha* to describe the old-style, dominant male. He's hard-edged and hard-driving. He's the one the word *macho* was invented to describe. He's often a good provider, but scores low when it comes to treating women as the equals they truly are.''

Ginger made a noise of agreement, then continued, ''Really, other than the way he simply *assumes* I'm going to ask how high when he says 'Jump,' Fred has been good to me. And my father would kill me if I broke off our engagement. But then I see myself ending up like my mother. A *function* instead of a person. Someone who keeps a beautiful house and gives fabulous dinner parties and always says the right thing. I can't do it. I just can't—''

''Then don't.''

''What?''

''Hey, gorgeous,'' Tully whispered through the speaker in Nevada's other ear. She turned and looked at him. He made the sign for twenty seconds until the next break.

''Look, Ginger. We have to go to a commercial. But I don't want to lose you yet. Will you stay on the line?''

''I . . . yes. Of course. I'll be here.''

''And Ginger?''

''Yes?''

''How about a free-for-all, after the break? Do you think you could take it?''

''A free-for-all,'' Ginger breathed, in combined awe and apprehension.

''We invite anyone to call in, give their slant on this thing. You know what I mean?'' Back at the board, Nevada sent Tully his cue for the next musical selection. Tully put it on: Annie Lennox, singing ''Sisters Are Doing It for Themselves.''

''Yes,'' Ginger said. ''Of course, I know what a free-for-all is.''

''Well?''

A pause. Annie Lennox filled the silence. Then Ginger made her decision. ''All right. A free-for-all. Okay.''

"All right, everybody. Ginger needs some input. Give us a call—555-2940...."

After the break, Ginger got her free-for-all.

First off, a caller who identified herself as Hildegard wanted to expand on "the alpha-male aspects of Ginger's predicament."

"I have learned from hard experience," Hildegard declared, "that there is no changing the alpha male. A man like you describe, Ginger, is great for fantasies and romance novels. But you're better off never to deal with one of them in real life. They're impossible to live with. Either you give in to them and become a professional doormat. Or you spend all your energy just trying to hold your own. Take it from one who knows. It ain't worth it. Sure, sometimes they're great in the sack. But you can't spend your whole life in bed, now, can you?"

"Er, right," Ginger murmured. "No. You can't. No way..."

Next, on line three, a caller who named herself Ladonna told Ginger, "Personally, honey, I think you're a fool. But go ahead and be one. Just give me that Fred's phone number, okay? I mean, you know, seein' as how *you* don't want him ..."

The next caller was a familiar voice. He went by Raymond. Between themselves, Nevada and Tully called him Rantin' Raymond. Rantin' Raymond started off shouting, as usual, "What the hell is it that you women want, anyway?"

Poor Ginger tried to answer. "Well, actually, I—"

But Ray was off and ranting. "Here you've got yourself a big, handsome rich guy who's willing to marry you and probably give you some babies that will significantly improve the gene pool, and you're on the phone to 'Honeymoon Hotline,' whining about how he isn't *sensitive* enough for you? He doesn't *listen* to you? He expects to *lead* while you *follow*. And I ask you, Ginger, doesn't *somebody* have to lead? Doesn't *somebody* have to get out there and earn the damn bread to put on the table?''

Ginger fell all over herself agreeing that somebody certainly did. But she still didn't love Fred. And what about that?

Nevada allowed Raymond to rant a little longer about the women of today and their mixed-up priorities, then she went on to the next call, a woman named Jane.

"This is so clear to me," said Jane. "You don't love him and you don't want to marry him. So don't marry him. What's the big conflict?"

Ophelia called next. She said Jane just didn't understand. "It's not easy for a people pleaser like you are, Ginger. I know. I'm a people pleaser, too."

"People schmeeple," argued a guy called Zeke. "You better get out, lady. You better get out now, before you get to the part where you already said 'I do.'"

"Ginger, you need time to nourish your own inner female self," the next caller, Sunflower, said. "You need a period of discovery—discovery of Ginger. You need to attain that moment of supreme self-understanding, when you find yourself reaching your loving arms toward the sun and calling out in ecstasy, 'I'm here, world! I'm woman! I'm *me!*'"

In the engineer's booth, Tully mimed sticking his finger down his throat.

They went through another commercial break before the controversy over Ginger's dilemma started to lose its edge. Nevada saw that it was time to move on and asked Ginger, "Well, have we helped you at all?"

"Yes. I was so scared to call. But I'm so glad I did. This has been...just what I needed. I see things so clearly now. I agreed to marry Fred for all the wrong reasons. And I'm going to break it off."

"Ginger," Nevada reminded her, "the choice, as I said before and will say again, is yours. It's a choice only you, the powerful, self-determined woman that you are, can make. I don't have all the answers. No one does. And 'Honeymoon Hotline' is only here as a place for you to lay out all your doubts and get some feedback."

"I know." Ginger's voice vibrated with new purpose. "But I really am sure, now, what I have to do."

"Check back with me, will you?"

"You know I will. After I've . . . done the work."

Nevada chuckled. "Well said."

"Fred's picking me up to take me to dinner at seven-fifteen. I'm telling him then."

A slight feeling of unease rippled through Nevada, although she wasn't sure why. "Take it at your own pace," she heard herself murmur. In the engineer's booth, Tully mimed dropping off to sleep, meaning that she should get on to the next call before she put her audience into a coma.

"This *is* my own pace," Ginger assured her.

Nevada took Tully's hint. "Good luck," she said, and punched in the next call.

Chase knew something was wrong when Virginia answered the door wearing yellow shorts and a tank top. Hardly an appropriate outfit for dinner at Marquessa, where they had reservations for eight o'clock.

Her blue eyes were wide and very serious. "Chase. Come in. We have to talk. . . ."

Half an hour later, Chase was back in his car on his way—hell—he wasn't sure where. From his car phone, he called the restaurant and canceled the reservation.

He drove west, out of Scottsdale, without really thinking about where he was going. Camelback Mountain rose up and passed away on his right. Just beyond the Biltmore Country Club, a series of malls appeared. He pulled into the parking lot of one of them.

An hour later, just as the store was locking its doors, he emerged from Sears Roebuck into the pleasant heat of the evening. He wore the clothes he had just bought: a Western shirt, Acme boots and 501 jeans. After tossing his Lombardo suit and Adam Derrick shoes in the trunk, he got behind the wheel again.

Forty minutes later, he found himself at Pinnacle Peak Patio Steakhouse, where his dad used to take the family on trips into Phoenix, back when Chase was a kid. He decided he could use a huge mesquite-grilled steak.

For the hell of it, he got his Robert Talbott tie out of the trunk and knotted it around his neck. They cut the tie off, of course, when he walked in the door. If he ever came back again, he could look for it, hanging from the ceiling with the million-plus ties that were already there.

He sat at a long table with a bunch of people he'd never met. His steak was as big as he remembered the steaks being here, and every time he crooked a finger, another shot of tequila appeared at his elbow. He got fed and he got blasted. And then, because he wasn't a complete fool, he called a cab to take him home.

The next morning, which was Saturday, he woke up with a nasty hangover. He crawled out of bed and dragged himself to the kitchen, where Lorelai, who was almost sixty now and had taken care of him for as long as he'd been on his own, had a fresh pot of coffee all ready for him.

Lorelai grunted. "You look bad, Mr. Chase. What'd you do last night?"

He slid into a chair at the breakfast table in front of a bow window that looked out on the pool. "Got the paper, Lorelai?"

She shuffled to the counter and gathered up the latest editions of the L.A. *Times,* the *Wall Street Journal* and the *Arizona Republic*. She carried them to him and plunked them down in front of him. "Good morning to you, too."

He asked for some toast. She poured his coffee and then went to take care of the toast while he stared blindly at the front page of the *Times*. He sipped from his coffee and reminded himself to see that the car he'd been driving last night was picked up at the steak house sometime today.

His head was pounding. Lorelai read his mind as always and put two aspirin beside his coffee cup.

He looked up into her wide, lined face. "Have I told you lately that I love you?"

Lorelai grunted. "I'll get that toast." She turned and shuffled off.

Chase looked out the window at the blinding morning sun glinting off the surface of the pool and wondered what the hell was wrong with him.

His fiancée had just called off the wedding. He'd been unceremoniously dumped. All last night, he'd tried to tell himself how outraged he was.

But now, in the bright light of morning, he had to admit what he really felt: relief.

Grant Frasier burst into Chase's top-floor office at the McQuaid building just after eleven on Monday morning.

"Chase." Grant waved what looked like a cassette tape in Chase's direction. "I'm as outraged as you must be."

"Sit down, Grant." Chase indicated a sand-colored couch and two chairs in a corner next to a floor vase from which golden stalks of pampas grass erupted.

"I *can't* sit. I'll go nuts if I sit." Clutching the tape in a white-knuckled fist, Grant paced back and forth in front of Chase's black marble desk. "Virginia only told her mother last night. And I went right over there. I kept after her until I had the whole infuriating story. I just can't believe it. I'm still in shock, I swear to you."

"Grant. Listen. It's all right."

Grant Frasier stopped pacing. He turned on Chase, his chiseled face red with fury. "It is not all right. You two were—are—a perfect match. I won't stand for her breaking it off."

"Listen. Grant. Are you listening?"

"Of course."

"I'm all right. And this is what Virginia wants. And it doesn't have to have any effect on the Club Paloverde situation, or the Sun Country Mall." He was speaking of two projects in which both he and Grant were currently involved.

Grant drew in a long breath. "Well. I'm glad for that, at least."

"Good. Now, settle down, will you?"

Grant dropped into a chair a few feet from Chase's desk. "I can't. Not completely. Not until I know that you two will work it out."

Chase ran a hand back through his hair. As he'd admitted to himself Saturday morning, he felt just fine about being dumped. The last thing he wanted now was for Grant to browbeat poor Virginia into reevaluating her decision. "Look. It really is over. I think you're going to have to get used to the idea."

Grant glared at Chase. "No. This didn't have to happen. It *wouldn't* have happened, if not for that talk-show redhead."

Chase's gut clenched. He didn't know of many talk-show redheads. "What?"

"That talk-show redhead, that friend of your sister's. She's responsible for this."

"What are you talking about?"

"Aha." Grant waved the cassette tape. "I knew it. Virginia didn't tell you, did she?"

"Tell me what?"

"*Why* she changed her mind."

"She said she'd given our relationship serious thought and—"

"Serious thought. Ha! She got on the phone to Nevada Jones. That's what she did. She called that damn radio show. Put her private business on the air."

"Virginia called—"

"'Honeymoon Hotline.' She talked to that mouthy redhead. And Nevada Jones told her to call off the wedding."

Chase turned away from Grant. He looked out the window behind his desk at the endless sprawl of Phoenix below him. He didn't trust what he was feeling: a kind of soaring, triumphant sensation.

Nevada.

He recalled the last time he'd seen her, just a little over a week ago on the gallery of the Bar-M ranch house, so smart and sassy, all in red.

And then, as if he'd read it this morning instead of a year ago, he remembered the note she'd left him after their one night in that run-down motel in Winslow.

It shouldn't have happened. And it won't ever happen again. Please don't call me.

The urge to go after her had been a powerful one. He'd longed to hunt her down. To pursue her relentlessly, to scale her every wall, break through each last line of defense. Until he had his hands on her again and she admitted that what had happened in that motel room damn well *should* have happened. And *would* happen again.

And again...

But he hadn't gone after her. He'd respected her wishes.

If she'd stayed clear of him, he would *never* have bothered her again.

But now Grant was saying she'd been mixed up in what had happened with Virginia. She'd *told* Virginia to call off their wedding. If she'd done that, then it would be a whole new ball game.

Chase turned back to Grant. "I assume that tape you're waving around is proof of what you're telling me?"

"You bet it is." Grant poked at the air with the tape, as if punctuating his sentences with it. "It ought to be illegal, the way Nevada Jones handles that show of hers. She thinks she's got a license to ruin people's lives. It's not right. And programming at KLIV should be going in a different direction anyway. I own shares in that radio station, you know. Major shares. And I sit on its board of directors."

"Grant, you own major shares in everything."

"Well. I paid KLIV a visit this morning. And I came away with a tape of the 'Honeymoon Hotline' show for last Friday." Grant put the tape on the edge of Chase's desk. "Your proof is right here. Virginia calls herself 'Ginger' and you 'Fred.' At least she had the good grace to keep your real names out of it."

Chase had an absurd urge to throw back his head and laugh. Fred and Ginger. Astaire and Rogers. Dancing in circles, looking great together. And not much else . . .

Hell. Maybe Virginia had a sense of humor, after all. He bit the inside of his lip to keep a straight face, glanced at the tape and then at Grant. "Thanks."

"Play it."

"I will."

There was a pause, then Grant was all solicitation. "Of course. I understand. You want to be . . . alone, when you hear it."

"Exactly."

"All right." Grant stood and straightened his jacket. "I'll be going, then."

"Fine." Chase came around his desk and herded the other man toward the door. "See you Thursday, at Club Paloverde." The grand opening of the huge nightclub-restaurant was slated for sometime in the fall, and they were negotiating certain aspects of interior design at this point.

"Yes. Thursday." Grant allowed himself to be pushed along, but dug in his heels as Chase opened the door to the outer office for him. "Look. Just give Virginia a little time, all right? She's . . . very impressionable, and—"

Chase put on a serious, regretful expression. "Give it up. Virginia's decided she wants out. And I think she's decided right. She's a sweet kid. And she deserves a kinder, gentler man than I'll ever be. Whatever made her change her mind, she did the right thing."

"Damn it, Chase . . ."

Chase put up a hand. "Let it go."

Grant sighed deeply and shook his head. "All right. But you will listen to the—"

"Grant."

"What?"

"Have a nice day." Chase pushed the other man gently from the room and closed the door behind him.

The cabinet that contained the wet bar had a stereo in it, including a tape player. Chase wasted no time in scooping the tape from the edge of his desk and putting it in.

Then, his heart pumping hard and fast with anticipation, he dropped to the sand-colored couch by the standing vase of pampas grass and listened.

"This is your own 'Honeymoon Hotline,'" Nevada said.

Chase couldn't believe his reaction. Now that he no longer had his relationship with Virginia to hide behind, he had to admit that just the sound of Nevada's husky voice did something to him.

A few minutes later, she laughed at an offhand remark Linda Lacklove had made. The sound pierced him in some deep and private place.

Gradually, as the tape played, he got himself under control enough that he could actually hear what was being said. He came to the part where Virginia called in.

From there on, he felt hooked. His secretary buzzed him. He stalked over to his desk and barked at her over the intercom not to bother him until further notice.

Then he listened, rapt, until the entire tape had played itself out.

When it was over, he was reasonably sure that Nevada had no idea who Ginger or Fred really were. Also, to be fair, he had to admit that Nevada really hadn't pushed Virginia into anything. On the contrary, she'd insisted more than once that the decision was "Ginger's," and "Ginger's" alone. She'd even advised, there at the end, that "Ginger" not be in such a rush to get rid of poor old "Fred."

Nevada had only been doing her job.

And hell, since Chase knew now that Virginia had made the right choice, maybe he owed Nevada a big thank-you, if anything at all. Without "Honeymoon Hotline," he doubted that Virginia would have drummed up the nerve to break it off with him.

Yes, Chase decided; Nevada deserved to know just how grateful he was to her. And he intended to tell her. Face-to-face. That very evening.

Chapter Three

After Monday night's show, Nevada met Ira Bendicks, KLIV's program director, for a quick bite and a beer at Ocotillo Slim's.

Slim's was a comfortable place not far from the station. Customers could choose to sit at heavy dark tables in studded, leather-padded chairs, or in the semicircular booths along the thick stucco walls. The decor ran to cowboy art and Navajo tapestries, while the jukebox played hard country, middle-of-the-road jazz and classic rock. The menu had a little of everything, from tender steaks to burritos to the best Caesar salad around.

But beyond the comfort and the casual atmosphere, there was a sentimental reason why both Ira and Nevada liked to eat at Ocotillo Slim's. Five years before, Ira had "discovered" Nevada there. Then, Nevada had been Slim's head bartender. Ira had hung on the long mahogany bar and eavesdropped while Nevada took care of her customers.

"You've got a talent, Nevada," he'd told her. "Ever thought of playing host on a radio show?"

The rest, as they say, was history. Her years behind the bar had taught her how to listen, and how to get people to figure out what they needed to do about their lives all by themselves. Nevada's real talent lay in her ability to nudge her listeners in the direction they'd wanted to go in all along.

When Nevada had started at the station, it had been a part-time thing. She hadn't quit her job at Slim's until two years ago. First, she'd proved herself with guest spots on other talk shows. Then she'd earned a cohost spot. And finally, she'd been given her own show.

It had taken three years to develop the "Honeymoon Hotline" format as it stood now. Nevada took pride in what she'd accomplished. Recently, a couple of other stations had tried to lure Nevada away. But she was loyal. To Ira and to KLIV. There had been talk of syndication lately—or at least, prerecording the show. But Nevada liked the live format. She felt that it kept her on her toes. And she had no driving need to get out into the wider marketplace. Not really. She liked things just the way they were.

As they drank their beers and ate melt-in-your-mouth roast-beef sandwiches, Nevada told Ira about some of the guests she wanted to try to get on the show. She also reminded him that she was still waiting for his answer about that raise she'd been pushing for.

Ira gave her the go-ahead on the guests and admitted he would probably have to pay her that raise. He would speak with Del Franco, the station's general manager, within the next week. And he would let Nevada know as soon as he got the approval.

Just as Ira was leaving, a couple of Nevada's old regulars showed up. Nevada scooted over in the booth and asked the waiter for a second beer. Her old customers ordered drinks and dinner and told her their troubles. One said she couldn't choose between a nice, steady guy who didn't excite her and an unreliable one who drove her crazy in bed. The other sighed and admitted that she and her husband of six years had decided to call it quits.

Nevada listened and nodded and laughed when they said funny things. They told her how they missed having her all to themselves. But they were glad she had found such success. If anyone deserved it, they both agreed, Nevada did.

She got up to leave at a few minutes after nine. Outside, the desert night felt close and hot, after the air-conditioning inside the restaurant. Nevada stood on the sidewalk for a moment, thinking about the two women she'd left inside. It was two years now since she'd completed the move from bartender to radio personality. But the problems her old customers confronted remained just about the same. They looked for love that would last, they said. But they never seemed to find it.

Nevada herself had no such difficulties—because she wasn't looking in the first place.

Whenever her two happily married younger sisters gave her a bad time about her single status, she would tell them, "I require the objectivity of total independence to be really good at giving advice about love."

Of course, her sisters would scoff and roll their eyes. But they knew, as she did, that she would never marry. Some women just weren't suited to getting along on a day-to-day basis with a man. And Nevada was one of those women. She liked living alone. She was content with her life. And she never had the slightest desire to change her single status.

Well. Almost never.

There *had* been Chase McQuaid.

He had pretty much knocked her idea of herself over backward. In one night.

And she had run from him....

Nevada was a little ashamed of that, of how she'd run.

But it had worked out all right. Her life had stayed the way she wanted it. And he would marry someone else.

And she had no idea why she was standing here on the sidewalk in front of Ocotillo Slim's, staring blindly at the glass-fronted building across the street and thinking about a man who was out of her life for good.

It was time to go home. Nevada dug in her purse for her keys, found them, and headed for her car.

Half an hour later, she turned onto her own street in the Phoenix suburb of Mesa. A brand-new gold Lexus sat in front of her house, but she didn't pay much attention to it. She assumed it belonged to the guest of a neighbor. And since her front door was surrounded by a small, walled-in courtyard, she couldn't see right away if anyone waited there for her.

Still blissfully ignorant of who owned the gold Lexus, Nevada turned into her driveway. As she rolled toward her detached garage, she glanced to the side and, through a break in the courtyard wall, saw Chase McQuaid sitting on her doorstep. He smiled at her.

She was so stunned, her foot stomped on the accelerator. The car shot forward. Reflex had her slamming on the brakes just in time to avoid a collision with her own garage door.

She bounced forward and backward as the car came to a halt. And then she just sat there, willing her heart to stop pounding so hard, realizing grimly who owned the Lexus. And wondering what was going on.

Had she conjured him up, put a curse on herself, by thinking about him earlier in front of Ocotillo Slim's?

Or, more likely, had something horrible happened—to Maud or to Molly?

Truly frightened now, Nevada jerked the keys from the ignition, jumped from the car, and sprinted for the tiny patio. There, she found Chase still sitting on her step, looking awfully calm for a man whose sister or mother was in terrible danger of some sort.

She halted several feet from him. "Is Maud all right?"

Lazily, Chase rose from her step and shook out the legs of the tan slacks he wore. "Last I heard."

"Is your mother well?"

"Healthy as a horse."

Relief made her knees shaky—but exasperation put the strength right back in them. She drew herself up. "Then if this isn't some emergency involving my friend or her mother, I can't imagine what you're doing here." She gave him a look of aloof disinterest and waited for him to either explain himself or get out of her way.

He did neither.

She was forced to demand, "Well. Why are you here?"

"I want to talk to you."

She didn't like the sound of that. Not at all. She tried a patronizing tone. "I really can't see that you and I have anything meaningful to say to each other."

Instead of explaining himself, he just stood there, smirking at her in the most infuriating way.

She commanded haughtily, "Excuse me. You're blocking my door."

"Oh. Pardon me." He stepped aside.

She moved in close to the door and stuck her key in the lock. Her plan was to shove it open, slip through, and shut it fast.

She managed the first two actions just fine. But when she tried to shove the door closed, there was something in the way: his boot.

"Get your boot out of my door."

Slowly, he shook his head. The porch light to his left picked up the streaks of gold in his hair. "We do have to... talk." He hesitated before that last word, as if to imply that talking wasn't all he thought they had to do.

She glared at him, totally bewildered and trying with all her might not to let that bewilderment show. What in the world was he up to? They'd had a tacit agreement for a year now. They avoided each other. And when they had no choice but to speak to each other, as had happened at Molly's party, they were polite and circumspect and they kept it brief.

But tonight, Chase didn't seem to be playing by the rules.

"Please, Chase. What could you and I possibly have to talk about?"

He raised his right hand. She saw, then, that he was holding a cassette tape.

"What's that?"

"A cassette tape."

"I can see that. Of what?"

"One of your radio shows."

"So?"

"Remember Ginger? Ginger and Fred?"

It took a moment, but then the names registered. "Yeah. So?"

"So call me 'Fred.'"

Her mouth suddenly felt as dry as the night air. "I... What?"

"*Ginger* was Virginia. My fiancée."

"I don't..." She began to get the picture. It wasn't a pretty one. "You can't mean..."

He nodded.

"Oh, God." Stunned at the possible ramifications of what he'd just told her, she fell back a step.

He used the opening to get into the house, boldly moving forward and pushing his way through the door, which he closed behind him. Then, casually, as if the house were his instead of hers, he reached for the wall switch and flicked on the light.

The house had no foyer. They stood in her living room. Eyeing him warily, Nevada backed to the center of the room, shivering a little—because the house was cool, she told herself; as always, she'd left the air-conditioning on when she went to work.

"Got a tape player?" Chase looked around. He spotted the stereo in the bleached-oak entertainment center on the far wall. "Ah." He started toward it, brushing past her in two long strides.

"Wait. Stop."

He turned back to her and arched a golden brow.

"I don't need to hear it."

He looked down at the tape, then up at her. "You sure?"

"Yes. I remember it."

"You remember how you told her to dump me?"

"I did not tell her that."

He lifted a muscular shoulder in a lazy shrug. "Let's say you implied it, then. Implied that it would be a good idea if she got rid of the Neanderthal. Me."

"I never said Neanderthal. I never said that word."

He tossed the tape on the coffee table, slid around behind it and dropped to the sofa.

"Wait. What are you doing? Don't sit down."

"Got a beer?"

"Absolutely not. You can't come in here."

"I'm already in."

"Well, I want you to leave. You've got absolutely no right to come barging into my house like this."

Instead of respecting her wishes, he made himself comfortable, stretching his big arms along the backrest, hooking one booted foot across a hard thigh. He even had the gall to let out one extended, self-satisfied sigh, while she stood on the other side of the coffee table, hands on her hips, feeling about as powerless as she'd ever felt in her adult life.

His expression went from self-satisfied to speculative as his gaze went roving. All over her. She could feel it, burning everywhere it touched.

"You are the sexiest damn woman," he murmured, more to himself than to her.

She should have been offended. She knew that. But somehow, his very boldness seemed to reach out to her, to stir things up inside her. He hadn't laid a hand on her. Yet she felt touched way down in the most secret part of herself.

Oh, this was bad. Standing here while he looked her over, all she could think about was the intimate things they'd once done together... and how disturbingly delicious those things had felt.

"There's unfinished business between us, Nevada." His voice was low. It seemed more a caress than a statement.

She sucked in a breath and mustered some outrage. "Don't you talk to me like that. You're... you're an *engaged* man."

He snorted. He sat there on her sofa and he snorted.

She didn't like that snort one bit. She feared that it might mean he *wasn't* engaged anymore. "You *are* engaged, aren't you?"

He shrugged. Those hazel eyes of his took everything in, from the new sofa he sat on, to the Sony Trinitron on the entertainment center. "The place looks good."

She made a noise of frustrated anger. In the old days, before that night in Winslow, when he was just her best friend's brother with whom she could never seem to get along, he'd been here once or twice. The way she remembered it, he'd made disparaging remarks about the house.

"It's the same place it always was," she told him. "Cramped, you called it, remember? A little 'stucco coffin,' you said."

"I was blind. But now I see it in a whole new light."

"What are you getting at?"

"Nothing. I only said your house looks good." His gaze moved over her once more. "*You* look good." He went on looking—slow, lazy passes, from her hair, to her face, lower, then back up again. "I don't know what it is about you. Maybe the way you keep insisting that you have no use for men."

"I *never* insist that. Men are fine. I have nothing against men. In fact, I make my living advising men and women how to better their relationships with each other."

He continued as if she hadn't spoken. "Or maybe it's purely physical. Those wide brown eyes. All that tangled, rusty hair. Those long legs and big—"

She threw up a hand before he could say the word *breasts.* "Don't you dare."

He shifted on the sofa, recrossed his legs. "Sorry. I got carried away." He leaned forward and faked a look of great sincerity. "It's because I'm a mess, emotionally. My heart is broken."

"Oh, please." She cast a glance at the ceiling, but there was no help there.

"Virginia dumped me."

Nevada looked at his smug face again. And she gulped. He'd just said what she'd been fearing he might say. "Er...she did?"

He made a nerve-flaying *tsk*ing sound. "Come on, Nevada. Don't pretend you're surprised. Like most of the misguided females in this city, Virginia looks up to you. And you told her to call off the wedding."

"I did not." She couldn't stand still. She paced over to the entertainment center, then turned on him again. "I never told her anything of the sort. I told her—"

"That only the powerful and self-determined 'Ginger' could make that kind of choice."

"What did you do, memorize that tape?"

"Just the best parts." He let out another of those big, fake sighs. "So now, once again, I am alone." He stood, held out his hands to the sides. "Abandoned." He dropped his arms. "Just like I was on a certain morning eleven and a half months ago. Because of you."

Nevada leaned on a bleached-oak shelf and forked some fingers through her hair. "Look. I'm sorry. I... Do you want me to talk to her or something?"

The rat appeared to be amused. "About what?"

"About how maybe she should reconsider the idea of taking advice from me. How I'm... How you and I were once... Oh, I don't know. How should I know?"

He took two steps and was out from behind the coffee table. "I thought you knew everything. You're *the* Nevada Jones, aren't you? The wise woman of the airwaves? Shamaness of Sun City?"

"You are despicable." She stopped leaning on the shelf and drew herself up to face him squarely down the length of the room. "What do you want?"

He was looking her up and down again.

"Stop doing that."

"What?"

"You know what. What do you want?"

That slow smile took over his face again. "How about a date—with you?"

"What?" The sound emerged as little more than a croak.

"You heard me. Go out with me."

From somewhere, she found her voice. "No, Chase. That's impossible."

"Nothing's impossible, Nevada." He sounded almost tender. "Not even you and me."

Suddenly, she wanted to cry. But she didn't cry. She was Nevada Jones and she was *objective* about things like this. "I want you to leave, Chase. I sincerely do."

She could hardly believe it when he nodded. "All right. I'll say good-night. But not goodbye."

"Goodbye would be better."

"Good-night's all you'll get."

"Fine. Then, go."

"I am."

But then, instead of turning for the door, he started walking toward her.

"Chase..." She backed up, but her heel hit the entertainment center on the first step. "Chase." It was a plea. "You said you'd go."

He kept coming. "I will. In a minute."

She pushed her shoulders back against the shelves and shook her head. "Stop. It's over. It hardly got started. It was only one night...."

He stopped inches from her and looked into her eyes. "It isn't over, Nevada."

"You're a pigheaded, heartless man. All you think about is... building shopping malls."

"Somebody has to build the shopping malls."

"Fine. Go do it. And leave me alone."

"I did that already. It didn't work."

"It worked for me."

His mouth did something funny at the corners, a smile that was not quite a smile. Warmth radiated from him. He smelled clean, like soap. And healthy. And... Oh, why was she thinking about the way that he smelled?

She shook her head. "No. It can't work. You... you were going to marry someone else."

"I was a fool."

"No..."

"But you saved me from that."

"Don't say that. I didn't. I never—"

"You told Virginia to dump me."

"I did not tell her that. And I didn't even know who she was. I swear to you, if I had known I would never have—"

"Shh. The point is, she *did* dump me. And I came here tonight to thank you."

"To thank me?"

"Uh-hmm."

"Don't thank me."

"Oh, yeah. You got me out of a marriage that never would have worked."

"It *might* have worked." She didn't sound convincing, even to herself.

"Uh-uh. No way. You know it. I know it. Virginia knows it. And now, that marriage is off. It's not going to happen. Now..."

Although it didn't seem he could get any closer without touching her, he managed it somehow. The shelves of her entertainment center pressed into her back. The heat of him seemed to swim around her, tempting, arousing....

"Now *what?*" she croaked.

"Why, now...I'm all yours."

His mouth hovered a breath's distance from hers. He was going to kiss her. She knew it. And the awful thing was, she longed for it. She could feel his lips already, settling over hers, stealing her breath and her will to resist....

That one night remained as fresh in her mind as if it were yesterday. She could taste him already, salt and sweet, all male and—he had just said it—all *hers*....

He lifted a hand, ran a thumb down her nose.

And then he backed away.

"I'll be in touch," he said.

He was at her door in four long strides, pulling it open, stepping out into the night. And closing it quietly behind him.

Nevada didn't move from her position at the entertainment center until long after she'd heard the smooth purr of his car's engine starting up out on the street. Then she went to the phone and called Maud.

Before her friend even got out a "Hello," Nevada was accusing her.

"Why didn't you warn me?"

"About what?"

"That Virginia and Chase are through."

"They are? No kidding?"

"You didn't know?"

"Do I sound like I knew?"

"All right. I guess not."

After a pause, Maud asked warily, "Okay. What's going on?"

Nevada let out a groan. "Your brother was here. At my house. He just left."

"Why was he there?"

"To thank me, he said. For wrecking his marriage plans."

"*You* were the one who wrecked his—"

"Never mind all that. It doesn't matter. The point is, he said he wants a *date* with me. He said he'd be…in *touch*."

Maud said nothing.

"Maud, are you there? Did you hear what I said?"

"Yes."

"Well. What am I going to do?"

Maud let out a long breath. "Nevada. I've told you for years. He's crazy about you. And *you're* crazy about him."

"No. He's not. *I'm* not. We never got along."

"Because if you admit you're crazy about someone, then you're not one hundred percent in control. And you're both so pigheaded, neither of you can stand not to be in control."

"No. What happened only happened because of you and Billy. It happened because Chase is your brother and I'm your best friend. Because we were both worried sick about you when you took off after Billy last year." A struggling songwriter and guitar player, Billy Mooney was Maud's ex-husband.

Nevada went on, "Chase and I were concerned about you. So we followed you. To Winslow. And Billy was playing in that seedy bar there. And we couldn't just leave you there and we couldn't get you to leave with us. So we stayed. We..."

"You had a few drinks and you danced a few dances. And you forgot for a while that you don't like each other?"

"Right. Exactly."

"So it's *my* fault that you ended up spending the night with my brother?"

"No. Of course, it's not your fault."

"You just said—"

"I'm upset. Don't listen to me. All I'm saying is, there's really nothing between Chase and me. It's over. It never got started. I want nothing to do with him."

Maud let out another long breath.

"What's that?"

"What?"

"That *sigh*. What did that sigh mean?"

"You don't want to know."

"Well," Nevada declared, "no matter what he does, I'm not going out with him."

"Did I say you had to? Settle down, will you? Take a deep breath or two."

Nevada did as her friend instructed, then asked, "Am I acting like an idiot?"

"Yep."

"You're right. I'm taking this way too seriously. It's not a big deal. If I'm not going out with him, I'm not going out with him. And that's that."

"Right on," Maud said.

"But I feel terrible about Virginia."

"Virginia? Why?"

As briefly as she could, Nevada explained how Virginia had called "Honeymoon Hotline."

"So, what do you feel bad about?" Maud asked, when Nevada was through. "It was an accident of fate that she called you, that's all. You didn't know who she was. And she didn't know that you'd once spent the night with Chase."

"I feel I should talk to her."

"God. What is with you tonight? That's an insane idea. Leave bad enough alone, I always say."

"Do you have her phone number, Maud?"

"Hey. What is going on? You're the levelheaded one, remember? *You* talk *me* out of crazy stunts like this."

"I just want to talk to her."

"Nevada . . ."

"Please."

There was a silence, then Maud muttered, "Hold on." She came back in a moment and gave Nevada the number. "I just want it on the record that I don't approve of this harebrained idea."

"Gotcha, and thanks," Nevada said.

"Are we still on for Friday?" They had planned a girls' night out.

"You bet. Why, had a better offer?"

Maud hesitated a fraction too long before insisting, "Of course not."

Nevada sensed what had happened. Billy Mooney had been on tour for months. Recently, though, he'd returned to town. And he'd started calling Maud. "Billy called and asked you out, didn't he?"

"Nevada . . ."

"Well, did he?"

"Yes. For Friday. I turned him down."

"Are you all right?"

"Sure. Billy and I are over. Finished. Kaput. Just like you and Chase . . ."

* * *

Virginia sounded thrilled when Nevada called her the next day. Nevada said she'd heard that Virginia and Chase weren't getting married after all.

"That's right," Virginia said.

"I'd like to talk to you, to meet with you."

"Sure. Come on over."

Nevada found Virginia packing for a long trip.

"I'm going to Brazil," Virginia explained. "Tomorrow. And after that, I'm going to France. I want to see the rain forest before there's nothing left of it. And I have a friend in Paris. An artist. I'll be staying with him. For a while. My father is furious. But he'll get over it. Eventually." Virginia's skin glowed and her pretty blue eyes shone. She didn't look terribly unhappy about the choice she'd made.

Still, Nevada had to say something about her part in that choice. "Virginia, I know you called my show."

Virginia blushed. "You knew... all along?"

"No. Chase came to see me. Last night."

Virginia's eyes went wide. "Nevada. I never told him I called in. I swear to you."

"It doesn't really matter how he found out."

"My father probably told him."

"Whatever. The point is, I don't give on-air advice to people I know personally."

Virginia bit her pretty lower lip. "I'm sorry. I shouldn't have. But... you helped me *so* much."

"Virginia. I wasn't... qualified to say a thing. Not in this situation."

"Because of you and Chase, you mean?"

It took about ten seconds for Nevada to believe what she'd just heard. Then she tried to speak. "I..."

Virginia smiled. "At Molly's party. That's when I realized. There was something in the air, between you, when Chase introduced you to me."

"Virginia, until that party, I hadn't exchanged ten words with Chase McQuaid in nearly a year."

"Oh." Virginia waved a slender hand. "Stop it. I know that. Chase would never fool around with one woman while he was engaged to another. It's not in him to behave that way. And I've listened to your show for four years. I don't believe you'd do a thing like that, either. So I know there was nothing funny going on. There was just . . . attraction. Something in the air, as I said. Something that never was in the air between Chase and me."

For once in her life, Nevada was at a total loss.

"Breaking up with Chase was *my* choice, as you told me," Virginia said. "And I made it. And I'm glad."

"So . . . it's all worked out just fine for you, then?"

"It's worked out perfectly," Virginia said.

Friday, after her show, Nevada walked over to Ocotillo Slim's to meet Maud. Maud hadn't arrived yet when Nevada got there, so she staked out their favorite booth, away from the small dance floor and the three-piece country band that played on weekends.

Ira Bendicks wasn't the only friend Nevada had made during her days as a bartender at Slim's. She'd met Maud there as well, eight years before. Maud, a CPA with a background in tax, had worked in one of the high-rise office buildings across the street. Maud still worked in that building, actually. But now she was the tax partner in her firm.

Maud came in at a little after seven, dressed in a lightweight business suit, her brown hair pulled back into a neat chignon. She took off her jacket and undid the top button of her blouse before she slid in next to Nevada. Then she helped herself to a margarita from the pitcher Nevada had ordered.

"God save me from the guys in auditing," Maud muttered. "Always making promises to the clients that *I'm* supposed to keep for them." She made a silly face, blowing out her cheeks and crossing her eyes. "But enough about the salt mines. How's your love life?"

Nevada shoveled a chip through the bowl of salsa in front of her. "I don't have a love life, you know that. And I like it that way." She put her hand under the chip to catch any drips and quickly brought the spicy, crunchy morsel to her mouth.

"Chase called me last night," Maud said.

"And?"

"He wanted to know if you and I still came here on Friday nights."

"Did you tell him?"

"Are you kidding? I know better than to get myself wedged in between the two of you."

"Good."

"Did you come to your senses and decide *not* to call Virginia?"

"Everything's worked out with Virginia."

Maud took a big sip from her margarita. "Was that an answer to my question?"

"As much of an answer as you're going to get."

"Gee. You *are* in a lovely mood this evening. I can tell already that we're going to have a really fun time."

Nevada opened her mouth to deliver a snappy comeback. And then she shut it without speaking. The hostess was just leading two men in from the bar: Billy Mooney and Chase McQuaid.

Chapter Four

"Do you want to leave?" Maud asked.

"Do you?"

Maud didn't answer. Billy and Chase approached, led by the hostess, Slim's wife, Nadine. Nevada cast a grim glance at the booth next to them. Sure enough. It was empty.

Chase and Billy slid into it. Nadine handed them menus, then promised that their drinks would be coming right up. Billy, who'd positioned himself in the curve of the booth so that Maud was almost directly behind him, turned around the moment the hostess left.

He pushed his white Stetson back from his forehead with a thumb. "It's good to see you, honey."

Maud granted him a single, icy, over-the-shoulder glance. "I told you I was busy tonight." Then she tried to ignore him.

But Billy Mooney wasn't easy to ignore. That was partly because of his flamboyant appearance: beneath the white

Stetson, his thick blond hair hung in gorgeous waves to his shoulders and his neat pointed beard and soft mustache drew attention to his sensual mouth. But beyond the fact that he bore a startling resemblance to George Armstrong Custer, there was also the way he refused to take a hint. "Honey. Come on. Give me an opening, here."

Maud faced resolutely front.

"Aw, honey. Haven't you missed me a *little?*"

Maud made the mistake of turning toward him again. Nevada stifled a groan at the look he gave her, a woebegone sort of look. The kind of look a sad old hound gives its master when it's been thrown out of the house on a stormy night.

"Billy," Maud said tightly. "Please. I don't want you here."

Right then, as if on a cue from some invisible stage manager, the three-piece band at the far end of the room started playing a certain Willie Nelson song: "Angel Flying Too Close to the Ground."

Nevada was looking at Maud's back. Even from that angle, she could see the softness claiming Maud, see the set of her shoulders begin to relax.

"Maud . . ." she warned low.

But it didn't do a bit of good.

"Dance with me, honey," Billy whispered.

"Damn you, Billy Mooney," Maud said.

Billy stood and held out a hand. Maud slipped from the booth and took it.

They moved off toward the small dance floor and into each other's arms.

Chase wasted no time in getting out of his booth and into the seat next to Nevada.

She gave him what she hoped was a hard, uncompromising glare, as she tried to ignore the sudden leap of her pulse at his nearness. "I could get up and leave."

He didn't argue, simply refilled her glass.

She didn't touch the drink. No way she was going to let down her defenses with another margarita now. Their waiter, someone new to Slim's, appeared. He set Billy's drink on the other table and then brought Chase's drink right to him. "Dinner?" he asked.

"Later," Chase said.

Nevada waited until the waiter was out of earshot, before accusing, "You shouldn't have come here."

Chase toasted her with his drink. "You're entitled to an opinion."

"And you shouldn't have brought Billy. Why did you do that?"

Chase drank. "I called him and asked him if you and Maud still came here on Friday nights. He said he didn't know, but he'd like to tag along if I wanted to find out."

"They're divorced, Chase."

He set his glass down firmly. "So what?"

"They've been divorced for a year. Maud has spent a lot of time crying on my shoulder. Until recently, I've been letting myself think that she's getting over Billy. But then he had to start calling her again. And now, *you* bring him here and drop him right in her lap."

Chase leaned back in the booth and watched his sister and her ex sway on the dance floor. "It's a beautiful song."

Nevada looked away. She and Chase had danced to that song. That crazy night in Winslow, when Billy kept signaling his band to play it over and over for him and Maud.

"Maybe we ought to let them make their own mistakes," Chase suggested softly.

"He's not good for her."

"In your opinion. But that's all you get when it comes to the two of them. An opinion. You know, you're really good, on that radio show of yours. You're . . . insightful. And pretty damned objective."

"Thank you," she sneered.

"But closer to home, your record's not so good."

"I knew there was an insult in there, somewhere."

"Remember that night in Winslow?"

Although she'd just been thinking of it herself, she didn't want him to know. "Let's forget that night in Winslow."

"No, let's not. That night proves my point—you can't live Maud's life for her."

"I'm not trying to live Maud's life for her."

He gave her a look of smug disbelief, then elaborated, "Your involvement that night had no effect on what happened between Billy and Maud. You remember how it was."

"Do we have to go into this?"

Her question didn't even give him pause. "It was a farce. Billy gets his final divorce decree in the mail and writes Maud some long, convoluted letter about how he'll end it all after his gig in Winslow if she doesn't come and stop him. So she calls you and tells you she's going to Winslow to keep Billy from killing himself over his broken heart. You beg her not to go, but she goes anyway. And then you call me and get me all stirred up over the whole mess. And then we both end up driving all the damn way to Winslow, where we find Billy and Maud acting like a pair of lovebirds in that two-bit honky-tonk bar where Billy's band was playing."

She couldn't stop herself from arguing. "And what came of it? Of that 'reunion' of theirs?"

She knew she'd put her foot in it when he answered, "*We* came of it." He lowered his voice to an intimate whisper. "One night. One damned unforgettable, beautiful night."

"Stop that. Stop it right now."

He looked off toward the bar, then back at her, but he didn't say anything more.

Somehow, Nevada just couldn't give it up. "Billy and Maud aren't good for each other. That's why they're divorced. It's over, between them."

Chase looked at the two on the dance floor and grunted. "I've seen 'over.' That's not it."

"Because you had to bring him here."

He shrugged. "He was bound to find her, one way or another."

He turned and looked at her. Their gazes locked. Nevada knew he was talking about the two of them as much as her friend and her friend's ex.

And he wasn't through. "You got to me that night. Really got to me. And then you got to my pride, with that damn note you left me. I should have tracked you down then, but you left me too raw."

"Did I give you the impression that I wanted to discuss this?"

"I did the classic thing, proposed to Virginia on the rebound. But you won't get rid of me so easily this time."

"We were talking about Billy and Maud."

"We were?"

"Yes. About how she's trying to forget him, but her own brother insists on making that impossible."

He asked, oh-so-gently, "What if she *can't* forget him—and he can't forget her?"

Nevada took a sip of that margarita, after all. "This isn't fair." She stared off toward the dance floor as one song ended and the next one began. It was another slow one. Billy and Maud just went on dancing. Nevada watched them for a while.

And then Chase whispered, "Dance with me."

The problem was, she wanted to say yes.

She made herself look at him again. This time, when she spoke, all pretense of belligerence was gone. "Oh, Chase. Don't do this to me. You don't need me. You don't need to waste your time on someone like me. I'll never be what you want."

His mouth was doing that thing again, that funny little smile that wasn't quite a smile. "It's only a dance."

"It's not. You know it's not."

"Someday you'll tell me, won't you, why you're making this so damn difficult?"

"There's nothing to tell."

"I don't believe that, any more than you do."

"It's just . . . not for me, this 'romance' thing."

"You make your living off this 'romance' thing."

"I require objectivity, to be really good at—"

He cut her off with a brief, ugly expletive. "Don't give me that crap. There's more. It goes deeper. I may be a Neanderthal. But I'm not a *stupid* Neanderthal."

"I never called you a—"

"Shh. Dance with me." He slid out of the booth and stood there, holding out his hand.

The music played on. And he looked at her so tenderly. So hopefully.

"Sit back down," she said.

But he didn't move. He stood so tall, his broad shoulders drawn back, somehow managing to look both earnest and uncompromising at the same time. Nevada thought that he had never been quite so appealing as he was right at that moment.

"Please." He mouthed the word. His hand remained extended.

And she was the one who blinked.

One corner of his mouth quirked up. It was only a minor skirmish. But the victory belonged to him.

With a sigh, she scooted out of the booth and laid her hand in his.

After midnight, the men walked the women out to Nevada's car. Maud, who was conservative and sensible in every way except her choice of Billy as a lifelong love, carpooled to work. Whenever they met for an evening at Ocotillo Slim's, Nevada drove her home.

As soon as they reached the KLIV lot, Billy lured Maud over to a cinder-block retaining wall that divided the lot from the next one over. Nevada reached her car to find that Chase was the only one still with her.

"Maud?" she called.

Maud gave her one of those "In a minute" waves.

"Give her a break," Chase said. "When can I see you again?"

Hoping that maybe he wouldn't ask a second time if she pretended she hadn't heard him, Nevada dug the small black control box from her purse and beeped off her car alarm. Then she felt around for her keys.

Chase propped an elbow on the roof of her car. "When?"

She pulled out her keys. "Why am I not getting through, here?"

"Maybe you're giving crossed signals."

She didn't argue with that; even she saw the truth in it.

His smile was dazzling. "There are advantages to being an 'alpha' male."

"Oh, God. My own show is working against me, now."

"I've been taping it. Every day. So I can listen when I want to. And I've learned that alpha males always get what they want."

"Not in this case."

"Yeah, in this case. In any case. The simple truth is, all your arguments are no match for the kind of testosterone levels you're dealing with, here."

"Chase, please. Give it up."

"No way. But I'll be subtle. I'll wait for just the right moment before I make another move."

"Ha."

"I mean it. Even an alpha male can make an effort at subtlety. And deep in the heart of every Neanderthal, there lurks a kinder, gentler man."

She found she was smiling. She'd been smiling too much tonight.

"Maud!" she called again. "Come on!"

Neither Maud nor Nevada said a word for the first few minutes of the ride home.

Finally, Maud spoke. "Okay, go on, say it."

Nevada shook her head. "Your brother said it was none of my business. And I'm trying to remember that."

"Just say it, all right? I can't stand the heavy silence in this car."

"Maud . . ."

"Just say it. Please."

So Nevada did. She reminded her friend how Billy lived on the road much of the time. How he was never there when Maud needed him. He was married to his music before anything else.

"I know," Maud said, as she always said whenever they had this discussion. "But I've loved him since I was sixteen. There's just . . . no one else for me, Nevada. I'm starting to see that now."

"So what are you telling me?"

"I'm telling you that for me, maybe ending it wasn't the right answer. Maybe I'm just going to have to learn to take him for what he is."

Nevada kept her eyes on the road as she shook her head. "That's *settling*, Maud. I hate to see you *settle*."

Maud reached across the seat to lightly nudge Nevada's arm. "Hey. It *is* my life. If you were me, you'd do things differently. But you're not me."

Nevada wondered for a moment why she felt so sad. Was it for Maud, who was determined to keep trying at something that had never worked yet? Or for herself, who refused to try in the first place? "So you're not in the mood for any expert advice tonight, is that what you're telling me?"

"You're a true friend, Nevada."

"In other words, butt out."

They laughed together at that.

Nevada turned into the wide residential street where her friend lived alone, then pulled to a stop in front of the sloping lawn that led up to Maud's big ranch-style house.

"Thanks," Maud said as she leaned on the door.

"De nada," Nevada said—and nothing more. Maud was right. It *was* her life.

The next day was Saturday and Nevada had no show to do. Since she hadn't agreed to emcee any community events, as she often did on weekends, the day belonged to her.

She lazed around the house in cutoffs and an old shirt, lingering over coffee and considering attacking the layer of dust on the furniture with spray polish and a cloth.

She thought about Chase a little, although she knew she shouldn't dwell on him at all. But she was honest enough to admit that she had enjoyed the night before. And dancing with him had been…well, the kind of mistake she rarely allowed herself to make.

As she'd swayed in his arms, she hadn't been completely able to block out the memories of that other night. Their one night.

And later, when she lay in her own bed, the memories had returned. She had ordered them away. But they were so clever. They waited until she slept. And then they'd come tiptoeing back to take over her dreams.

Now, this morning, she really hoped he wouldn't call. Because, no matter how fast her foolish heart beat at the thought of him, she would not go out with him.

Around nine-thirty, the phone rang. Nevada jumped at the sound, then forced herself not to answer until it had rung three times.

But it wasn't Chase. It was her sister, Evie, who lived in the small northern California town of North Magdalene with her housepainter husband and his three children by a previous marriage.

"How are you feeling?" Nevada asked. Evie was expecting a baby in the fall.

"Good. Really good," Evie said.

Nevada knew right away that something wasn't right. "What is it? You sound worried."

Evie laughed. "As usual, you're on to me. You and Faith always figure out something's wrong before I even say a word about it."

Faith was their middle sister. There was a very strong bond between the three of them, forged during their childhood years, when they had lived a life of wandering, sleeping in cramped motel rooms or the back seat of a car—the years when they'd had only each other to cling to.

"Tell," Nevada demanded.

"All right. It's Father."

"You're worried about dear old Dad?"

"Yes, I am."

"You have such a full life. Why waste any of it in concern over Gideon Jones?"

Evie sighed. "Oh, Nevada, don't be sarcastic. He *is* our father. We can't turn our backs on him, no matter what he's done."

Nevada saw nothing at all wrong with turning her back on Gideon Jones—except, perhaps, the danger that he might stick a knife between her shoulder blades. His sins were legion.

She and her sisters had escaped him the day Evie had turned eighteen. They'd longed only to be free of him. But he'd lurked in the shadows of their lives for fifteen years after they left him behind. And then, a year and a half ago, he'd emerged to create havoc once again, kidnapping Evie, and almost causing her death.

Now he lived in a high-security mental institution in Oregon. Nevada refused to go there. But both Evie and Faith had visited him. They said his mind was pretty much gone.

"He's dying," Evie said. "Cancer. It's all through him. The doctors give him a few months at the most."

Nevada felt nothing. A vague sadness, perhaps, as one might experience at the news that a stranger was terminally ill.

"Nevada, did you hear me?"

"I heard. Don't suffer over him, Evie. He doesn't deserve it."

"Oh, but he does. Everyone does. We can't know what he lived through in his life. We can't know what made him what he became. But we can...remember that he did keep us all together, after Mother died. And we can forgive him. And be there for him. We can do that much. He's so totally powerless now."

Nevada had carried the remote phone into the living room. Now she flopped onto the couch. "You're an angel, Evie. Always have been. And Faith, too. Both of you are...better than this mean old world deserves. I wish I could be like you. But I'm not."

"Stop it, Vada." Evie used the name she used to call her big sister when she was hardly old enough to stand on her own. "I'm no angel. And neither is Faith. And you're just...the strong one. Always the strong one. Too strong, maybe sometimes, don't you think?"

"Naw. You're lots tougher than me."

Evie laughed, then grew serious again. "You should go visit him. Before he's gone. For your own sake as much as for his."

"No, thanks. I'm ... sorry he's dying. But he's out of my life. I don't want to see him."

Evie changed the subject after that. They talked of Faith and the progress Faith and her new husband, Price, were making toward repairing their huge old house in the San Francisco Bay area that had been badly damaged by a big earthquake a few months before. And then they discussed the possibility that Nevada might take a few days of vacation and visit North Magdalene again in the next month or two.

Just as they said goodbye, there was a knock at the door. Nevada's pulse zinged into high gear. It would be Chase, and she would have to firmly send him away.

But it wasn't Chase. It was her elderly next-door neighbor, Mr. Alphonse. He said he wanted to borrow milk for his coffee, but Nevada knew that he really wanted company. She invited him in to share the pot she'd already made. They chatted for an hour, then he toddled on home.

The rest of the day wasn't as relaxing as she might have hoped. Nevada felt edgy. She jumped every time the phone rang, then silently called herself a fool when she found out it wasn't Chase.

As night drew on, she realized that spending the evening alone would drive her up the wall. She called Maud, but Maud said she had other plans—Billy, Nevada felt sure. But she didn't express her disapproval. She let it be, although that feeling of sadness came over her again.

After she talked to Maud, Nevada called a few other friends. But everyone had made plans. So she went out to dinner alone and told herself she enjoyed it. She stopped to rent a movie on the way home. But it turned out to be a loser. She switched it off halfway through and went to bed.

Sunday was the same. She just couldn't get comfortable inside her own skin. She waited. For *some*thing to happen. But nothing in particular did.

By Monday morning, she had begun to despise herself a little. Well, more than a little, actually. In Nevada's opinion, there was nothing more pitiful than an ambivalent woman. A woman who waited for things to happen to her—rather than *making* things happen.

But what, exactly, could she do? Chase was giving her just what she'd asked for: he was leaving her alone.

If she'd *wanted* to see him, she could have called him and asked him out. But since she supposedly wanted nothing to do with him, the fact that she couldn't stop waiting for his call didn't make a lot of sense. And really, it had only been two days since she'd seen him. It only felt as if it had been years.

She needed advice—a "Honeymoon Hotline" to call. But the number wasn't going to work for her, she knew. If she called, she would only have herself to talk to.

The phone rang just before noon. It was Ira. After she got over her absurd disappointment that he wasn't Chase, she agreed to stop in his office right after her show that evening. He seemed a little distracted, but she knew that he must be intending to formally offer her that raise she had asked for.

She would focus on that, she decided—on all the uses she had for the extra money she would be making—rather than mooning over Chase McQuaid and praying that he would call.

But the news from Ira was not what Nevada had expected. She should have known there must be something grim in the offing, she realized in hindsight, when Ira didn't suggest they go on over to Ocotillo Slim's. He'd chosen his office. *After* her show was over. He was taking no chances as to how she would react.

As soon as she had taken a seat in the chair opposite his desk, Ira told her how much he'd enjoyed the years they'd worked together.

"Ira," Nevada joked, "you sound like you're *firing* me, not giving me a raise."

Ira rubbed his hand over the bald crown of his head, the way he did when he was nervous or uncomfortable.

Nevada felt her stomach lurch. "Ira. Talk to me."

And he did, after moving the brass paperweight on his desk from one corner to the other and clearing his throat as if a Volkswagen had gotten stuck in there. "Nevada, I'm afraid that raise you hoped for is out of the question...."

It got worse. KLIV, Ira explained, was changing directions in its programming, going for more of a political slant. Actually, in his meeting with Del Franco this morning, Del had told him he wanted Nevada's show phased out altogether, eventually.

Nevada had the ridiculous urge to pinch herself, just to be sure this was only a nightmare.

Because it *had* to be a nightmare. It couldn't really be happening.

She hadn't come prepared for this. Not in the least. But still she valiantly tried to defend herself. "Ira. This is nuts. People love my show. My show is hot. Last week you were talking syndication. And now—"

Ira shook his head and then rubbed it some more. "Nevada. It's the nature of the beast. We're just going in a new direction, that's all. Yes, your show is doing fine. But it's not going to fit in with the kinds of things we're going to start developing now."

"*What* kinds of things?"

"Issue shows. News of the hour. Talk shows with a current-events slant."

"Ira..."

He stopped rubbing his head long enough to raise a hand. "Look. This is nothing that's going to happen overnight. It'll be several months before we'll actually be discontinuing 'Honeymoon Hotline.' But I wanted you to know what's really going on. So you'd have time to start evaluating your options."

For one of the few times in her life, Nevada Jones was completely at a loss. She felt as if Ira had pulled a two-by-four from behind his desk and whacked her between the eyes with it. She reeled.

She thought of the offers she'd had from other stations. More than likely, one of them would still give her a job. But Ira had *discovered* her. He was her mentor. And her friend. And she couldn't comprehend how he could do this to her. She'd been *loyal* to him. And to the station. Her show was a genuine hit, but she still operated under a verbal agreement. She'd never asked for a contract, because she'd put her trust and loyalty into KLIV. And look where trust and loyalty had gotten her. Nowhere.

"I think you're making a huge mistake here, Ira," she heard herself say in a voice that sounded amazingly calm and self-assured, considering that she felt like shattered glass inside.

Ira went on rubbing his head. "The board and the major shareholders made this decision. Del and I are just the messenger boys."

"You say it'll be months before the show is actually cut?"

"Yes." He stood, leaned forward and put his knuckles on his desk. "Nevada. Listen. I'm in a tough spot, here."

She leaned forward, too. "Then talk to me."

"There's only so much I can say."

Nevada saw, then, how upset he really was by this. And it occurred to her that maybe he was doing the best he could for her, in this situation—whatever the situation actually was.

Ira went on, his tone pitched low and confidential: "I can't give you a raise. But sometimes decisions get made that shouldn't be made. Sometimes the people who have the power to make the decisions don't know what they're doing. Are you with me?"

"Not really."

"What I'm telling you is that maybe, if you hang in there, I can turn things around in the next few months. This'll all blow over."

"*What'll* blow over?"

He was back to rubbing his head. "I can't tell you. Hell. I don't really know myself. All I've been told is that your request for a raise is denied. And I'm to start thinking in new directions, to work on 'phasing out' everything that isn't politics- or news-oriented."

Nevada thought she understood, then. "You weren't supposed to tell me that I was being 'phased out,' right?"

"No, that's not so. No one said I couldn't tell you. The truth is, *I* wanted to keep it from you. Me, personally. Because I really am going to put everything I've got into turning this mess around. But that doesn't mean I'll succeed." He looked away, out the window at blue sky and tall buildings and the top of a palm tree. "You deserved that raise, Nevada."

She took his meaning: she would put herself in a weakened position if she didn't get the raise and yet stayed on anyway.

He looked at her again, a pointed look. "Do you hear what I'm telling you?"

She did, loud and clear. He was telling her that as her mentor, he would advise her to move on, even if, as her boss, he didn't want to lose her.

He didn't—but the people who made the big decisions at KLIV did.

And that was enough for her.

"You'll have my notice on your desk in the morning. Two weeks, Ira, and I'm out of here."

He nodded. "I'm sorry. But I do understand."

Chapter Five

It took Nevada a few days to really accept the fact that she was leaving KLIV behind. During that time, she moved through life on automatic pilot.

But by the end of the week, she'd started making herself think about looking for another job. She called the two stations—one in Tucson and a rival of KLIV right in Phoenix—that had approached her before. They were eager to talk to her. She made appointments for early in the following week.

The Tucson station came up with an excellent offer. But when she thought about it, she realized she had no desire to move to Tucson right now. The Phoenix station's offer was more modest; she turned it down on principle. She took care to leave the door open at both stations, although she had the feeling that neither of them was the right place for her.

And besides, she just didn't feel ready yet to decide where she would go next. She had some money saved.

Once her final two weeks were up, she would take that vacation in North Magdalene that she'd promised herself. She would admire her baby sister's expanding tummy and play computer games with her nephew and go swimming with her two little nieces in the cold mountain river that ran along the outskirts of town. And by the time she returned home, she would be over getting the shaft from KLIV and ready to get on with her life.

Chase never did call. And she tried to tell herself that she accepted his not calling. After all, it was better for both of them if he just let the whole thing slide.

But as her last day at KLIV approached, she felt—well, there was no other word for it—she felt *forlorn*. Each night she went on the air and gave her all for the lonely and lovelorn. She started to realize that her regular callers—from Linda Lacklove to Rantin' Raymond—were like old friends to her. And she would be sad to leave them behind.

She never breathed a word on the air that she was leaving. She and Ira had decided that if she told her listeners of her imminent departure, then they would talk about nothing else until she was gone. And "Honeymoon Hotline" was not about the job prospects of Nevada Jones. She would tell them on her final night, and no sooner.

Maud and Billy were seeing each other steadily. More than once, when Nevada called her friend, Billy answered the phone. Nevada learned a hard lesson: she'd grown accustomed to turning to Maud whenever she was lonely or wanted to talk. But now, much of the time, Maud wasn't available.

Actually, Nevada's life seemed to have barreled right into a major crossroads. Somehow, in the years she'd worked to develop "Honeymoon Hotline," she'd managed to allow her job and her faceless listeners to become like her family. Soon, now, she would be walking away from them, losing them, as she felt that she was losing Maud.

And for some insane reason, in all this upheaval, she couldn't stop thinking about Chase, wishing he would call, wishing he would show up at her doorstep...and for what?

So she could hang up on him? So she could order him to go away?

She wanted no man in her life, anyway. But if she *did* change her mind and decide to seek a partner in life, Chase McQuaid would be the last guy on earth she would go looking for. He was much too overpowering a man. A woman could be submerged, annihilated, reduced to a quivering, hopeless shadow of herself, if she were to care too much for someone like Chase.

No, Nevada understood why she kept obsessing about Chase. She maintained enough objectivity to see just what she was doing. For years, she'd been nobody special—a good bartender, a supportive sister, a friend you could count on. But not many people had known her name. She'd more or less come to accept that she would never set the world on fire.

And then, at the age of thirty-two, she'd been hired by KLIV. She'd created "Honeymoon Hotline." Five years later, she was a celebrity. And she'd made the mistake of identifying herself with her job.

Now, she was losing that job. Her life was changing. She had a secret fear it might be starting to come unraveled, so she was clutching at straws. Her listeners did this kind of thing all the time. They put all their focus on a man, so they wouldn't have to think about the real issue: what to do with their own lives.

Hey, wait a minute, a small, traitorous voice in the back of her mind whispered. *You were obsessing about Chase* before *you found out you were losing your job....*

"Shut up," she told that voice. She said it aloud, while she was out in her front yard at seven in the morning, watering the marigolds she'd planted a few weeks before.

"What was that, Nevada?"

She looked up from the flower bed to see Mr. Alphonse, in his robe and slippers, standing on his front porch with his morning paper in his hand.

"Nothing. Want some coffee?"

Mr. Alphonse looked so sweet and grateful when he smiled. "I'd love a cup." She turned off the hose and led him inside.

That night, after the show, Ira caught her as she was leaving and asked her to join him at Ocotillo Slim's. Over fat chili-*verde* burritos, he asked her how she was doing and if she was still sure she wanted to quit her job, as planned.

Some scared little girl down inside her wanted to scream, *No, I'm not sure! I want my job back! I want it back right now!* but she heard herself asking, "What about that raise?"

Ira shook his head. "Sorry. No can do."

"Then on Friday, I'm outta here."

"I bet we get lots of letters," he said, smiling a little. "A whole hell of a lot of outraged letters. It could be bad. I might have to end up offering you a bigger raise than you asked for in the first place, just to get you back."

Nevada put her hand over his. "You're a good friend, Ira. Thanks."

"Eat your burrito. I'll see about getting us another beer."

Just a few days before her job ended, Nevada called Evie and told her sister that she planned to leave the station. Evie was stunned. She knew how Nevada loved her job.

"I was thinking I'd come up there," Nevada said, "to North Magdalene, for a week or two, as soon as I'm free."

"Oh, yes. That's a great idea. Come as soon as you can."

It did Nevada's heart good to hear the eagerness in her sister's voice.

The more she thought about it, the more she felt certain that a vacation in North Magdalene was just what she needed. Besides Evie and her husband and kids, there were any number of Joneses there, offspring of Oggie Jones, Nevada's uncle and a charming old curmudgeon who had fathered five children. Now most of those children had children of their own. And they all lived in that tiny town. It would be good, Nevada decided, to have all that family close by for a while.

Evie mentioned Gideon again before they said goodbye. "He's much worse, Nevada. We've been talking about flying up there in the next few weeks."

"Who's 'we'?"

"Me. Faith." She mentioned their respective spouses, "Erik and Price. And Uncle Oggie, too. I have this feeling, I really do, that it will be the last time. If you change your mind about—"

"I won't. When you go, give him . . . my regards."

Evie said nothing for a moment. Nevada could picture her beautiful sad smile. "All right. I will."

On the last night of her show, Nevada told her listeners that she was leaving. She did it right up front.

"Tonight, I have some sad news. Sad for me, anyway. And I don't know how to give it to you any way but bluntly. So, here goes.... Tonight is my last night on KLIV."

Nevada glanced at Tully, behind his wall of glass. For once, he was making no faces and giving no hand signals. Ira had squeezed in there next to him, as he used to do when Nevada first started out. Then, she and Tully had needed him to actively play producer and keep the show on track.

But tonight, Ira was here for old times' sake. He'd wanted to be on hand for this last go-around. Nevada raised her eyebrows at him in a "How'm I doin'?" expression. He flagged her a big thumbs-up.

She continued, "I want you all to know that I haven't made the decision to leave lightly. Changes at the station have forced me to reevaluate my position here. I really believe that, for me, this is the best choice. I've had a great time at KLIV, developing this show, talking to all of you—helping you a little, I hope. Hey, it's been just grand. And what I'll miss the most is each and every one of you. Whether you've ever called in or not. I know you're out there. And I've had a ball...."

She looked at Tully and Ira again. Tully was taking calls. Ira looked down at the row of lights, then back up at her with a roll of his eyes; they were coming in fast and furious.

Nevada turned to the computer screen where Tully posted the calls. Already, every line was on hold.

"I see you all want to talk," she said, smiling. "And so do I. Let's do it." She punched in line one. "Mary Contrary, what's up?"

After that, it was two and a half hours—minus commercial breaks—of irate listeners.

They told her she *couldn't* leave. They begged to know why. They wanted details of where she would go next, and when she would be on the air again.

And would the show be the same? Would it still be live? Would they be able to call in like they could now? Was she going off to do some TV talk show or something, like everyone else in the country was doing lately?

Nevada fielded the questions as best she could. She couldn't say much—and she didn't have much to tell them, anyway. She listened and she reassured and she even managed to get one or two of the callers to recap his or her own major issues and talk about the ways they'd been working on them.

Then, half an hour before the end, "Fred" called.

Line 5—Fred. Ginger dumped him, because of your advice. It's worked out great. He wants to say thanks.

When those words came up on the screen, Nevada was saying goodbye to Hildegard on line three. Hildegard, normally a very tough lady, was actually in tears.

"You have saved me, Nevada. Time after time." Hildegard paused to sniffle and sob. "When things get rough out there. When I know I'm going to do something pitiful, like giggle when a man tells me I'm cute, or say yes when I really want to shout no, I think to myself, 'What would Nevada do in this situation?' And you know what?"

All Nevada had to say at that point was, "No, what?" But she was too busy staring at the word "Fred" on that computer screen.

"Nevada? Are you there?" Hildegard sobbed again, pitifully.

"Of course. Yes. Right here."

"Do you know what?"

"No, what?"

"I just… I feel better, that's all, just by thinking of you. And the minute I do that, I can always figure out what to do."

Nevada thanked Hildegard and wished her well.

And then they took a break. As Roy Orbison sang "The Only One," Nevada sank back in her chair and tried not to wonder if "Fred" was still waiting there, on line five.

The break seemed interminable. But at last Tully muttered in her ear, "Ten seconds, Nevada."

She looked up as Tully counted it down.

And then she was back on, with all six lines full. She could choose any one of them....

"Hello, everybody. We're back for our final half-hour together on your 'Honeymoon Hotline.'"

Her hand hovered over the line of little buttons. "I'm saying goodbye tonight. This is my last show, for those of you tuning in late. And I want to talk to as many of you as I possibly can."

She shouldn't, she knew it. But her heart was beating like a trip-hammer.

"Right now, we have..."

She couldn't stop herself. She just had to know if the call she'd waited two weeks for—the call she swore she didn't want to get—had come through at last.

She punched in line five. "Fred, is that right?"

"Hello, Nevada."

Something shot through her at the sound of his voice. It might have been joy. Or relief.

But whatever it was, she refused to examine it.

He shouldn't have called. But he had....

She shouldn't be talking to him. But she was....

"Nevada?" he asked. There was such teasing humor in the single word. "You still with me?"

"Yes," she said, a little breathless. "Hello, Fred."

"I can't believe you're leaving," he said. The words seemed to have a thousand meanings.

And her usually glib tongue felt like a slab of wood in her mouth. "Well, I am."

"You all right, gorgeous?" Tully's voice came in her other ear.

She looked through the glass at him and Ira. They gazed back at her with concerned expressions. They knew her too well. And they could see something wasn't right. She gave them a double thumbs-up.

"Fred" spoke again. "Do you know who I am? This is my first actual call to your show."

Nevada drew herself up. "Of course, I remember. Your fiancée, Ginger, inspired a lively discussion centering around the two of you, just three weeks ago." Had it really only been three weeks since Virginia called in? To Nevada, it seemed like half a lifetime had passed.

"Ginger dumped me," "Fred" said, as if Nevada didn't already know.

But then, her audience *didn't* know. So Nevada played along with him. "And how are you taking it?"

"Being dumped?"

"Is that how you feel—dumped?"

He gave that some thought. "No. I feel pretty good, to be honest."

"You do?"

"Yeah. I feel great. I...got a hold of a tape of that show. The one where Ginger called in."

"And?"

"I played it. Several times."

"For those who didn't tune in that evening, Ginger called because she and Fred were getting married very soon and—"

"It would have been tomorrow, if we'd gone through with it. Can you believe it?"

"No, I can't, Fred. But thanks for filling me in."

"You're welcome."

"Where was I?"

"Ginger said she didn't love me and I didn't love her and we were getting married in three weeks. And then, after just about everyone in Phoenix called to tell her I was an alpha-male idiot who would never learn to treat her as the equal she really was, Ginger decided not to marry me after all."

"And she stuck by that decision?"

"Right. She left the country."

"No kidding?"

"No kidding. But I'm still here. And I've been listening to your show every night it's been on since then."

A warm glow was lighting her up inside. A ridiculous warm glow. "You have?"

"I love your show, Nevada."

"You do?"

"There's nothing like it on the air."

"Thank you."

In her ear, Tully made a choking sound. Nevada looked at him and Ira. Simultaneously, they crossed their eyes at her, meaning, "Where are you taking this?" She gave them a "Wait and see" signal, by patting the air with a hand.

Of course, she had no idea where she was going. But they didn't have to know that. It was her last night, for heaven's sake. What would they do, *fire her* if one of her calls rambled a little?

This was just so...magical. And fun. And somehow *safe*. To be talking to Chase who pretended to be Fred on her last night on KLIV.

In the engineer's booth, both Tully and Ira made "Pick up the pace" hand signals.

Nevada simply swiveled her chair so she looked away from them, at the far wall.

"They're fools to let you go," said "Fred."

"They are?" She spoke softly into her remote mike. That warm glow that had started a few minutes ago seemed to have spread to every inch of her body.

"Is this what you want, Nevada?"

"You mean to leave the station?"

"Yes."

"I think it's for the best."

"Meaning you're not at liberty to say."

"Yes."

"Come on, gorgeous," Tully warned in her ear. "Bring it on back around."

Grudgingly, Nevada said, "Tell me more about Ginger, Fred."

He sighed. "All right. If that's how we have to play it."

"That's right."

"I'm glad Ginger dumped me."

"You are?"

"She wasn't the woman for me. I know that now."

"You do?"

"Nevada, I really have been listening."

"You have?"

"Every night. Without fail. I'm trying my darnedest to figure out where I've gone wrong in my relationships with women."

"And what have you learned, Fred?"

"Nevada, sometimes I'm a little relentless, when I want something. A little . . . heavy-handed."

"All right. I can believe that."

"I'm trying to develop a lighter touch about things."

"And how are you doing with that?"

"Better, Nevada. Much better, I think."

"And what else?"

"Well, I like to be the boss, I honestly do. But I think I'm going to have to learn to follow, now and then. It's not going to be easy. I like to be the boss for a reason— I'm good at it."

"I'm sure you are."

"But sacrifices have to be made—if I ever want a woman who's my equal. And I do want that woman, Nevada. Do you understand?"

A little shiver started at the base of her spine and slithered its way up until it raised the tiny hairs on the back of her neck.

"Nevada?" he prompted silkily.

"Yes," she replied. "Yes, Fred. I heard what you said."

"That's why you can't quit. Because I need you to keep me...on the right track. Without you to listen to, I could be in trouble all over again."

"Sorry. The decision's been made."

Nevada turned her chair enough to glance at the booth. Ira and Tully looked more relaxed now. The call from "Fred" had moved in a direction they could understand. Ira caught her eye and made the signal that she should wrap it up, but not because he didn't know what she was up to. The call had simply run its course.

She knew Ira was right. The time had come to move along.

"Listen, Fred..."

"Gotta go, huh?"

"I'm glad to hear that things are working out for you."

"Every day's an adventure, I'll say that much."

She thanked him for calling. He said the pleasure was all his.

And then she went on to the next line.

"And now we have Linda Lacklove. Hello, Linda. How are you?"

"I'm in shock, that's how I am. This can't be happening. And just when I was starting to think I might get my life together, too. I've been doing the work, I really have. Last Friday night, I actually had a date with a nice guy. We went to dinner and a show and I didn't even sleep with him."

"Did you have a good time?"

"It was bearable. Not exciting, but I got through it. I kept thinking I'd learn to really enjoy evenings like that. With your help."

"You're doing just fine, Linda. You'll continue to do fine."

"No, I will not. I'll... I'll end up running out and begging some loser to make me his wife for a night. You know I will. I just can't make it without you, Nevada. Tell me it isn't true...."

In the end, Nevada had to ask Linda Lacklove to stay on the line for a referral to a good psychiatrist. Then they cut away for another series of commercials.

After that, the remaining fifteen minutes went off just fine. And when it was over, the receptionist out front paged her to say she had some fans who'd shown up outside.

She went through the front doors, where she signed a few autographs and repeated how much she would miss them all. After a half hour or so of listening to them tell her how she couldn't leave, the fans dispersed.

When the receptionist buzzed her back inside, Tully was waiting for her. He lured her to one of the meeting rooms. There, a few of the office people, and Del Franco, the general manager, were waiting with a cake and champagne.

They all toasted her and wished her well, and she found she couldn't be mad at Del, although he still wouldn't be straight with her when she got him off to the side for a moment and tried to find out just what all this "new directions" talk amounted to.

"Listen up, troops." Ira raised his plastic glass in a salute. "Here's to Nevada. We're fools to let her go."

"To Nevada," the others repeated with quite a bit of feeling, and they all drank.

Nevada left KLIV for the last time at a little after nine. Under her left arm, she carried a box containing a few personal belongings that she'd dug out of the desk she'd rarely used. In her right hand she held a potted African violet, which had belonged to one of the secretaries and which Nevada had often admired.

She pressed her hip against the metal bar that opened the rear exit, slid out into the hot June night, and waited for the door to swing shut and lock behind her. Then she turned for her car, which she'd parked in its usual space, not far from the door.

Three steps later she saw that Chase McQuaid was waiting for her, leaning up against the building, his arms crossed over his chest.

Chapter Six

He pushed himself away from the wall as she approached him. "All right. What the hell's going on? You love that damn job of yours. Why are you leaving?"

She stood there, with her half-full box of unused office equipment and her African violet, staring into his eyes that looked more green than brown in the halogen parking-lot lights. "How long have you been waiting here?"

"About an hour and a half."

For some ridiculous reason, she was moved. "You . . . called my show."

"Yeah." The word was soft.

"It's been two weeks."

"Two weeks tonight."

"I thought you'd given up."

"On you?"

"Yes."

His lips formed their almost-smile. "I gave up once. It didn't work. This time, I was giving you some space."

"Gee, thanks."

"Isn't that what women want these days? Some space?"

"Don't ask me. I'm too...ambivalent lately."

He shook his head. She watched the hot desert wind ruffle his hair a little. "You're a problematic woman, Nevada."

She didn't argue with that. She would either end up lying like crazy—or conceding the point. So instead, she shifted the box under her left arm enough that she could beep off her car alarm with the device she already held in her hand. Then she fumbled with her keys.

He took pity on her. "Here. Give me the box and the plant." She handed them over, then he followed her to the trunk, where she stuck her key in the lock. "I'm hungry," he said as he waited for her to open the trunk. "Let's go get something to eat."

She lifted the lid. "Chase, I just want to go home."

"Fine." He put the box in the trunk for her.

"I'll take the violet."

He gave it back to her, then gestured toward the edge of the lot. "My car's over there. I'll follow you."

Nevada knew very well that she should tell him no. She shut the trunk lid and heard herself say, "I suppose I could throw a couple of sandwiches together."

At her place, Nevada put her violet in the kitchen window and began assembling what she would need to make turkey-and-cheese sandwiches. Chase brought in a bottle of vodka, along with the box from her trunk. Nevada eyed the bottle.

"I picked it up before I staked out the parking lot at KLIV," he explained.

"Strange things happen when I drink vodka with you." It had been **vod**ka that they had drunk that night in

Winslow—not that she should be referring, even obliquely, to that night now.

He looked at her levelly—a look that stole her breath. "In Winslow, we drank cheap vodka."

She kept her voice cool and offhand. "As if that explains anything."

He chuckled. "This vodka isn't cheap. Quality makes all the difference."

"So, what are you saying? If I have a drink with you tonight, nothing . . . out of the ordinary will happen?"

"No, I'm not saying that. I'm not saying that at all." He turned and began opening her cupboards, looking for glasses.

"Well, then, what?"

"I'm saying, if something strange *does* happen, at least we won't have headaches in the morning."

"Well." The word was heavily weighted with irony. "That's a load off my mind."

"I figured it would be. Where are the damn glasses?"

"In there." With the knife she was using to spread the mayonnaise, she pointed at the cupboard he sought.

He brought down two rocks glasses, then held one up, a question in his eyes.

Was it more than a drink he offered? Probably. She hesitated, knowing the answer she *should* give—and yet, tonight, wanting nothing so much as to give him the answer she shouldn't.

"Well?"

She shook her head.

With a rueful shrug of wide shoulders, he started to put the glass back in the cupboard.

"Wait . . ."

He lifted a brow at her.

"All right. Over ice, please."

He didn't leer. He didn't even smile. He simply turned and carried both glasses to the refrigerator, where he dropped three ice cubes in each one. After that, he returned to the counter and poured the drinks.

Nevada finished making the sandwiches. Chase cleaned up after her as she worked—which surprised her. He'd always seemed such a big-time guy. A major mover and shaker. Someone who would consider straightening up the kitchen as utterly beneath him. But he seemed perfectly at home with screwing the lid on the mayonnaise jar, and sticking the deli-sliced turkey back into the meat drawer.

When he picked up the sponge to wipe up the bread crumbs, Nevada found herself watching his hands. They were strong, tanned hands. The little hairs on the backs of them were silky looking, bleached golden by the desert sun.

Another memory of that night in Winslow came sneaking into her mind. After the first time he'd made love to her, he'd rested his hand on her stomach. She'd looked down at it, and thought how very tanned it was against her own paleness. He'd seen where she was looking. And his strong, brown hand had slid upward, to cup her breast—a caress that was at once cradling and possessive. . . .

On the counter, Chase's hand had gone still. She looked up to meet his eyes.

"What?" he asked.

"Nothing," she lied. "Let's go out in back and sit by the pool. I like it outside this time of night." She grabbed their sandwiches and a bag of tortilla chips and headed for the back door. He followed with the drinks.

The pool took up most of the small backyard, but there was room for two padded loungers, a few chairs and a round glass-topped table. Tully had come over one day and hooked up outside speakers for her, so as soon as she'd put the food down on the table, Nevada excused herself to go inside and put on a little soft music.

Of course, as soon as she put the music on, she wondered if Chase would think she was trying to set some kind of seductive mood or something. She almost turned the music off, but then felt silly for making a big deal of it in her own mind.

She went back outside to join him, pausing in the kitchen to decide whether or not to switch on the light by the back door. She didn't do it. The pool lights created a soft glow, and she'd left the kitchen light on. It shone out the window, golden and bright.

Chase had already made himself comfortable in one of the loungers. He was munching chips and making short work of his sandwich. Nevada joined him, picking up her plate and stretching out in the other lounger parallel with his, her feet in front of her and the table at her side between them.

"So." He picked up his drink and sipped. "You haven't told me yet why you're leaving KLIV."

She sighed. "Do we have to talk about that? It's such a gorgeous night."

And it was. A half moon hung, pale and soft and silvery, high up in the sky. Close to the earth, the city lights bleached the night. But up there with the moon, it was ebony velvet, and the stars, pinpricks of glittering brightness in the black.

"The night will still be gorgeous," he said, "even after you tell me what's going on."

She sipped from her own drink, found it dry and astringent, yet silky as it slid down her throat. "I don't really know what's going on, to tell you the truth."

"On your show you mentioned changes at the station."

"Yes. Or so Ira Bendicks—he's the program director—told me. I had asked for a raise. Ira pretty much promised it to me. Then, two weeks ago come Monday, Ira called me into his office and told me my raise was denied and they were phasing out my show. Some changes in 'direction.' From the top, evidently. I decided not to hang around to be phased out, and gave my notice right then.''

''What 'direction' are we talking about, here?''

''Ira said they're going more toward news and politics.''

''I see.''

She looked at him across the glass table. His expression was puzzling. ''What is it?'' She canted sideways in the lounger, leaning a little closer to him. ''What do you know?''

''I can probably get your job back, and your raise. If you want it.''

For a moment, she just gaped at him, her sandwich forgotten in her lap. Then she commanded, ''Explain.''

And he did. ''Grant Frasier, Virginia's father, is a major shareholder in KLIV. He's also on the board of directors, from what I understand. And he's good friends with the owner, Bud Traverse.''

''You're saying Grant Frasier has enough clout to—''

''Turn things upside down at KLIV? Yes. *If* he wanted to put some effort into it. Apparently, you made him mad enough that he did.''

''But that's crazy. I didn't do anything to him.''

Chase was giving her one of those patient looks of his. ''Nevada, the way Grant looks at it, Virginia and I would be getting married tomorrow if it wasn't for you.''

''That's not fair. Virginia made her own decision.''

''We're not talking about what actually happened, Nevada. We're talking about the way Grant *sees* what happened.''

Nevada tried to absorb all this. ''How do you know about what Grant Frasier thinks?''

''He told me. In no uncertain terms, while he was trying to convince me that I should give Virginia another chance. He's the one who provided that tape I had of the show. Grant thought Virginia and I were the perfect couple. In fact, he introduced us. And he created a lot of opportunities for Virginia and me to get to know each other. Everything was working out just fine, as far as Grant saw it—''

''Until Virginia called 'Honeymoon Hotline.' ''

''Right. And he never liked your show, anyway.''

''Well, that's nice to hear.''

He was grinning. ''You can take it.''

''Right. I'm used to abuse.''

''It's a question of taste.''

''You're making it worse, McQuaid.''

He didn't look contrite in the least, but he did clarify even further: ''All along, from what I've heard, Grant's wanted the station to go to the news-and-information format you just mentioned. I think, when Virginia threw me over after talking to *you*, Grant decided to put some energy into getting the format changed. He went to work on old Bud. And that's why you didn't get your raise.'' Chase took the last bite of his sandwich and set his empty plate on the table between them. ''So. Do you want your job back—*with* that raise?''

''You really could . . . *fix* it?''

He laughed then. ''You make me sound like some wise guy.''

''Well, but could you?''

''If Grant's the problem—and I'm sure he is from what you've told me—then, yes. Grant and I have a lot of things in the works together. He wants to get along with me. Probably *more* than he wants to get even with you.''

''Well. That's . . . encouraging.''

''Do you want me to talk to him?''

She didn't even have to think about it. ''No, thanks.''

He frowned at her. ''Nevada, I'd be glad to do it. It's not a big deal.''

"Yes, it is. I said, no thanks. I'll find another job, don't worry."

"That's not the point."

"I beg to differ. It is very much the point. If I can't keep my job on my own, I don't want it."

Now he was looking even more patient than before. "Nevada, this is the way things work—when people have clout, they use it. Grant used his clout to get things his way. End of story—unless you've got clout, too. Which you do."

"Meaning you?"

"Yeah. In this case, meaning me."

"And then I'd owe you."

"No. You'd owe me nothing."

"You can say that. You can even mean it. But it's how I would _feel_ that matters. And I'd feel that I owed you."

"So, don't feel it."

She glanced up at the moon. "Is that just like a man, or what? 'Don't feel it,' he says."

He rattled the ice cubes in his glass. "Since you're down to talking to the moon, I guess I'll back off. For now."

"Thank you."

"Refill?"

"No, I'm fine."

He got up and went in the house. She picked up the second half of her sandwich, took a bite, and decided she'd had enough. So she left it on the table, sat back with her drink and enjoyed the soft music she'd chosen.

About three bars later, the music stopped.

And fifteen seconds after that, Willie Nelson began, "If you had not fallen, I would not have found you...."

Nevada sighed and set down her drink. Then she leaned back, closed her eyes and waited to hear the sound of the kitchen door closing.

The sound came—a soft, very definite _click_.

She felt Chase's approach. And then she heard the small *clink* as he set his fresh drink on the table beside her.

She opened her eyes and looked at him.

He held out his hand.

She almost spoke.

But he put a finger to his lips, and she understood. She and Chase were always using words on each other: words as weapons, words as play, words as a way to dance around each other without getting too close.

Maybe, right now, they could get along without any words at all.

He was looking at her the way he'd looked at her two weeks ago at Ocotillo Slim's—so earnestly and uncompromisingly. With such tenderness. And hope . . .

At that moment, there really was nothing else to do but to dance with him.

She laid her hand in his, swung her legs to the side of the lounger and rose to stand before him. His arms went around her. And the song seemed to fill up the night, soft and low—seductive in that sincere way that only a Willie Nelson song can be.

Slowly, they danced around the pool. Nevada felt his warmth. And the broadness and strength of him, so close, caressing all along the front of her.

And she thought again of that night two weeks ago, when they had danced together.

And then, although she shouldn't have, she thought further back than that.

To the night in Winslow that had started it all. They'd danced to this song then. And later, much later, deep in the night, they'd danced in another way, that most intimate of ways.

That certain moment crept into her mind again, the way it had in the kitchen; that moment after the first time they'd made love. His hand, on her belly at first, then moving up to cup her breast. And his lips nuzzling her tangled hair away from her ear.

He had whispered to her....

"Anything else I ought to know?"

His voice was teasing.

But she was feeling very fragile right then. Much too fragile to take any teasing. She stiffened and tried to pull away.

He didn't allow that. His hand slipped up to close over her shoulder. "Hey, easy. It's all right. You just...surprised the hell out of me, that's all."

It had been such a crazy night. She couldn't quite take it all in. They had driven for hours through the desert, bickering most of the way. And then, when they'd reached Winslow at last, they had seen what fools they'd been: Billy didn't look suicidal in the least. And he and Maud had no time for Chase and Nevada. They were too wrapped up in each other.

Chase said he wasn't getting in her car again and submitting himself to another four hours of her mouth and her driving until he'd had a good, stiff drink. So they'd stayed for a drink, which became two drinks.

And then they'd danced. Together. He had teased her that at least she knew how to follow on a dance floor, if nowhere else.

The hours had melted away. And later, there had been one of those sudden, vicious desert rainstorms. They'd stood out in it, and gotten drenched to the skin.

And Chase had kissed her.

And after that kiss, they'd come here, to this motel room with the orange spread on the bed and the single print on the wall—of an adobe shack with a saguaro beside the door.

They had made love.

And now, unwelcome tears were pooling in her eyes. She kept her head turned away from him and blinked furiously, not wanting him to see.

"Nevada . . ." His voice was gentle, coaxing.

She tried for bravado. "The last woman in the world you would have pegged for a . . . virgin. Right?"

"Hey . . ."

"A thirty-six-year-old virgin. Bet you thought there weren't any of those left."

"Stop it."

She blinked one more time, then made herself face him. She felt kind of hazy, from the vodka. And she felt scared, of what she'd just done with him. And she felt . . . a little wild, too.

"I liked it," she heard herself whisper, the words barely making a sound.

But he heard them. "So did I." The hideous light fixture near her side of the bed—an orange plastic ball hung from the ceiling by an iron chain—showed her his eyes. They looked almost brown right then; no green in them at all. Brown and very deep.

His face was so close that their noses almost touched. She thought that she liked the way he smelled. Like . . . geraniums. Not the flowers, of course, which didn't really have a smell. But like the plant itself. Green and woody and a little bit musky.

She put her lips on his neck, tasted him with her tongue: salt and sweet. Then she whispered, "I always wondered if I'd like it."

He chuckled—a pleasant rumbling sound. "You must not have wondered too hard. Since you never did it. Until now."

She pulled back enough that she could look at him. "It all seemed too dangerous, when I was young. And then I got older. And it just got . . . unlikely. I'm so . . ."

"Independent?" He traced the shape of her collarbone, leaving pleasant little tingles, tiny afterimpressions of feeling, behind.

"Uh-hmm. It's always seemed like it would only...complicate things. But now, since I've been doing 'Honeymoon Hotline,' it *has* bothered me a little."

His hand slid downward. She shivered in response.

"Why has it bothered you?" He touched her, in that private place.

She gasped, then explained in a voice that sounded like a purr to her own ears: "Well, an expert on love—who's never made love herself? Is that fair?"

He started kissing her shoulder and his hand went on with its play down below. "Well, now you don't have to worry about that anymore, do you?"

She moved, in a slow rhythm against his hand. His lips went roving. Up over the swell of her breast to her nipple that was already hard and aching for him to...

His mouth closed over her breast. She gasped again. He sucked, gently, then harder. She lifted herself up to him.

And then she tangled her fingers in his hair. She pulled his head up.

He looked at her, his eyes greener than before, a little dazed, hungry. "What?" Down below, his hand left off tormenting her. "Did I...hurt you?"

"No. It's not that."

"I want you. Again."

She could feel the proof of that, against her thigh. And she wanted him, too. But bewilderment was washing over her in waves. She felt that she was floating—in a sea of confusion. And burned by a sun called desire.

"Chase? What are we doing? Don't we despise each other?"

He went very still in her arms and his gaze didn't waver. "No. It's just strong, that's all. Too strong. Neither of us likes that. We both like to be . . . on top. So we never got along."

"Until tonight."

He smiled at her then, slowly. "Until tonight."

"What will happen in the morning?"

He considered the question, then shrugged. "Worry about the morning when it gets here."

"But I don't—" The sentence stopped on a sharp hitch of breath as he shifted his body, so that he lay full-length upon her, his hard legs between her soft ones, and that hungry part of him pressed at the vulnerable juncture of her thighs.

"I like the way you fit against me." He slid inside. She gasped again. "Yeah . . ." He sighed. And then he started to move. . . .

The song ended.

They had danced to the far side of the pool, near the back fence. They stood there, swaying without moving their feet, as the next song began. Nevada's head rested on Chase's shoulder.

He took her chin, guided her face up, so he could look into her eyes. "We weren't careful, that night."

She knew then that he'd been remembering, too. "No. It was a crazy night. *We* were crazy."

"And irresponsible."

"Yes. Yes, we were."

"I thought, for a few months, that maybe you'd call me and tell me you were pregnant."

"No."

"No, what?"

"No, I didn't get pregnant."

His hand was cupping her chin, his palm against her throat. "I want a kiss."

"Yes," she said.

His hand slipped around to caress her nape under the wild fall of her hair as his mouth gently closed over hers. His lips covered hers as if he'd been made to kiss her.

That was the thing that scared her, the thing that moved her. That it was so natural. So right. To have his mouth against hers.

They stood, on the edge of the pool, wrapped in the hot, seductive embrace of the desert night, kissing for the longest time. Lazily, now and then, Chase would lift his head and smile at her, then lower it again, his mouth slanted the other way, to kiss her some more. His tongue played with hers, teasing and coaxing at first, then growing more bold, more like the man himself, exploring and taunting, getting to know her all over again.

Nevada pressed herself to him, clutching his hard shoulders. And she felt how he wanted her, as well as the answering liquid heat down inside her own body.

The pool lights in the water not far from their shoes played upward, the gentle glow spilling over them as it passed by on its way toward the night sky. The water rippled a little and so did the light, so that once when Nevada opened her eyes she felt that they were kissing underwater. She could see waves moving on his shoulder, and on her hand that clutched that shoulder.

At last, when she'd begun to hope they might simply keep on kissing, right there by the pool, forever and ever, he broke the kiss just enough that he could whisper against her lips, "Tonight?"

She didn't answer, only stood a little taller, trying to capture his mouth again.

"No." He pulled back a fraction more. His hands clasped her waist firmly. "Answer me."

"Oh, Chase..."

He looked at her for a long moment. His eyes, in the watery wavery light from below, were exactly hazel right then; both green and brown equally.

Nevada dropped back on her heels, feeling a little foolish. "What? Why are you looking at me like that?"

"I don't think I want an ambivalent woman in my arms tonight."

A tart remark rose to her lips. She held it back, settling for a meaningless, "I see."

He chuckled, the sound warm and good-humored. "You could beg."

"Excuse me?"

"Something like, 'Make love with me, Chase. Carry me off to bed and drive me crazy until the morning comes.' That might convince me that ambivalence won't be a problem."

She pursed her lips, since he wouldn't kiss them. "I'm not going to say that."

"I know." He bent close again—but only to kiss the tip of her nose. Then he put her away from him and sauntered around the pool and back to the table where his drink was waiting.

She hovered where he'd left her for a moment, feeling foolish. And bereft.

And then, dragging her feet a little, she went to join him. He watched her approach, setting down the drink as she reached his side.

They looked at each other, then he asked, "Are you going to be all right?"

She studied his face. It was a fine-looking face, square-jawed with a good, strong nose, straight brows and a sensual mouth. He lifted one of those straight brows, since she hadn't answered him.

She did answer. "I'm fine. I'm...glad you...staked out the parking lot, waiting for me. Tonight would have been grim. But you made it good. Thank you, Chase."

"*De nada*. I'll see myself out."

* * *

After she'd carried the chips, plates and glasses inside and turned off the stereo, Nevada took a long shower. The water felt good, running down her body.

But not as good as Chase's touch would have felt.

She wasn't really sure why she hadn't stopped him from leaving. She did want him. And at some point that evening she had accepted the fact that their making love again was more a question of *when* than of *if*.

But he'd been right. She remained ambivalent about what was happening between them. Making love again would be such a major step. And she just wasn't ready to take that step yet.

After their one night together, it hadn't been easy to put him from her mind. But slowly, with great effort, she'd managed it. By the time she'd been introduced to his fiancée a month ago, she'd even succeeded in convincing herself that she was over him for good.

That, evidently, had been a delusion. She wasn't over him, as he had so relentlessly and effectively set out to prove to her. Yet, as long as they didn't make love again, it seemed possible to hold on to the frail belief that she could stop this thing any time she chose to.

Yes, there lay the basis of her fear: that when she let him into her bed again, some major bridge would have been crossed. She would no longer be able to tell herself that she could be free of him just by walking away.

Nevada stepped from the shower, dried herself off and slathered lotion on her legs and arms. Then she pulled on the T-shirt and bikini pants she liked to sleep in, brushed her teeth and went to bed.

She tossed and turned for a while, thinking of Chase, thinking of her beloved "Honeymoon Hotline" that was lost to her now. But at last, she felt herself settling in, relaxing, drifting toward sleep.

Her last waking thought came with a resigned little sigh: she would probably end up dreaming of Chase.

But she didn't dream of Chase. Or if she did, that wasn't the dream she remembered when she awoke.

The dream she remembered was of her childhood. Of her mother's house in Kenosha, Wisconsin, where she'd lived until the age of eight, when her mother had died and her father had sold everything and taken his daughters into his wanderer's life with him.

The house had been a big wooden house, with a wide front porch and pillars and dormer windows upstairs. There had been enough rooms that each of the sisters—Nevada, Faith and Evangeline—had her own bedroom.

Most of the time, it had been a house of women. Gideon was always off, gone, away somewhere. And the house smelled good, of orange-and-clove sachet and freshly baked bread. The house was truly her mother's house, left to Mary Keyes Jones by Grandma Keyes. And Mary had money of her own from the Keyes family, too. Nevada knew this because sometimes, when he came home, her father would yell at her mother to give him some of that money she had squirreled away. He swore he could double it in six months. But her mother wouldn't do that. And Gideon would storm out of the house and not come back for weeks—which was just fine with Nevada. Secretly, Nevada didn't care if he never came back.

In front of the porch, in summer, a hydrangea bloomed, huge clusters of pale purple flowers. Nevada had loved that hydrangea. That hydrangea seemed a mirror of her life, full and beautiful and softly violet in color—except when her father was home.

Once, when he was home, he had gotten drunk and fallen into the hydrangea. The pale violet petals had scattered everywhere and the green stalks had snapped.

That was what Nevada dreamed: of that hydrangea, so full and heavy with blooms at the height of summer. And of her father, tumbling into it in slow motion, smashing it, the petals flying, the big green leaves crushed and ruined.

And she dreamed her mother's death, just as it had happened. Late in the night.

It had started with one of their arguments: her father's raised voice, talking about the money again; her mother's hushed, intense one. And then her mother had come out of their bedroom, her bare feet *shush*ing on the rug of the landing.

Her father came out of the bedroom, too, right behind her. "Where the hell do you think you're going?"

"To the spare room downstairs."

"Get back here."

"No, Gideon. And keep your voice down. You'll wake the girls." Mary's feet went *shush*ing on toward the stairs.

That was when Nevada had opened her door just a crack and peeked out of her room. She saw her mother rushing by in her pretty floor-length violet-colored robe. And then her father, pounding after her. "I said, get back here—"

He caught her at the top of the stairs, grabbed her arm.

"Let me go!" she whispered, low and so very angry.

Nevada saw it all. Her mother's feet caught on the hem of her robe; her mother jerked away from her father—forever.

Down she went, tumbling, over and over, knocking and bouncing against the wall and the stairs.

Her father screamed, but it wasn't really a scream. His voice came out a terrible, torn whisper. "Mary... No, Mary..."

And then there was no more knocking and bouncing. Nevada pulled open her door and tiptoed out onto the landing.

"Mary! God, Mary!" Her father ran down the stairs.

Nevada stopped at the top step and looked down, at her mother lying there, absolutely still, her violet robe spread out around her in a fan, her head turned to such a funny angle. And her father, bent over her, rocking on his knees, begging, "No, Mary. Come back. I love you. You're the only thing I've ever loved. Oh, Mary, I'm sorry...."

And the robe turned to flower petals, a thousand violet blooms, spilling across the floor. Her mother's lifeless body disappeared. And her father sat in the middle of all those petals, rocking, crying silently, his shoulders shaking.

And then he looked up. And he was old—an old, sick man. He grinned up at Nevada, his cracked lips parting to reveal crooked, yellowed teeth.

"Not much longer," he whispered in a voice that sounded like corn husks rubbing together. "Not much longer now..."

Nevada was awake before dawn. She made coffee and drank more than she should have, sitting at her kitchen table, staring at the African violet on the windowsill.

She made herself wait until eight to call Evie.

"You ready for a visitor?" she asked.

"You're coming right away, then?" Evie sounded glad, which created an answering feeling of warmth inside Nevada.

Yes, a trip to North Magdalene was just what she needed....

"I'll leave this morning," Nevada said. "As soon as I can get packed."

"Will you fly or—"

"Please." Nevada hated to fly.

And Evie knew it. "I know you hate flying, but it's such a long drive. You flew here for my wedding and survived."

"Only because I had no other choice. I was strapped for time. You know that."

Evie sighed. "Don't push yourself too hard. Stay safe."

"I'll check into a motel if my eyelids start drooping."

"You'd better."

"And I'll see you before noon tomorrow, at the latest."

"Great."

Nevada had meant to say goodbye then, but somehow, one last question slipped out. "Any more news, on Gideon?"

"No, we're still more or less on standby here. We call the hospital every day or two, just to check on him. And they've promised to call us, if he takes a turn for the worse." Evie paused, then spoke reassuringly. "Look, Nevada. I understand how you feel. And if we get that call while you're here, no one would expect you to go along with us if you didn't want to."

"I know that."

"So there's no problem, then?"

"No. I just wondered . . . how he was."

"The same." Evie's voice was so gentle.

There was nothing more to say then. Nevada told her sister that she loved her and got off the line.

As quickly as she could, she packed enough clothes for a two-week stay in North Magdalene. By nine o'clock, her two suitcases were locked up and ready to go.

She had a great feeling of urgency to get in the car and away—one that she absolutely refused to examine. She told herself it was natural. She had a long drive ahead of her and she wanted to get on the road.

She called Mr. Alphonse next door and asked him if he would look after her house for a while. He came right over and she gave him coffee and made out a list of things he would need to do—from watering the African violet to putting the chemicals in the pool to setting out the garbage when he set out his own. He wished her well before he trundled back across the lawn to his own house, carrying a final cup of coffee, a set of her house keys and the list of duties she'd assigned him.

Nevada went outside and put the padlock on the back gate, then she double-locked the back door and checked all the windows. She set her air conditioner for eighty-two degrees and then left by the front door. She got in her car and backed it from the garage halfway down the driveway, so she could load it from the front patio. She locked up the garage as she had everything else. And then she started packing the car.

She was almost finished; she had her head in the trunk and was trying to wedge her makeup case in so that it wouldn't tip over between her two full-size suitcases and her overnight bag when Chase spoke from behind her.

"On the run again, I see...."

She whirled around, bumping her head on the trunk lid in the process and letting out a small cry of pain.

He stood less than a foot from her, wearing tan slacks and a polo shirt, a white bakery bag in one hand. Not fifteen yards away sat one of his cars, a sleek gray Mercedes. She had no idea how he'd pulled up and gotten out of it without her hearing him.

Her gaze found its way reluctantly to his face. He looked perfectly calm. But his eyes didn't. Right then, they were neither brown nor green. They seemed black.

Black and smoldering with carefully controlled rage.

For several weighted seconds, they regarded each other. Then Nevada couldn't stand the silence.

"I've made some plans for a trip. I have to go."

"What plans?"

She glared at him. "I don't have time right now to—"

"*What* plans?"

The absolute command in his voice had her answering automatically, "I've decided to visit my family. In California."

Chase cast a glance at all the luggage in the open trunk behind her. "It looks like a long visit."

She turned and shut the trunk with more authority than she felt. "Probably, yes. A long visit."

"How long?"

"I'm not sure."

"To the best of my recollection, you failed to mention any trip last night."

She felt totally defensive. And she knew exactly why: because he had her nailed. She was running from him every bit as much as she was running toward the comfort of her family.

"Do I owe it to you, now, to tell you if I'm leaving town?" She cringed at her own words; they betrayed her defensiveness so completely.

He smiled—a cold smile. "It would have been . . . thoughtful of you, if you had."

"Well, I didn't."

"Right. State the obvious for me. That really helps."

Every moment she stood here, she despised herself more. "I have to go." She started to turn.

"Stop."

And she did. She froze where she stood. His eyes bored into her. She felt that they pierced her, right into the heart of her, where she knew herself to be a coward, and dishonest, as well.

Oh, what was happening to her? It seemed her whole world, her whole *idea* of who she was and what she stood for was crumbling to nothing.

"Please, Chase . . ." she began, and then didn't know how to finish. What *was* she trying to say? *Please forgive me? Please let me go . . . ?*

His eyes changed, softened just a little. He shook his head. Then he held up the bakery sack. "I brought some croissants."

"Chase..."

"I thought you could supply the coffee."

"I've had too much coffee already this morning."

"Fine. Just make some for me, then."

"I said, I have to go."

"I won't keep you long, don't worry."

There was another extended, tension-filled silence. And then Nevada turned and led him into the house.

Chapter Seven

Inside, she headed straight for the kitchen. She got half-way there, as far as the dining room, which lay just past the living room. Then Chase caught her hand.

His touch seemed to burn her. She gasped, turned on him, and tried to jerk away.

He didn't let go. They stood by her teakwood dining table. He set the bakery bag on it.

"What?" she demanded, defiant.

"On second thought, you can skip the coffee."

She was wearing a sleeveless tunic over a pair of stretchy leggings. His hand slid slowly up her bare arm, leaving those tingly, shivery sensations behind it. He cupped her chin. His eyes burned into hers, as his touch brought goose bumps to her skin.

Nevada knew that he meant to kiss her. And that she should stop him. But she didn't.

His mouth came down, it covered hers. And he did kiss

her—a long, slow, lazy, all-the-time-in-the-world kiss. He tasted fresh and his skin smelled so good and clean.

And to Nevada, it was as if the kiss last night was merely continuing. Everything else flew away as she kissed him back, lifting her arms to curve around his neck.

After the longest, most exquisite time, he raised his head and looked down at her. His eyes were hazel again, and full of rueful tenderness. "Let me come with you."

Her heart missed a beat as it occurred to her that she wanted him to come with her—almost as much as she wanted to escape him. "Oh, you can't...."

"Why not?"

"I don't know how long I'll be gone. Maybe two weeks, or even more."

"So?"

"So, how can you possibly leave for that long on such short notice?"

"Let me worry about how I'll do it. Just tell me I can come with you."

"But what if... it doesn't work out?"

"Nevada. I can manage to find my way home if it comes to that."

What else, she thought grimly, *could* it come to? She and Chase were a volatile combination. True, of late he'd been infinitely patient with her, but he wasn't a patient man by nature. And she was still sitting on the fence, straddling the line, playing all those *yes-no* games she'd always rebuked her "Honeymoon Hotline" listeners for indulging in. She would drive him up the wall eventually. There would be some kind of major battle. And they would both be the losers.

"Say yes," he prompted.

"Don't you have a mall or two to build?"

"Take me with you."

"It's a very long drive, Chase. To a little town called North Magdalene."

"Never heard of it."

"It's a couple of hours from Reno, in the Sierra foot-hills."

"Take me with you, Nevada." His gaze wasn't quite so tender, and his voice had a thread of steel in it now.

Somehow, the way he was looking at her made all of her reasons why he couldn't possibly come with her seem like nothing but excuses—which, she had to admit, they probably were.

"All right," she heard herself say. "You may come."

He grinned then. "Oh, I'm so grateful."

She shook her head. "This is crazy. You'll be sorry."

"Let me be the judge of that."

She felt breathless. She couldn't think.

He suggested, as she might have guessed he would, "Instead of driving, let's fly."

She shook her head. "I hate flying."

"I know that." The look on his face said he was remembering that infamous drive to Winslow last year. He'd wanted to fly them there, in his Cessna something-or-other. She had flatly refused to do anything but drive.

"I want to take my own car."

"You can rent something when you get there."

"Rent something where? I told you, it's a *very* small town, Chase. There *are* no rental-car places there."

"Come on, a nearby town will have a Hertz office."

"Renting's expensive. Have you forgotten I'm unemployed?"

"Flying would be faster."

"No. I'm driving. You can fly to Sacramento, if you're determined to, and I'll give you directions on how to get to North Magdalene from there."

"That's ridiculous. The whole idea is, we're going together."

"Fine, then. If you really want your own car, we can caravan. That would be all right with me."

''What? Think of all the arguments we'd avoid if I took my own car.''

''Exactly.''

''All right.'' He let out a long, put-upon sigh. ''Have it your way. You always do. We'll take your car.''

Before they left, Nevada called Evie again to ask if it would be all right if she brought a guest.

''Your friend Maud?'' Evie asked brightly. Both she and Faith had met Maud more than once over the years.

''Er, no. Not Maud.''

''Nevada, is something wrong?''

''No. No, of course not.''

''Then who's your guest?''

She said it quickly, to get it over with. ''It's Maud's brother.''

''Maud has a *brother?*''

''Gee, haven't I ever mentioned him?''

''I . . . Not that I recall.'' Evie sounded totally bewildered. ''What's his name?''

''His name's Chase.''

There was a long pause. Then Evie said, ''Nevada. Is this . . . a romance?''

''Oh, Evie . . .''

''Look, if it is . . .''

''Yeah?''

''Well, I just think it's wonderful, that's all.''

Nevada felt her face flaming. Luckily, she'd made the call from the bedroom and Chase was in the kitchen drinking a can of cranberry juice in lieu of coffee and eating one of his croissants. ''I don't know if it's so wonderful,'' she told her sister. ''But the man just will not go away.''

''Is that bad?''

''Oh, Evie. I don't know.''

''Nevada, are you okay?''

Nevada held back a groan. "No, probably not. But I'm on my way. And I'm bringing Chase McQuaid."

Once Chase had finished his juice and Nevada had completed her call, they proceeded to his huge Spanish-style house in Scottsdale, where he parked his car with the rest of the fleet, packed a bag, grabbed a cellular phone and told his housekeeper, Lorelai, that they were on their way to North Magdalene, California. He had Nevada give her Evie's number for emergencies.

When Nevada handed Lorelai the information, the housekeeper looked her up and down. "Hey. Now I remember you. You're that friend of Maud's, right?"

"Yes."

Lorelai spoke to Chase. "There might be hope for this one. She's no baby like that other one. And I can see in her eyes that she's got a quick mind. A woman's got to be quick to keep up with you."

Chase looked pained. "Thank you for sharing, Lorelai."

"Any time," Lorelai muttered, then turned and shuffled away.

Next they headed for the McQuaid building downtown where Chase had some papers to pick up. As she drove, Chase used his phone. He canceled some meetings and penciled in others for later dates. He called a cement contractor and yelled at him for a while, then called someone else and told him what a great job he was doing on the advance advertising for something called Club Paloverde.

By the time they'd made the stop at Chase's office and were on their way out of town, Nevada remarked that a lot of people Chase worked with seemed to be in their offices on Saturday. He cast her a glance, chuckled and said he was calling people where he knew he could reach them—whether that was at home, or at their weekend retreats. Then he punched in the next number and started giving orders again.

They got along great through the early afternoon. But by then, Chase had finished his calls. He suggested that she let him drive.

"I'm doing fine," she told him.

Soon after that, they stopped at Kingman to fill up the car and get something to eat. Chase wanted to find a "decent" restaurant. And Nevada just wanted to grab a fast-food burger and keep moving.

Since she had the wheel, she won. They were out of there by a little after two, munching burgers and fries as the high desert rolled past.

Chase sipped his root beer and wondered aloud if Nevada would ever get over her incredible compulsion to be in control of all situations at all times.

She exercised great restraint and quelled a remark about how it takes one control freak to recognize another. All she said was, "I want to get there."

"You will. But you could also enjoy the trip."

"I'm enjoying the trip." She kept her eyes on the road and popped a french fry in her mouth.

He made a disbelieving sound. "You're running."

She reached for her diet cola, which waited in the little beverage tray slung over the hump between the seats. "Oh, really?" She brought the cola to her mouth and sipped from the straw. "What am I running *from?*"

"Me."

She slid the cola back into its spot in the tray. "Well, I'm doing a lousy job of running from you, considering I'm taking you with me where I'm going."

"You're running," he repeated, infuriatingly smug. "You're afraid to slow down. If you slow down, you'll have to deal with me."

"I *am* dealing with you, right now—and not enjoying it one bit."

"Sometime you'll have to stop," he warned, still so smug she wanted to pop him one. "And I'll be there."

She stifled a groan. "I know that. Oh, boy, do I ever know that."

They drove in silence for a while as they finished their lunch. And after that, Chase stretched out as best he could in the passenger seat and closed his eyes. He slept for well over an hour. Nevada enjoyed the stark scenery, including stunning views of distant mesas, which appeared vibrant orange and streaked with purple—and she also enjoyed the silence.

She cast more than one glance at Chase. She thought he looked very sweet when he slept. He looked almost *soft*—a word she'd never have imagined herself using to describe him. His lashes lay like tiny silk fans against his cheeks. And once he sighed and rubbed his nose and then yawned. He looked so cute, she smiled—and almost hit an armadillo that was lumbering across the highway in front of her. She managed to swerve and miss it, but she said rude things about it under her breath as she rolled on past. An armadillo crazy enough to cross the highway in the hottest part of the afternoon probably shouldn't be allowed to live, anyway; it would only produce crazy offspring like itself to be killed on highways by women who should have been watching the road.

And it *was* hot out there. Thanks to the modern miracle of air-conditioning, they were nice and cool in the car, but she could see the heat waves rippling up from the highway.

"Everything *under control?*" a sardonic voice asked from beside her.

He was awake. Nevada replied in a noncommittal tone, "So far, so good," and wondered grimly how she could ever have thought him cute—and what had possessed her to let him come along with her.

At a few minutes past four, they topped a rise and saw Las Vegas spread out below them. Chase mused aloud about how much fun they could have there if she would only slow down. She stopped long enough to top off the tank and make use of the rest room. Chase called her heartless under his breath.

He suggested again that she let him drive.

Again, she insisted that she was doing just fine.

It was eight-fifteen in the evening, nearing sunset, when she hit the poodle. They'd just filled up again and left a town called Tonopah. The poodle was the same story as the armadillo.

Chase had stopped making snide remarks long enough to take another nap. And she couldn't help sneaking glances at him, thinking how peaceful he looked and hoping she could make it all the way to North Magdalene before she had to stop and sleep. She had a very strong feeling that, if they stopped somewhere to spend the night, they would spend it in each other's arms.

And, in spite of the fact that she found herself perversely contented to have him along, she remained no more ready than she had been last evening to make love with Chase.

But if she could just get him to North Magdalene before the question of sleeping came up, she could see that they slept separately. Evie and Erik had three children, after all. No doubt, they would prefer it if their unmarried guests didn't share a room.

Of course, she could just let Chase drive. But she suspected, with good reason from all his groaning and grumbling the past several hours, that as soon as he got control of the car, he would be headed for the nearest hotel. He would be low-key but determined about the whole thing. He would get them two rooms—with a door between. And in the morning, they would wake up on the same side of that door.

But then she shook her head. Last night, he hadn't pushed her. Why should she believe he would push her now? Maybe the real truth was that she feared what she herself might do, more than she feared a possible seduction by Chase.

She should just stop thinking about it. For whatever twisted reason—and her reasoning had grown quite twisted of late—she intended to do everything in her power to see that she didn't spend a night in a hotel with Chase. And that was that.

And now, she should keep her mind firmly on the road ahead. Because she *did* feel tired. Twilight was a tricky time. And she had to be careful not to let her attention stray from—

That was when she saw it, in her side vision: a flash of dirty white, like a big ball of filthy cotton. It seemed to shoot up from the right shoulder of the highway and bounce against the right-front bumper of the car. She would have thought it was only her imagination, but she did hear a very distinct and dreadful little *thud* right at the moment when the dirty white ball disappeared again.

Luckily, they were nearly alone on the highway right then—very few cars in either direction. She slammed on the brakes and swerved to the side of the road, causing the car to kick up a cloud of dust and make a lot of awful screeching noises.

Chase shot straight up in his seat, swearing. "What the hell! Are you crazy? What's going on?"

The car reached a full stop right about then. "I hit something. Some kind of animal, I think." She leaned on her door to get out, but before she could do that, a semi whooshed past, making the car sway.

Chase reached across and grabbed her door handle, so she couldn't get out. "Do you *want* to die, is that it?"

"Chase. I hit something. A cat or something."

He was shaking his head. "So. Not a very bright cat, obviously. It's better off dead."

Although she had entertained similar thoughts concerning the armadillo that afternoon, she hadn't actually *hit* the armadillo. That made all the difference.

"I have to go back and see," she said in her best don't-mess-with-me tone. "Now, let go of my door."

He didn't move.

"I mean it, Chase. Let go of my door."

He glared at her for another three or four seconds, then he heaved one of those sighs common to men who deal with strong-minded women. "Stay here." He released her door handle and got out on his side.

She sat still for a count of ten, then she knew that staying there just wasn't going to work for her. Two more semis had thundered past since the first one. So she didn't even try to open her own door. She scrambled over the gearshift and across the passenger seat to alight on that side.

A hot wind blew road dust into her face as she ran to catch up with Chase, who strode briskly back the way they'd come, eyeing the shallow ditch beyond the shoulder as he went. The wind and the traffic created enough noise that he didn't hear her until she caught up with him.

"Don't you ever stay where you're put?"

"A thoroughly sexist remark if I ever heard one."

Something whined right then—a pitiful sound. They both heard it and turned to look farther along the ditch.

The dirty white poodle lay, half hidden beneath a big tumbleweed, about thirty feet away. It lifted its head, looked at them, and whined again. The wind caught the tumbleweed and moved it on down the ditch, leaving the small dog in plain sight.

And a sad sight it was, too. The thick, woolly fur, trimmed by some dog groomer not too long ago into a classic "poodle" cut, had turned gray with dirt, and studded with burrs and sticks. It wore a beat-up collar with some kind of glittering stones in it. Someone had tied pink ribbons to its ears, ribbons streaked with dirt now, and drooping forlornly. And blood matted the hair on its right temple, above one soulful little eye: the place where it must have run into Nevada's car.

"Oh, the poor thing..." Nevada stumbled down the side of the ditch, slipping a little because her thin sandals gave no traction, getting dirt between her bare toes.

"Nevada. Wait." Chase came right after her. He caught her arm.

"Let me go, Chase. That dog needs help."

"Wait. Listen."

The poodle whined again.

"Chase, please..."

"Listen. You don't know where that animal's been. It could be diseased. And it's injured. You don't know how it will react if you touch it."

"It's a *poodle,* Chase."

"Nevada, poodles get diseases, too. And they also have teeth."

"I'm going to help it."

"I don't like it at all when you get that look."

"What look?"

"That damned *determined* look."

The poodle whined again, but this time the whine was much closer.

Chase and Nevada glanced down to see the dog standing at their feet, wagging its filthy pouf of a tail and gazing up at them through the gathering gloom as if they were just the folks it had been looking for.

Chapter Eight

Chase insisted on driving when they got back in the car. "If you're taking that damn animal," he said, "then you're the one who's going to be looking after it."

Since she didn't trust him not to toss the little pooch out the window the moment he got a chance, Nevada let him have his way. She sat in the passenger seat, cradling the dog, which curled up in her lap as if it had been sleeping there its whole life. It really was dirty, but Nevada didn't much care. At least she hadn't killed or maimed it when she hit it.

"That animal smells," Chase muttered.

"Drive," she said.

The dog made no objection when Nevada took off the collar. It was pink, like the bedraggled ribbons in the animal's ears. Even Nevada, who knew little of gems, could tell that the stones were just bits of colored glass. She turned the collar over. She saw a name and phone number written there in permanent marker.

She told Chase, "There's a phone number here."

For an answer she received a disgusted-sounding grunt.

"And a name. Babette. She's obviously a girl."

Chase shot her a look, one that clearly said, *As if I care.* "What about a dog license?"

She fingered a broken hook on which the dog's tag had probably hung. "It looks like she might have lost it."

That was when Chase swung a U-turn. Right there in the middle of the highway. Before Nevada could finish shouting in dismay, they were going the other way.

"Are you crazy? What are you doing?"

"Going back to Tonopah."

"But I want to get to North Magdalene."

He cast her another look, this one laden with long-suffering exasperation.

Nevada shut her mouth and said nothing more. He was right. They would find a phone and call the number and reunite Babette with her owner.

The first gas station they reached, he got out and made the call. It took no time at all. In minutes, he returned to the car and sank into the driver's seat.

"Well?"

He pulled his door shut. "The line is no longer in service."

Babette looked up at Nevada, whined and then licked her hand.

Nevada frowned at the red-stained fur over the dog's eye. "She needs medical attention."

Chase leaned over the console and peered at the injury. "There's no swelling to speak of and hardly any blood. The dog is fine. Dirty, but fine."

"But, Chase—"

He refused to listen. "We'll stay here till morning. And then we'll take the dog in."

"You mean to a vet?"

"No, I mean to an animal shelter."

She shook her head. "This dog is not going to any animal shelter."

"Why not?"

"If they don't find her owner, you know what they'll do to her there."

"It's always possible that they'll find her a new home."

Nevada shot him a disbelieving frown. "Not a poodle."

After a moment, he asked, very carefully, "Why not a poodle?"

"Nobody wants poodles these days. They're not a popular breed anymore. People want shepherds and Labs and miniature collies these days."

"Nevada. How do you know this?"

"I read it somewhere."

He leaned his head back on the rest and muttered something crude at the roof of the car. Then he turned to her. "Do you think maybe you're cracking up a little, here?"

"What do you mean?"

"I mean, you're acting very strangely. So obsessed with getting to this town where your family lives that you'd barely stop long enough to fill up the tank. And now this dog."

She pulled a burr from Babette's tail. "What about this dog?"

"You're behaving all out of proportion about it. It makes no sense. You're not exactly an animal lover by nature. You don't even keep a *goldfish,* as far as I remember."

"I like to be able to get up and go when I want to. Pets tie a person down."

"So, why all the concern about this dog?"

She glanced down at Babette, who looked up at her trustingly. "She's defenseless. It's not fair." For some reason, tears were blurring her eyes.

"Hey."

She blinked the tears back and lifted her chin to face him. "My father's dying." She had no idea she would say that until it was already out. "I've ... cut him out of my life. But now he's dying. And it's ... It's on my mind."

Chase's eyes changed; something that looked very much like compassion came into them. "Is that what all this ... erratic behavior is about?"

"I don't know...."

"Why didn't you say something about your father before?"

"I... Oh, I just don't know. I kept hoping I'd stop caring, I guess."

"And *have* you stopped caring?"

"Once, I really thought I had."

"And now?"

She lifted her shoulders in a baffled shrug.

"Why did you cut him from your life?"

She looked out the windshield at the gas pumps and the convenience store. The sign in the window read, Try a Super-Gulp: Sixty-four Satisfying Ounces.

"Why did you cut your father from your life?" Chase asked for the second time.

She made an attempt to explain. "He's a horrible man, Chase. If a person can be evil, he is. It's ... It would take hours, *days,* to tell you all the awful things he's done. To me. And to the people I love."

He reached across the space between them and took her chin, guiding her head around so she had to look at him. "*Will* you tell me?"

She cast her glance down. "Not now. Please ..."

Chase rubbed her cheek with the pad of his thumb. She felt moisture; he was wiping away a tear—one she hadn't even realized had fallen.

"Is your father why we're racing to California?"

She shook her head, turning into his hand a little. It did feel good when he touched her. "He's not in California. He's in Salem, Oregon. There's a state hospital there, for people who would be in prison if they didn't have psychiatric problems."

"Your father should be in prison?"

She nodded.

He rubbed the side of her neck very lightly with the back of his index finger, a touch that was somehow both arousing and reassuring at the same time. "I seem to remember something about that. Maud mentioned it, I think. Quite a while ago."

She dragged in a breath and told him what Gideon had done. "He kidnapped Evie, my youngest sister, almost two years ago. Literally chained her to the wall in a basement room for a week. She got pneumonia and almost died. You bet he should be in prison."

"But why would a man do something like that?"

"It goes back years. He'd been . . . obsessed with Evie from the time Evie got to be ten or eleven and he discovered she had certain—oh, how can I say this? He learned she had certain 'talents.' "

"Talents?"

"Yes. Certain special abilities to see things others couldn't see. And to know things no one else knew. To soothe the sick and ease people's pain. He was always one for far-fetched moneymaking schemes that never worked out. But when he discovered Evie's talents—her 'gifts,' he used to call them—he came up with a scheme that *did* work."

"What kind of scheme?"

"He set Evie up as a 'psychic locater.' And it worked. Because Evie did seem to have an uncanny ability to make sick people well, and to find the missing. Gideon exploited her 'gifts' and we all lived a better life than we had up until then. But Evie hated it. We *all* hated it. And we waited for Evie to turn eighteen. And when she did, we ran away...."

"Are you telling me that this sister of yours, the one we're going to stay with, is a *psychic?*"

Nevada sighed. "I'm not telling you anything except what happened in the past. If you asked Evie now, she'd swear it was all a fake, that she never had any psychic gifts at all, only a talent for reading faces and an ability to pick up the clues in people's gestures, in their body language."

"But what do you believe?"

"Please, Chase. It just doesn't matter anymore. Evie's a nice pregnant lady who owns a shop in a small town and loves her husband and stepchildren more than anything in the world."

His expression was bemused. "The more you explain, the more confusing it gets."

"I know."

Gently he suggested, "Let's find a place to stay. For the night."

She wanted to ask, *Will you try to make love with me?* but didn't dare. He might say yes.

And worse than that, he might say no....

Instead, she wondered aloud, "And what about tomorrow?"

"In the morning, we can call the local vets and dog groomers. Maybe one of them can tell us something about your precious Babette."

"But tomorrow's Sunday."

"Nevada. We've been on the road all day. We both need rest. We'll do what we can about the dog. Tomorrow. All right?"

What could she say? His suggestion made sense; and she had nothing better to offer.

"Well?" he prompted.

"Yes. Let's find a place to stay for the night."

* * *

It took a while, but Chase found them a decent motel where dogs were permitted in the rooms. Nevada sat in the car with Babette while he checked them in. He returned with keys to separate rooms.

Babette jumped to the ground when Nevada opened the car door. The dog sat on the pavement, watching intently, as Nevada collected her makeup case and overnight bag from the trunk. When Nevada went into the room, Babette trotted right at her heels.

Inside, Nevada set everything down on a couch near the door, then straightened to look around.

The walls were papered in dusty rose and the quilted bedspread displayed a blue-and-rose geometric print. The furniture was of oak, or at least a credible imitation. Over the headboard of the bed hung an Impressionist print, a soothing Monet of water lilies in a pond. To the right of the print, between the bedstand and the room's small table and chairs, loomed the door she'd expected would be there—the one that joined her room to Chase's.

From behind her, she heard Babette whine.

She turned to the dog. "What's the matter? Thirsty?" She went and filled the sink, which, along with the vanity counter and mirror, stood against the far wall by the door to the bathroom. Then she lifted Babette onto the counter, where the dog lapped the water eagerly.

"My mother always taught me that animals don't belong on counters," Chase said from several feet away. Nevada looked up to see him standing just where she thought he would be: in the now open door between their rooms.

"It's the best I could do without a bowl," she said.

He nodded. "Yeah. I was just thinking that maybe I ought to go see about picking up a few doggy supplies."

"Good idea. Get some dog food. And a leash. Maybe a blanket. And a dog comb and brush, if you can."

"Yes, ma'am." He looked her up and down. Poodle hairs covered her rumpled tunic. A layer of grime, acquired during her scramble into the ditch back there on the highway, coated her sandaled feet. She knew she smelled of dog. But none of that mattered. She felt warm all over when Chase looked at her—warm all over and sexy, too.

He was grinning, as if he knew just how she felt. But all he said was, "So much for the dog. What do *you* want to eat?"

She heard Babette's toenails scrabbling on the counter, so she turned and helped the poodle to get down. "It doesn't matter. Whatever you get will be fine."

"Let that dog out in a few minutes," he warned. "All that water has to go somewhere."

She promised that she would.

Once Chase had left, Nevada decided she should probably clean Babette up a little. So she filled the tub and removed the dog's ruined pink bows.

After a trip outside to relieve herself, the poodle went eagerly into the tub. She sat there, panting, actually seeming to smile, as Nevada washed her with the complimentary motel shampoo and worked out as many burrs and brambles as she could with the comb from her makeup case. She took special care of the injured area above the dog's eye, though it appeared that Chase had been right about it. The wound was a little swollen and Babette whined when Nevada pressed it lightly, but the cut was a shallow one and the blood washed right out.

Finally, after two shampooings and a thorough rinsing, Nevada drained the tub and dried the dog, first with a towel and then with her travel blow-dryer.

Babette didn't even flinch at the loud sound the dryer made. Nevada wondered if her owner had used one on her in the past.

By then, Babette was looking pretty good. Nevada put her on a dry towel in the main room and the dog lay down with a little whuff of contentment.

Nevada returned to the bathroom and rinsed out the dirty tub, then sat back on her heels with a sigh. The thought of a shower right then was so tempting. She glanced quickly at her watch, which she'd set on the toilet tank while she bathed the dog. Chase had been gone about forty-five minutes. If she hurried, she could surely have a shower before he returned with their dinner.

She hurried out to the main room, pulled her light cotton robe from her overnight bag and grabbed her makeup case. Then, peeling off her rumpled clothes as she went and pausing at the mirror over the sink long enough to remove the gold hoops from her ears, she returned again to the bathroom and stepped into the tub.

The water felt wonderful. She washed every inch of herself, including her hair. When she got out, she swiftly performed her ritual of spreading on lotion. Then she wrapped her hair in a towel, turban-style, and pulled on her robe.

She emerged from the steamy bathroom to find Chase setting a bowl of canned dog food in front of Babette. He'd already put a blanket down under the towel to make a softer bed. And he'd filled a second bowl with water, which he'd placed not far away. The dog, her head tipped to the side, watched him put the food before her with a great deal of interest. But when Chase stood from the task, the dog just sat there, looking up at him hopefully.

"All right, go ahead," he said.

And Babette bent her poufy little head to the bowl.

"She has excellent manners, don't you think?" Nevada asked, setting her makeup case on the counter and then unwrapping the towel from her head.

"She's not bad, for a poodle." Chase continued watching the dog for a moment, then he turned.

At the sight of Nevada, he stopped. His gaze made a slow pass from the top of her head to her bare toes. "Well. Hello." The slight huskiness in his voice caused little shivers to travel along her arms and down the backs of her legs. She wondered if she should have dressed in more than her robe.

Yet, she *was* covered all the way down to mid-calf. And it was too late to worry about it now, anyway.

She turned to the mirror and began rubbing her still-wet hair with the towel. "I gave Babette a bath."

"I noticed."

"And then I decided I could use one myself."

"Hey. Fine with me." She could see him in the mirror, still watching her, and she paused for a moment. They shared a long glance, one that had shivers moving through her again.

That night in Winslow, they had showered together, in the tiny cell of a bathroom where the tile was peeling off the walls of the shower stall and the faint odor of mildew permeated everything. But of course, that night, she'd brought no robe.

Not that she'd needed one.

Chase kept watching her face in the mirror. The look in his eyes was probing, questioning.

Nevada broke the hold of his gaze and set the towel on the counter.

She thought he shrugged, but the movement was very slight. Then he was gesturing at the table across the room, where two large white bags waited. "I got Chinese. That okay?"

"That's great." She spent a moment more finger-combing her wet curls. Then, trying not to be too obvious about it, she retied the sash at her waist so that when she sat down, nothing would show that shouldn't.

When she joined him at the table, Chase was already pulling the white cartons out of the bags. "I seem to recall that you were pretty good with chopsticks.'' He held up a pair, still wrapped in paper.

''Thanks.'' Nevada took the chopsticks and peeled off the paper, feeling pleased that he'd remembered she used them. After all, they'd only eaten Chinese food together one other time.

It had been three or four years ago. And, really, they hadn't been *together*. They'd just been in the same party, which had included Maud and Billy. In fact, Chase had brought a date, hadn't he? A pretty, soft-spoken brunette.

But actually, looking back now, it seemed that Chase hadn't been paying much attention to the brunette. He'd spent most of his time making caustic remarks to Nevada. And she'd been caustic right back at him. Everyone had thought they were very amusing.

Everyone except possibly the brunette...

''No plates?'' Nevada asked now, waving her chopsticks.

He looked up as he pulled a second pair of chopsticks from one of the bags. ''I knew I forgot something.'' Swiftly, he peeled the paper from the chopsticks, separated them, opened a carton of sweet-and-sour pork, and dug in.

Nevada could hardly believe her eyes. She grabbed one empty bag and then the other, and peered into the depths of them. ''I don't believe it. Where's your plastic fork?''

He finished chewing and swallowed. ''Impressed?'' He chopsticked up another morsel and neatly poked it into his mouth.

''You're using *chopsticks*.''

''You bet.'' He opened one of the two little cartons of milk he'd bought and took a big gulp.

''But you *never* use chopsticks. You think people who were brought up using forks should go right on using them.''

"I still think so. But I've got a right to be as silly and pretentious as the next guy. Now, get busy on this food."

Nevada gaped for a moment more, then started on the cashew chicken. As she ate, she wondered about him. She could never pin him down. And sometimes she had the scary feeling that he was smarter than she was.

Nevada had no false modesty about her intelligence; she knew that she was head and shoulders above most men when it came to brains. She'd never gone to college; she'd earned a GED rather than actually finishing high school, but she read widely and kept up on current events. She could hold her own in almost any company. In a way, she supposed, it was her mind that had always kept men at bay. They knew after a short conversation with her that they could never keep up.

Except Chase. *He* kept up. And sometimes he just forged ahead and left her behind in the dust.

"Finished?"

She drank the last of her carton of milk, then sat back and sighed. "That was just what I needed. Thanks."

"My pleasure." He dropped his chopsticks into one of the bags and sat back, too.

He looked across the table at her. Then he smiled—a slow smile. Again, she thought that maybe she should have put on something other than her robe.

His gaze moved lower. She resisted the urge to look down and be sure the robe wasn't falling open in the wrong place.

"Okay, what now?" His voice was husky and low and weighted with equal parts humor and heat.

She glanced over at Babette. The dog had finished her meal and now lay on her towel, apparently asleep.

"What now, Nevada?"

Suddenly it seemed terribly important that she close up the cartons and put them back in the bags. She started to do just that.

But then Chase reached across the space between them and snared her hand.

She froze.

"What now?" he asked for the third time.

She forced herself to meet his gaze. "Chase, I don't—"

"Stop."

She said no more.

He released her hand and stood. "Good night," he said. And then he headed for the door to his own room.

And she knew she should simply let him go. But the problem was, she *couldn't* let him go.

She caught his arm as he went by. "Chase, please..."

He stiffened, and she thought he would pull away. But then she took his wrist, laid her cheek against his hand and looked up at him.

"What do you want, Nevada?" He sounded wary, but some of the stiffness had left him.

"I want you to understand why I'm giving you all these mixed signals."

He studied her for a moment, then muttered grudgingly, "I'm listening."

"You know that I'm attracted to you."

He almost smiled. "I thought maybe you were."

"You *know* it."

"All right, Nevada. I know you want me. And I want you. It isn't news."

"We want each other."

"Right."

"But I'm... I just don't seem to know how to be with you. I feel that I'll... lose who I am, if I give in to what I feel for you."

"That's in your own mind."

"Which makes it real. To me."

"If your mind's in your way, then change it."

She sighed. "Spoken like a man."

"You want me to be something else?"

"No. No, I don't."

"That's a relief."

"Oh, Chase. If I could only make you understand. I don't trust this thing between us. And besides that, well, I'm just not a woman who'd make a good wife. I...I don't see how it could last between us."

A long breath escaped him. That elusive smile appeared on his lips and then vanished, only to appear again. "We're in a motel room in Tonopah. On our way to God-knows-where, just the two of us and a runaway French poodle named Babette. Is permanence really the issue here?"

She rubbed her cheek against his hand. "Oh, I don't know. I suppose not."

"Then what is?"

How could she make him understand? She turned her head, so she could place a kiss on the back of his hand. It was a strong, well-formed hand, dusted with silky golden hairs. "I'm so afraid." She breathed the words against his skin.

"Did someone say you couldn't be?" His fingers curled, reaching, brushing at her hand.

She knew what he wanted, and entwined her fingers with his. "No. I know it's all right to be scared." She let out a small, pained laugh. "I used to tell my listeners that on my show, 'It's all right.' I'd say, 'Being scared is all right.' But now, *I'm* the one who's scared. And it's awful. Because I'm supposed to be the woman with all the answers. And suddenly, I...don't know anything." She closed her eyes, dragged in a breath, then looked at him once more. "Everything's changing. My sisters are *married.*"

His eyes were very dark and soft. "Sisters sometimes do that."

She let go of his hand. "Not *my* sisters. They were never going to get married. They were independent, like me. They were never going to let a man gain that much importance in their lives."

"Why not?"

"It was bad, Chase. When we were kids."

"The awful father . . . ?"

"Yes. After we were grown, for years, all three of us stayed completely away from romantic entanglements with men. But then Evie—"

"The one we're going to visit?"

"Right. Evie met Erik."

"How long ago was that?"

"About two years ago. Evie and Erik Biggins fell in love. And suddenly, she was getting married. And then, just this last April, Faith married her boss. Price Montgomery's his name. Faith was his housekeeper for so long—years and years. It really was just a business relationship. And Faith had never even been on a date in her life. But then she quit working for Price. She struck out on her own. And Price suddenly realized he couldn't live without her. And now they're married. Like Evie and Erik."

"Do you think your sisters *shouldn't* be married?"

"No," she admitted softly. "It was the right thing for both of them, I know it. They're both truly happy." She shook her head. "But it's a lot to take in."

He muttered something under his breath that sounded both tender and exasperated. Then he took her by the shoulders, pulled her out of her chair and over to the bed.

"Sit," he said.

She dropped to the edge. He sat down beside her, put an arm around her and pulled her close.

She sat stiffly at first, and then she relaxed, although she probably shouldn't have. But he offered just what she needed, a comforting touch. She rested her head lightly on his broad shoulder. "It's just all too much." She sighed. "My sisters getting married. And then Maud takes up with Billy again. My father is dying, which isn't supposed to matter to me. But somehow, it does. And I've lost my job...."

He smoothed her hair. "And then there's me, who won't leave you alone."

She sighed. "That, too." It really did feel good, to lean against him. And there was the scent of him, which she'd always liked. Masculine and healthy smelling. A little musky now, at the end of a long day. But even the muskiness drew her. She snuggled closer still, closing her eyes, breathing him in, nuzzling her head against his chest.

His body tightened a little when she rubbed against him, but she felt no alarm. He really was being so kind and understanding about all of this. She opened her eyes and glanced up, smiling. He met her gaze. The hand he'd wrapped so comfortingly around her moved. She turned her head enough to see that he'd captured a stray lock of her hair. Idly he coiled it around his index finger.

"Chase?" Her voice sounded husky to her own ears.

He said nothing. He finished coiling the damp lock around his finger. Then he smoothed it with his thumb. She watched, leaning fully against him, as he pulled his finger free, leaving a ringlet behind, which he smoothed so it fell back over her shoulder.

Then, with his other hand, he took her chin and turned her face so they were looking at each other once more.

His eyes had changed. They were heavy-lidded, more intent than a few moments ago.

But his voice was low and soothing when he spoke. "You worry too much."

"I know. But I..."

He touched his finger to her lips. "Shh. Listen. You can be scared. And confused. And not have the answers. And make love anyway."

"But..."

"But what?"

"It isn't wise."

"Nevada." He traced her eyebrows, one and then the other, as if smoothing away troubled thoughts. "What's going on here has nothing at all to do with wisdom."

"I know that, I suppose, but—"

He moved swiftly, then, to cup her face in both of his hands. His fingers slid backward, into her hair. "At some point, we just have to move on to the next step. I think you know that. I think you *want* that. So, please. Take the plunge."

"Chase..."

He tipped her face up fully, and brought his mouth right against hers. Then he whispered, his lips caressing hers as they moved, "You're. Driving. Me. Nuts." He made each word a sentence in itself.

She had nothing at all to say to that.

He dropped his hands, stood, and looked down at her. "It was bad enough just sitting across from you, in your thin white robe, with your hair all wet, getting a faint whiff, now and then, of your soap and your shampoo and whatever else it is about you—that *scent* that only you seem to have. I know you belted that robe tighter so I wouldn't see anything. But I *can* see. Way too much." His gaze traveled down, as it had when he was sitting across from her.

She started to fiddle with the sash, thinking she would retie it again, but then realized she would only be proving his point.

He was still looking, standing there above her, his eyes dark and hot and heavy-lidded. "I can see the shadow between your breasts. Did you know that?"

"I..."

"And your nipples..."

She swallowed, but didn't speak. Any words she might have uttered died unborn in her constricted throat.

He explained further: "They...push against the cloth, when you move."

She licked her lips, embarrassed—and aroused. "I should have worn more than a robe...."

"Right. But you didn't."

"Chase, really, I—"

"But the final damn straw was just now, rubbing against me like that. Looking at me all dreamy-eyed."

"I, uh, I don't seem to be behaving the way that I should."

"Right." He turned, took a few steps toward the table, then faced her again. "And I've been patient. Damn patient. More than a year's worth of patient, if you get right down to it."

She just couldn't let that go without dispute. "That's not fair. We avoided each other for almost a year. By mutual consent. And let's not forget Virginia."

"Why not? *I* have. And Virginia's forgotten me. There never should have *been* a Virginia. You know it. I know it. Even *Virginia* knows it."

She cast desperately about for more excuses, for one more marginally acceptable reason to keep the inevitable from taking place. "But the fact that there *was* a Virginia counts for something."

"Really? What?" He waited a few beats for her to come up with an answer, but she just couldn't think of one. So he went on, "Don't throw Virginia up at me. I've already admitted I was with her on the rebound. From you. What the hell more do you want? Blood?"

"No. Of course not."

He shook his head, turned away.

"Chase, I'm sorry, I—"

He faced her again and put up a hand. "I'm not after apologies. Let's get down to present time, here."

"All right. Fine."

"I walked away last night, when we both knew it wouldn't have taken that much convincing to get you into bed."

"Yes. And I'm grateful, I truly am."

"Get this. I am not after your damn gratitude, any more than I want you telling me you're sorry. I'm not even sure exactly what I *am* after, to tell you the brutal truth. But I know a major part of what I'm after. And that's you and me. Together. Naked."

She found she had absolutely nothing to say. Never had she been left speechless so many times in one night.

He moved in on her again. "I had some damn politically correct idea that I was going to wait—for you to make up your mind without any help from me."

She looked up at him, wide-eyed. "And I appreciate that, Chase. I do."

He bent down, so his lips hovered right above hers. "But Nevada..."

"I... What?"

"To hell with waiting." His hands cradled her face once more. His mouth was so close.... "I want you and you want me and at least that's one thing we're both sure of. I say we act on that. I say we take a big risk and do what we both want to do. Now."

"But..."

"Nevada."

"What?"

"Let me give you a suggestion."

"A suggestion?"

"That's what I said."

"All right."

"Are you with me, here?"

"I am, yes."

"Untie the sash of that damn robe."

She blinked. "Uh, I . . ."

"Do it. Now."

He spoke with such absolute command that her hands moved automatically to the knot at her waist. "Yes . . ." His gaze stayed locked with hers. "Do it. . . ."

"Oh, I don't . . ."

He took her lower lip between his teeth, very lightly, then released it. Her lip burned as if he'd hurt her. But he hadn't hurt her. The burning came from pleasure.

She felt her own breath, shallow and hot. It mingled with his, he was so close.

"Do you want me to go?" he asked.

She made a small, frustrated sound in her throat.

"Do you?"

"No . . ."

"Then do it. Untie the robe. Do it, or . . ."

She remembered the night in Winslow, his hand sliding up to cup her bare breast. And her breasts were suddenly aching, her whole body tingling.

"Do it, Nevada. I want to see you. I want to see you now."

Her fingers were moving—swiftly, urgently.

The sash dropped away.

"Yeah," he whispered.

"Oh, now will you kiss me?" she pleaded.

He answered with action; his mouth closed over hers.

Chapter Nine

Chase kissed her slowly, his hands cupping her face, his mouth moving on hers, urging her lips to part. And when they did part, his tongue claimed her, sweeping her mouth, tasting her and taunting her at one and the same time.

His hands slid down, over her throat. Still kissing her, he found the sides of the robe and peeled them slowly outward, over her shoulders and down her arms. She felt the coolness of the air on her bare breasts and belly.

And then his hands were sliding farther down to clasp hers. He pulled her up, not breaking the endless kiss, so she stood before him. He pushed the robe off and away as his mouth went on toying with hers. She heard the robe drop, like an exhaled breath, around her bare ankles.

Without the robe, she was totally nude. But he wasn't giving her a chance to think much about that. He was still kissing her.

He put his hands on her hips for a moment, hands that felt slightly rough against her tender skin. She wanted to break the hold of his lips just enough to look down, to see the tan against the white. But before she could, those hands went roving upward, over her rib cage, to the side slopes of her breasts. They rested so lightly there, against her fullness. And then they moved around to the front of her.

He cupped her breasts. She felt her nipples, hard and aching, in the center of his palms.

She gave an urgent little cry into his mouth. He made a sound in response; a satisfied, masculine sound. And then his hands slid farther up. He took her shoulders.

And he broke the kiss. She blinked, bewildered, as he stepped back from her. He looked into her eyes. And then lower. He looked at all of her.

Her body burned as if he touched it everywhere.

And then he was meeting her eyes again. "Hi, there," he said.

She felt a wavery smile bloom on her lips. "Hello."

"I remember you."

"Oh, Chase . . ." She just knew she was going to cry.

But he gathered her close. "It's okay. Hey, it's okay." His hands stroked her back; long, soothing strokes. She melted into him. He felt so good, so right.

And suddenly, she couldn't wait another minute to have him as naked as she was herself.

She pulled away and gazed directly into his eyes.

He saw the change in her right away. Some of the tenderness melted from his expression, leaving unabashed desire. "That's better."

"I do want you, Chase. You're everything I swore never to want. But I do. Heaven help me, I do."

"Show me." His voice was low, husky. "Show me how much."

She guided him around, until his back was to the bed. And then she pushed him down. She knelt before him and, with some effort, pulled off his boots. His socks came next. She threw them over her shoulder, one at a time.

He laughed then; a pleased, very masculine sound.

"Don't just sit there," she said. "Help me."

And he did. He unzipped his slacks, shoving them down and off, right along with his briefs. And then he yanked his shirt over his head and tossed it across the room, where it landed on a swag lamp and set it swinging.

She sat back on her knees and looked at him. At his broad shoulders and washboard belly and long, hard legs. He was thoroughly aroused.

"I brought protection with me this time," he said. "In my suitcase in the other room."

She wasn't surprised. He'd made his intentions quite clear all along.

He reached down and snared her hand. "Let's go." He stood, pulling her to her feet and then starting for the other room.

Dazed, yearning, totally willing, she stumbled behind him through the door that divided his room from hers, leaving Babette alone, sleeping soundly on her towel.

In the other room, which was just like hers only green where hers was dusty rose, Chase got the condoms from his bag. And then they started kissing again. They were so eager, their noses bumped.

They fell across his bed, laughing, and he tossed the box onto his nightstand. She levered up on top of him and he wrapped his arms around her and kissed her some more. She kissed him right back, twining her tongue with his, tasting him as he tasted her. They rolled, so that he took the top position.

When he lifted his face to look down at her again, he lay cradled between her thighs. She could feel him, intimately pressing against her.

He closed his eyes, tipped his head back and groaned deep in his throat. She knew he wanted to slide into her, right then. And she knew that she would welcome him, that she was wet and ready for him already.

But he didn't slide in. He held very still. They waited together, in an agony of anticipation that was a game, really; a game that they shared.

He pulled back a little, so he didn't press so temptingly against her entrance.

"I think—" he ground out the words "—maybe we'd better . . ."

She knew what he meant. She reached for the box of condoms and managed to flip back the lid and pull one out. But then, before she could open the packet, he started kissing her again, a deep, hungry kiss. His body pressed her down into the mattress, demanding, heavy, so good. . . .

His mouth left hers. He began kissing his way down, over her chin and her jaw, along her neck to her collarbone and then over the slope of a breast. His cheek was rough with a day's worth of beard, but the roughness delighted her. He took her nipple in his mouth and began to suck.

She moaned and clutched his head, pressing him close to her, offering herself up.

He took what she offered, drawing deep. She felt the pull that went down into the heart of her. And she lifted herself higher toward him.

His hand found her, parted her. She cried out. He took her mouth again, drank the hungry sounds from her lips as down below he was doing magic things, forbidden things.

Her body was gathering, readying, moving toward fulfillment. She would shatter soon....

And then he pulled back. He looked at her. She knew what she must look like—flushed, her still-damp hair all tangled against the pillows, her eyes heavy with need of him.

"Put it on." His voice sounded harsh, hungry.

She fumbled with the condom, but found she was all thumbs. "I don't... I never..."

He took it from her, tore it open and rolled it down over himself. She watched, fascinated, excited, yearning. She couldn't resist. She reached out, touched the now-covered tip.

He groaned. "It's been too long. I can't wait."

She held out her arms. He came into them, settling with a heavy sigh between her thighs. And then, with a quick thrust of powerful hips, he was inside her.

"Oh!" It was a shock, a thoroughly delicious one.

Once again, she thought of *rightness*. It felt so right, to have him inside her. It shouldn't. But, oh, it did.

"Don't move."

She didn't, although she wanted to. Oh, she wanted to....

He got himself up on his elbows and rested his hands along the sides of her head, in her tangled hair. Slowly, he pulled back.

"Don't move," he warned again, this time in an agonized whisper.

She bit her lip. But that was the only movement she made. Where they were joined, she remained absolutely still, although he had pulled back from her and her body yearned to have him fill her again.

And he did, but in his own time, watching her face the while, pressing slowly, slowly in, until he was buried all the way inside her softness once more.

She tossed her head from side to side, nipping at his hands, begging without words for him to...

"What?"

"I want..."

"Tell me."

"I want... to move."

He pulled out and thrust in. "Like this?"

"Oh, Chase."

He did it again, harder. "And this?"

"Yes."

"And this, and this, and this, and this..."

With a deep cry, she thrust her hips up to meet his. And then there was no stopping her. Or him. They rode each other wildly, rolling across the wide bed, each claiming the top position, then surrendering it, then rising to bid for it once more.

They were on their sides, facing each other, when the end came. They stopped. And then in unison, they pressed their striving bodies together, so close and tight. She felt him, felt the pulse of his release. And her fulfillment bloomed from that. Her body clutched him and released him in an internal explosion that she wished might never end.

She called his name.

He whispered hers.

And they went limp in tandem as the aftershocks rolled through them, sweet and stunning and finally fading away to a tender glow.

He fell apart from her, to sprawl on his back across the bed. And she fell the other way. For a long, sweet moment, she stared at the mint-green ceiling. There was the sound of their breathing and the cooling warmth of their bodies.

He stirred, eventually, and left her briefly, to get rid of the condom. When he stretched out beside her again, he laid his hand on her belly. She looked down at it, so tanned and lean against her white softness.

And the night in Winslow came to her, the night she'd run from. The night, she was learning more poignantly with each day that passed, that she had not escaped at all.

Chase leaned over her and kissed the tip of her nose. She smiled at him, a languorous smile.

"So sweet now," he murmured against her cheek. "So soft and sweet."

She felt tired in the most lovely way, her body heavy, deliciously boneless. He lowered his head and took the nipple of her breast between his lips, very lightly. She moaned a little, enjoying the sensation, but feeling too marvelously quiescent to do much more. He kissed her other breast. She sighed in lazy delight.

And then his mouth moved lower. He kissed her belly. She idly laid her hand on his head and stroked his hair.

And then he went lower still.

"Oh, Chase..."

"Shh..." He breathed the soothing sound against the soft nest of auburn curls at the apex of her thighs.

And then he moved around, nudging her legs apart, settling himself between them. He dipped his head and he was kissing her intimately, his tongue probing her most secret places.

The languor that had claimed her turned to need all over again as his kiss deepened, stroking, laving, knowing her as she had never, ever meant to be known.

She reached down, shoved her fingers into his gold-streaked hair. "Chase, oh, Chase..." Her body rose and fell, and his kiss went on and on.

The completion broke upon her like a wave. She lay beneath it, swept under to the blackest depths by its power. And then lifted high, on its crest, crying out, pushing herself shamelessly against the hungry mouth that pleasured her.

At last, she fell back limp. His kiss continued, gentle now, warm and slow and easing, soothing. Good.

After a time, she reached down and stroked his hair. He moved, pulling himself up her body enough that he could lay his head on her belly, where he rested, sighing.

He muttered something.

"Hmm?" she asked.

He looked up, along the white length of her body, into her eyes. "No one tastes like you," he said.

She smiled, feeling dreamy and content, drugged with satisfaction. "I'd say the same to you. But I have no basis for comparison."

He brought up both hands, laid them on her belly, propped his chin on them and went on looking at her.

She frowned a little. "What?"

But he just shook his head, that almost-smile of his coming and going on his lips.

They heard a whine.

Babette was standing in the doorway to the other room, a pleading look in her soulful black eyes.

"She needs a few minutes outside." Chase was already levering himself up and off the bed.

"I'll take her out," Nevada volunteered, rolling to her side and propping herself on an elbow.

He was already yanking a pair of slacks from his bag. "No." His gaze caressed her. She smiled in response, allowing herself to take pleasure in the desire that smoldered in his eyes. "Stay right there. Get your strength back. I'm not through with you yet."

And he wasn't kidding. When he returned, they made love again. Then they showered together. Then he backed her up against the counter by the sink and kissed her until she could hardly stand.

When she told him that her knees were giving out on her, he muttered, "No problem," and hoisted her onto the countertop. She fumbled behind her for the condom she herself had brought over from the table by the bed.

She slid it on him herself this time. Then, slowly, with tender but relentless hands, he parted her legs and moved between them.

"I love a woman who comes prepared," he whispered huskily as his mouth closed over hers once again.

They ordered room service from the motel's café the next morning. And as soon as they'd eaten, Nevada called Evie.

"Where are you?" her sister asked.

"Not as far along as I wanted to be. In Tonopah."

"Where's that, exactly?"

"The middle of Nevada."

"Is everything . . . all right?"

"More or less. I ran into a poodle."

"You what?"

"I hit a dog, with my car. The dog's okay. But we're trying to find the owner before we go on."

After a significant pause, Evie said, "Is Maud's brother a big animal-lover, then?"

She glanced at Chase, who sat with his back to her on the end of the bed, talking into his cellular phone and finishing up a third cup of coffee. He had on a pair of jeans, but no shirt. The muscles of his back were hard and sculpted, his skin so firm and tan. Something tightened deep inside her as she thought of the night before.

"Nevada?" Evie said in her ear.

"Hmm?"

"Is Chase a real animal-lover?"

"Uh, no. Not particularly."

"Well." Evie's silence said everything. She knew very well that her big sister was no animal-lover, either. She asked, "What's going on?"

"Nothing. Really. I feel guilty about the dog, that's all. I want to do what I can. And I wanted you to know that I'll be later than I expected to be." She thought of her father, but remained reluctant to ask about him outright. "Any... news on your end?"

"No. Nothing to speak of. Are you really okay?"

"I'm fine." She promised they would be there by that evening sometime, and got off the line.

At nine, she started calling veterinarians, most of whom were off for the day. The two she actually reached had no recollection of having treated a white poodle named Babette. A quick search of their computer records turned up nothing, either.

After she'd tried all the vets, she moved on to dog groomers.

It was the same problem as the vets; none of them were open.

But when she reached the second-to-last listing, someone actually answered, "Pretty Pet, Donna Lynn speaking."

Nevada introduced herself and asked if Donna Lynn had ever groomed a white poodle named Babette.

"A toy?"

"Excuse me?"

"Is the dog a toy poodle? About ten inches tall, not the tiny 'teacup' variety, but small enough to fit comfortably in your lap?"

"Yes. Yes, that's right."

"Continental cut?"

"I don't—"

"It's the classic show cut. Poms on head, legs, two on the main part of the body. Around the feet, too."

"Yes. That's her. We found her yesterday, out on the highway."

"Aw, the poor little sweetheart."

"Do you have a phone number for the owner?"

Donna Lynn hesitated. "Look. I should probably call first, if that's all right. You know how people get sometimes, when you give out their phone numbers."

"Of course." Nevada gave the woman the motel's number and the number of the room and said she would wait right there by the phone.

"That Babette's a sweet little dog," Donna Lynn said. "I'll call you back if I can't reach the owner."

Nevada thanked her and hung up.

"Pay dirt?" Chase asked. By then, he was stretched out on the bed with the television remote in his hand, channel-surfing.

"I think so."

The phone rang a few minutes later. In a flat voice, a woman asked if the poodle Nevada had found had been wearing pink bows in its ears and a pink collar with vari-colored glass stones in it.

"Yes. Yes, she was."

"All right. You might as well bring her on back here." The woman gave Nevada an address and then hung up before she could ask for a phone number just in case.

"Well?" Chase asked, once Nevada had put the phone back in its cradle.

"That was the owner. She says we can take Babette to her." She glanced at her watch. "It's a little after ten. Let's get packed up and check out. We can drop Babette off on the way out of town."

"Yes, ma'am," Chase said, and swung his legs to the floor.

As it turned out, the house was easy to find. A big, re-verse-floor-plan wood-sided ranch house in a nice neighborhood.

When they knocked on the door, a dog started barking from somewhere in back. A deep, menacing bark.

In Nevada's arms, Babette started quivering.

A middle-aged woman with gray hair cut in a severe chin-length pageboy opened the door. She looked at Babette and then briefly at Nevada and Chase. "Yes," she admitted wearily. "That's my mother's dog."

The woman made no move to invite them in. Nevada didn't mind. What she could see of the dim hall behind the woman looked dark and uninviting, anyway.

In the back, the loud barking went on. The woman yelled over her shoulder, "Quiet, Max!" The barking stopped for a moment, then started up again. The woman looked at Nevada. "As you can hear, I've already got a dog. A purebred Rottweiler. Max." The woman shot Babette a look of distaste. "My mother died a month and a half ago. She left me Babette. I've done my best for her, I really have. But this isn't the first time she's run away."

Max was still barking. The woman yelled at him again, achieved a brief silence, and turned back to Nevada. "Max doesn't care for Babette."

In Nevada's arms, the quivering Babette let out the tiniest of whines. In the back of the house, Max started up again. Nevada experienced a quick, ugly vision of powerful black flanks, of long, sharp teeth and beady black eyes.

"Look," she heard herself say. "I'm willing to keep this dog, if you really don't want her."

Chase jabbed her in the ribs. Nevada shot him a glare and then forced a smile for the woman with the Prince Valiant hair. "So, what do you think?"

The woman looked at her sideways. "Listen. I won't kid you. My mother had pretensions. But that's about all. That dog's got no papers. She's not a purebred. She came from a litter of mutts, each one different from the next. For some reason, she looks exactly like a toy poodle. But she's not. She's just a mutt."

Nevada wanted to feed the woman to her own Rottweiler. But Max probably wouldn't eat her. He only ate mutts who had the temerity to look like real poodles.

She kept on smiling. "It's all right. Really. I'd like to have her."

Chase didn't speak to her until they were back on the highway with Babette settled comfortably on her blanket in the back seat. And then all he asked was, "What's your sister going to think of your bringing a dog along?"

He sounded aloof and disdainful and irritated, too, all at the same time. She answered too sweetly, "She won't mind. She said I could bring *you*, didn't she?"

"Very funny."

"Chase, I couldn't just leave her there. With that heartless woman and that awful, howling dog."

He gave her another glance, as superior as the last one. "The woman was clearly willing to take care of her."

"Babette hated it there."

He lifted a hand from the steering wheel and waved it dismissively. "Now you can read that dog's mind." He kept his eyes on the road.

"Well, she kept running away, didn't she?"

He made one of those grunting sounds he liked to make when a question was just too ridiculous for him even to bother with.

She started to say something provoking, but then she had a better idea. She reached across and touched the side of his neck, just a light, quick caress.

He looked at her again, another swift glance. But this time the glance wasn't aloof or disdainful or any of those things. This time, all of last night could be seen in his eyes. Nevada was suddenly aware of the beat of her own heart and of the slight, not-unpleasant soreness between her legs.

"If you don't stop being so superior," she said softly, "I won't let you drive."

He had his gaze on the road again. She could see that he was trying to stay irritated, but a smile played at the sides of his mouth.

"Come on," she said. "You like Babette, too. You know you do. At least, just a little..."

He grumbled and muttered. Then he admitted, "It has occurred to me that you might never have stopped driving yesterday, if it hadn't been for that mutt."

"That's true."

"And last night wouldn't have happened." He swiftly looked her way again. They shared a glance that was stunning in its intimacy.

Then he turned his attention to the road again. He drew in a breath. "All right. So you've got yourself a dog."

She looked back at Babette, who raised her head and panted happily at her. "Yes. I suppose I do."

They rolled into Reno at a little past three that afternoon. Chase pulled into a gas station and filled the tank. Nevada took Babette to the Doggy Comfort Station someone had set up at the edge of the lot, then put Babette in the back seat again and went to the rest room herself.

Chase was parked by the phone booth when she rejoined him in the car. "Call your sister," he said.

"Why?"

"We'll stay here tonight."

"But we're less than two hours from North Magdalene."

"We'll stay here. I want one more night with you, at least."

"But, Chase—"

He cut her off. "How many kids does this sister of yours have?"

"Three, and one on the way. Why?"

"Will you and I be sharing a room?"

"Well, I don't know."

He wasn't buying. "You know."

She wrinkled her nose at him. "All right. Probably not."

"Is there a decent hotel there? Where we could get a nice suite?"

"Please. I told you, it's a very small town. There's one motel. My sister, Faith, owns it. And it's closed down right now for major renovations."

"Fine. I've made my point. Call your sister. Now."

Chapter Ten

Chase felt a distinct sense of relief when Nevada said, "All right."

He waited in the car with the dog while she went to make the call to her sister, thinking with some satisfaction that they were finally getting somewhere.

Last night had been very much to his liking. And he wanted another night like that—at least one—before he had to deal with all of her family and a house full of kids. It was good to know he would get what he wanted.

Of course, the minute she got back in the car, she started giving him instructions about where they would stay.

He patiently explained what he wanted in greater detail, mentioning the name of one of the finest hotel-casinos and the penthouse suite he had in mind.

She sighed and bit her soft lower lip. "Chase, I'm sorry. But I just can't afford something like that right now."

He shrugged. "No problem. I'll pay for it."

In the back seat, the dog whined. She reached back there and rubbed the fuzzy pouf on the top of its head. "I want to pay my own way, Chase."

He tried to stay reasonable, but *he* wanted the best and was willing to pay for it. It should be a night to remember, and damn it, it *would* be. Even he heard the impatience in his voice when he spoke again. "Don't make a big deal out of this. We've got something good going on here between us, right now. Why the hell shouldn't we enjoy it while it lasts?"

She gave him one of those looks that made him nervous—a defiant, chin-high look. "It'll cost too much, Chase. And what about Babette? A lot of places don't allow dogs in the room."

"I'll worry about Babette." A dog in a room was like anything else: no problem—for a slight fee.

"Chase, I just don't—"

He whispered, "Please?"

And that did it. He saw the softness come over her. When he made demands, she would always fight. But when he said "Please," that was something else again.

"Oh, all right, then," she said. "Waste your money if you have to."

He spoke gently, soothingly. "I don't consider it a waste."

She granted him a smile. "Well. That's nice to hear."

He started up the car and pointed it where he wanted to go before she could figure out something new to argue about.

They took a three-room suite on the twentieth floor of the casino-hotel he'd chosen. The big sliding-glass door of the sitting room opened onto a balcony, one that looked out over the city of Reno and the high, stark mountains, still capped with the last of the winter's snow.

It was just four in the afternoon by the time they'd checked in. He threw their suitcases in the dressing room and turned to her.

She read his look. "Oh, Chase..."

He turned again and fumbled in a zippered compartment of his bag until he came up with a handful of small foil packets. Then he held them out and tried to look hopeful.

She laughed that husky laugh of hers.

And then she came into his arms, a damn miracle of a woman, long-legged and slim-hipped, with those round, heavy breasts that drove him out of his mind. He felt those breasts now, against his chest, and he pulled her tighter to him, so he could feel them even better.

They kissed their way through the sitting room and into the bedroom, where he tossed the packets on the little table by the bed and pulled her down across his lap in the big easy chair there.

Her sweet mouth moved, eager and hungry, under his. He drank from her, starved for her, although it had been mere hours since the last time he'd had her. This thing he had for her was getting stronger. Wilder.

Half incoherently, as he fumbled with the buttons of her shirt and kissed her hard and deep, he remembered how it had been just the other night, in her backyard. They'd danced and he'd kissed her. And then he'd walked away, because she hadn't been willing enough for him then.

Could he walk away now?

Did it matter? The way she was kissing him was plenty willing. The scent of her swam all around him, driving him nuts. The right kind of nuts.

He had her shirt open, at last. He felt around for the hook of her bra, found it and took care of it. She helped him. Then the shirt was gone and so was the bra, and her breasts filled his hands. He bent his head and took one sweet peak into his mouth, sucking deep. She writhed and moaned and pressed herself closer, giving him more of her.

There really was nothing like the taste of her. He tangled his fingers in the silky red coils of her hair and pulled her head back, lifting his head from her breast so that he could take her mouth again.

She sighed when he kissed her, and suddenly he knew he couldn't wait anymore.

He reached down and unzipped his fly. And her eager, soft hands were there, helping, getting him free.

She slid the protection down over him. He moaned deep in his throat at the feel of her hand closing on him. And then, still wearing her skirt and panties, she straddled him. He touched her, sliding his finger beneath the elastic of her panty leg. And she was as ready as he was. He pulled the elastic out of the way and with a quick thrust of his hips he was inside her, where he'd longed to be.

She rode him then, for a long, sweet time. And when she reached the peak, he went over with her, letting her body milk him, until there was nothing left and he lay back in the chair, spent.

After a while, they got up and showered, which presented another opportunity for love play. She teased that they needed to have protection ready—anywhere they were.

He laughed when she said that, but then he got out more condoms and put some in each room of the suite. Eventually, they dressed again and went down to the casino. They played blackjack and backgammon. Nevada even picked a lucky slot machine that showered quarters on her the second time she dropped a coin in the slot.

By the time they visited the change cage and traded in all those quarters, it was early evening. They went up to the room and put the leash on the poodle and took her for a walk through the streets of Reno.

When they returned, they fed the dog and Chase asked Nevada where she wanted to go for dinner. She said she wouldn't mind room service at all.

He picked up the phone and ordered their dinner.

When he hung up, Nevada was standing at a gilt-framed mirror near the door to the outer hall, fiddling with the posts of those gold hoops she always wore in her ears. He moved up behind her and put his hands on her shoulders.

"I forgot to ask. When you talked to your sister, was there any news about your father?"

Her reflection in the mirror looked a little pinched, suddenly. The father was a big issue with her, he knew, although it was like pulling teeth to get any details out of her.

"Well?" he prompted, careful to keep his voice gentle.

"No. There was nothing." She turned and wrapped her arms around his neck. Her breasts brushed his chest.

And he felt himself getting hard again, like some sex-starved kid.

Strange, what she could do to him. A woman near forty, just like he was. A strong-minded woman with a sharp tongue and a mean streak. An *independent* woman. Stubbornly single. A woman who would have been called an "old maid" not fifty years ago.

She was smiling now—that smile that really got to him. A smile both innocent and knowing at the same time. She pressed herself against him, feeling what she did to him. "Again?" she asked, her breath hitching just a little.

They started kissing—slow, long, deep, drugging kisses. Within minutes, both of them were out of their clothes. They went on kissing. And touching.

It amazed him how well they got along when neither of them was wearing clothes. She never argued when he had her naked, when he touched her in all the places no other man had ever touched her before him.

Somehow, when they were naked, she let herself be open to him. Be vulnerable. Be all those things she never trusted herself to be under ordinary circumstances. She was all woman when she was naked. Sometimes it occurred to him that if he could only keep her that way, they would never have any problems.

By then, he had her backed against a wall, her hands above her head, her fingers entwined with his. And he wanted to claim her again. Fully.

She moved her head, breaking the hold of his kiss. And her dreamy, heavy-lidded eyes met his. "Over there. In that drawer by the wing chair..."

He chuckled, a sound that came out like a growl. And he rubbed his chest against her beautiful, full breasts. "I know where I put them."

"You'd better go and..." The words died on a groan.

He kissed her some more, teasing her, and himself. It was so good. And he wanted it to last. To go on and on. Never to end; although he feared, with the two of them, that an ending was probably inevitable.

But not now. Not for a long while, not until he'd had his fill of her.

If such a thing was possible.

He lifted his mouth from hers and slanted it the other way. And the moment came when he realized he had to have more than just teasing. He backed up and released her hands, expecting her to move, to follow, or to suddenly play shy.

But she didn't move, except to lower her hands to her sides. She waited. There. Against the wall. While he went to the drawer and took care of the problem.

When he returned to her, she was pressed there, her back against the wall, just as he had left her. The wall was covered in some nubby brocade fabric, and her hair clung to it, fanning out around her flushed, finely chiseled face. He put his hand beside her head, rubbing the already-electric strands. They crackled in response. He took a handful of the silky stuff and bent his head close and buried his nose in it. It held the scent of her. Musky and spicy. Sugar and cinnamon. And something tart. Lemons, maybe. No. Oranges...

She watched him, her eyes sleepy and soft, her warm breath fanning his neck. He took her hips and lifted her, guiding her long legs around him. And he slid inside.

She gripped him. And he pushed into her. She threw her head back against the wall, crying out. The gold hoops danced against her white neck. The cinnamon hair frothed against the brocade-covered wall.

It ended too quickly. He braced a hand on the wall and reluctantly allowed her to slide her feet to the ground. There was a sofa nearby. As soon as he'd disposed of the condom, she took his hand and guided him to it. She sat and he sat beside her. She smiled at him and pulled him down to rest his head in her lap.

He had almost dropped off to sleep there, with his cheek against her belly and her soft hand stroking his brow, when the discreet knock came at the door.

"Dinner," she whispered.

He forced his eyes to open.

She looked down at him, all soft and pliant and just the way he liked her best.

She suggested, "I'll put my robe on and—"

He was already sitting up, reaching for the slacks he'd discarded a while ago. "No way. Stay naked."

She rolled her eyes. "What will the bellman think?"

"He'll never know." He gestured toward the bedroom. "Wait in there."

She rose lightly to her feet and sketched a bow. "Yes, my lord."

"Hmm. I like the sound of that."

"I believe it." Her voice dripped irony.

The discreet knock came again. "Now, get going," he told her.

With a put-upon sigh, she went to wait in the other room.

He called her as soon as the food had been wheeled in and the bellman, well tipped, had been sent on his way.

Naturally, she'd put on her robe. They ate, and then he took the robe off her again.

It was late when they walked the dog one more time.

The next morning, she got up before him, to take the dog out. Feeling totally content, he rolled back over and dozed off again.

The next time he woke, he heard the shower going. He climbed from the bed and joined her.

Quite a while later, when they were both dressed and ready to go down and hunt up some breakfast, she said she thought they ought to just pack up and check out.

He suggested they stay another night.

She said she couldn't.

"Why not?"

And she had no real answer for that. He kissed her, whispering, "Please," against her mouth.

After they finished making love again, she called her sister Evie. From what he could piece together from Nevada's end of the conversation, the sister seemed surprised at this turn of events—but not particularly bothered. Maybe Evie thought Nevada was long overdue for a stay with a man in a penthouse suite.

While Nevada was still on the phone, he got behind her, smoothed her hair out of the way and put his lips on the back of her neck. He felt a shiver move through her, and knew she held back a sigh.

"Hold on a moment, will you?" she said into the phone. Then she put her hand over the mouthpiece and turned her head to look over her shoulder at him. "What are you up to?"

"Give her the number here. And the number of my phone. And tell her we'll stay a few more days."

"Chase. That's not what we agreed on." She tried to sound firm.

He started rubbing her shoulders. "Please?"

"We can't just—"

"Why can't we? I can make the time if you will."

"But this is just crazy."

"This is just wonderful. Let's not give it up. Not yet." He didn't want to use the magic word too often; it could lose its effectiveness, so this time he settled for just looking at her as if he would kill or die for another few glorious nights.

He knew when she sighed that he had won those nights and the days that went with them.

She turned to the phone again. "Evie, listen. Chase and I were just talking...."

Five minutes later, after giving her sister the numbers and requesting that she call if there was any news about their father, she hung up and turned to him.

"I can't believe I'm doing this."

He pulled her into his arms before any second thoughts could find their way out of her mouth.

Over that day and the next, Nevada had the time of her life. She and Chase gambled in all the casinos and sampled the food in a couple of Reno's best restaurants. They swam in the hotel's heated pool, listened to a free noontime concert on the banks of the Truckee River and toured the rose garden in Idlewild Park.

And they made love every single chance they got.

Their only real responsibility was Babette. And aside from regular walks and a little dog food, Babette made few demands.

Although Chase wouldn't admit it, he actually seemed to be growing fond of the dog. He even bought her a new collar. This one was black and decorated with steel studs. Babette held her head high and pranced around the sitting room when he put it on her.

"See?" Chase said. "She likes it. No more wussy little pink bows for this pooch. Am I right?"

And Babette barked in what actually did sound like total agreement.

It was a magical time. They spoke of nothing beyond the moment, and they never argued. During those too-brief days, they wanted exactly the same thing: fun. And each other. And they got both.

The only serious moment in that time of pure delight occurred very late Tuesday night. They'd made long, beautiful love together and then dropped off to sleep.

For a while, Nevada's dreams were sweet. She dreamed of her mother's house, back when she and her sisters had been little girls. She heard childish laughter, and then her mother's womanly chuckle echoing through the rooms. And she herself was some disembodied spirit, floating near the ceiling, looking down.

In the living room, she saw Faith at about the age of five. Faith was playing with her favorite doll—a bride doll that Faith had always called Jonesie. Jonesie possessed an extensive wardrobe beyond her white satin-and-lace bridal ensemble. Right now, Faith was dressing her in her roller-skating outfit, which came complete with miniature skates. Faith hummed as she worked, although Nevada couldn't identify the tune.

Nevada wondered where Evie was. And as soon as the question came into her mind, she found herself floating toward the kitchen. There she saw a four-year-old Evie seated at the table, her tongue caught between her teeth as she struggled to draw a picture of a sunflower on a big sheet of construction paper. At Evie's feet sat their mother's dog, a little white terrier, Lillie. Lillie panted up at Evie, and whined hopefully. Evie reached down and patted the dog on the head.

Then Nevada floated away again, through the rooms and out the front door, where she hovered, looking down at the hydrangea in front of the porch. It was heavy with blooms, glorious and full beneath the summer sun.

And then the house and the porch and the heavy pale purple clusters of blossoms faded away.

She found herself dancing with Chase in a meadow high in the mountains. The meadow was one Nevada remembered from a painting that hung above the mantel in Evie's living room. Evie's husband, Erik, had painted it. It was a beautiful scene, with the sky like a blue bowl and the mountains looking so near, stark and jagged and tipped with snow. Bleeding hearts and buttercups and Queen Anne's lace brushed their calves as they swayed to Willie Nelson singing "Angel Flying Too Close to the Ground."

Chase's arms cradled her close, and she smiled, her head on his shoulder.

She wanted to tell him how happy she was, to explain how she'd never thought of feeling like this, never imagined that she ever would. She lifted her head and opened her eyes.

And all the beauty blew away. For a brief and horrible moment, Chase's face was her father's face.

And then all signs of Chase flew away. The meadow had vanished.

And she stood at the top of the stairs of her mother's house, staring down at her father, who looked up at her, old and ill.

"Not much longer," he whispered through dry, cracked lips. "Not much longer now..."

"No," she heard someone crying. "No. Oh, no..."

* * *

"Nevada. You're dreaming. Wake up...."

She opened her eyes and saw Chase bending over her.

"Hey. You were crying in your sleep."

Her heart was beating hard and fast. She lay there, waiting for the heavy pounding in her chest to slow, looking up at Chase through the darkness, reassured by his presence at the same time as it struck her how odd it was, to wake from a bad dream and find a man in bed with her.

He touched her face, brushing away tears. "Okay, now?"

She nodded, but without much conviction. She kept thinking of Lillie, the little white terrier that had been her mother's. After her mother had died, Lillie had disappeared. Her father had claimed he'd found the dog a new home. But Nevada had never believed anything her father said.

"Want to talk about it?" Chase asked.

She didn't. All she wanted to do was forget. She pulled him down. "Kiss me, Chase...."

At first he resisted. "Are you sure you're all right?"

"Yes, just kiss me. Kiss me, please...."

At last, he lowered his mouth to hers.

After a time, she dropped off to sleep again, held close in Chase's arms. Lovemaking had soothed her. And as unconsciousness claimed her again, she had no thought of her father or of the past.

Still, she wasn't at all surprised when the phone rang at a little after nine the next morning.

Chapter Eleven

Nevada said goodbye to Evie and hung up the phone.

Chase was sitting up in bed. "Well?"

"It's my father. He had a really bad night, evidently. The hospital called Evie and said that if she wants any chance of seeing him before he dies, she should come immediately. They're all on their way there."

"Who?"

"Evie and her husband, Erik. Faith and her husband, Price. And my father's brother, my Uncle Oggie. By some miracle, Evie got three seats on a flight out of Sacramento for Portland that will be leaving in a couple of hours. And Faith got something out of San Francisco for herself and Price. They're all meeting at the hospital as soon as they possibly can."

"And what about you?"

She saw her father, as he'd looked twice now, in her dreams—old and sick. She heard his rough, sad whisper. *"Not much longer. Not much longer, now..."*

"Nevada?"

Could there be some value in seeing him? And what could she possibly say to him? Evie had said that the times she'd visited him in the past months, he'd been off in his own world somewhere; he hadn't even seemed to know her.

"Nevada." Chase's voice finally got through to her. She looked at him. "You're going, aren't you?"

"What makes you think that?"

He released a long, slow breath, then picked up the pad she'd scribbled on while she talked to Evie. "You wrote down the way to the hospital. And what looks like the name of the hotel where your sisters will be staying."

"Evie insisted."

He swore; a harsh, frustrated sound. "This is your *father*. And I think you want to go, even though you *say* you don't."

She rubbed her eyes. "I don't see how I could get there in time, from what Evie just said."

"You could fly, the same as they are."

Shouldn't she have known he would suggest that? "Yes," she answered grudgingly. "But there's no major airport there. If a flight was available, we'd be flying to Portland or Eugene. And then it'll take an extra hour or two to get to Salem."

"These are all just excuses. And flimsy ones, too. Are you going or not?"

"Chase..."

"A simple yes or no will do it."

She glared at him. "Yes, then. *Yes*. Are you satisfied, now?"

He grinned at her. "Attagirl." He looked at the clock. "I'll call my travel agent and see what she can come up with."

But on such short notice, the travel agent couldn't come up with a flight until the next morning, unless they wanted to try standby. Nevada was just about to suggest they go ahead and drive the distance, and hope that her father held on.

But Chase had another suggestion. "I can fly us there myself. I can have it all set up in the next couple of hours. How far is Salem?"

"Chase, I really—"

"How far?"

She raked her tangled hair back with a hand. "I'm not sure. Maybe five hundred miles, in a car."

"I can get us there in three hours, max, from takeoff, I promise you. And I'm sure there's at least an airfield in Salem where we can land."

As he spoke, her stomach seemed to rise to her throat. "Exactly how big is this airplane you're talking about, Chase?"

"I'll try to get my hands on a Cessna 340, like my own. It's a twin-engine eight-seater."

"Chase. No."

"Nevada..."

"Please. I hate flying in *big* planes. In little planes, I could claw out the windows to escape."

He was shaking his head. "So you've told me. And I went along with you last year, when you insisted on driving to Winslow rather than letting me fly us there. But this isn't just Billy and Maud having marital problems. This is a man dying, right?"

Nevada thought of the one time she'd been up in a small plane—twelve years ago. It was supposed to have been a treat; herself and a girlfriend on one of those little charter flights to see the Grand Canyon from the air. She never should have tried it; she'd always disliked flying, after all. But her friend had been persuasive.

And Nevada had ended up losing her lunch in a plastic bag and wishing she had a crowbar so she could shatter a window and leap gratefully into the Colorado River far below.

Chase kept on, relentlessly logical. "There's only one question—do you want to get there fast or not?"

The man was like a heat-seeking missile. He homed in on the real issue and wouldn't be deterred.

Because if she intended to go, she *did* need to get there fast. Judging by the warning the hospital had given Evie, she'd *better* get there fast or Gideon would be gone.

"Nevada." Now Chase sounded impatient. "Are you in a hurry or not?"

She dragged in a long breath and let it out slowly. "All right. If you can find a plane to fly, we'll do it your way."

"Good."

"But you'll have to let me pay my share of the flight."

He swore, succinctly. "Just let me do this for you, dammit."

"But it isn't right that—"

"Nevada. It's not a big deal to me. It's pocket change. And you are out of work. Just say thank-you and let's get the hell out of here."

"All right. Fine. Thank you."

"You're welcome."

"One more thing, though . . ."

He looked as if he might resort to violence if she came up with another excuse. "What?"

"We'll have to stop at a drugstore first, so I can buy out their supply of Dramamine. You don't want to get in that plane with me if I don't have Dramamine."

He relaxed. "No problem. Start packing. I'll get dressed and then line up the plane." As he spoke, he was up and out of the bed, headed for the shower. She sat there amid the rumpled bedclothes for a moment, staring somewhat dazedly after him as he strode so purposefully away from her. He was in his element now: in complete control of where they were going and how they would get there.

Babette, who lay curled into a ball beside the bed, looked up and yawned as he stepped over her on his way out.

Nevada showered after Chase, then ordered them breakfast from room service. Chase made an endless string of calls, hunting up a plane and clearing a flight schedule for them, making hotel reservations in Salem, pausing now and then between punching out numbers for a bite of toast or a sip of coffee.

Once she'd finished her own breakfast, Nevada took Babette down for a walk, then packed their bags and checked them out of the room using the automatic checkout service.

They left the suite for the last time at a little after eleven. On the way to the airport, they made only one stop: at a drugstore, where Nevada bought her motion-sickness pills. She immediately gulped down double the recommended dosage.

At the airport, they parked Nevada's car in the long-term lot. By half past noon, they were in the air. The flight wasn't nearly as bad as Nevada had thought it would be. She slept through most of it, which was just fine with her.

Chase had a car waiting for them when they touched down at McNary Field in Salem. It was one of those luxury 4X4's, shiny and black. Leave it to Chase to handle everything, Nevada thought woozily after a man in a canvas jumpsuit had escorted her and Babette from the plane to the car.

Idly, she opened the glove box. Sure enough, along with the rental-car registration she found a map of Oregon and one of Salem. Chase McQuaid thought of everything, no doubt about it. She snapped the compartment shut. Then, with a sigh, she sat back to wait as the man in the jumpsuit moved their luggage from the Cessna and Chase made arrangements for the plane to be hangared there at the field until they needed it again.

"The hotel—or straight to the hospital?" Chase asked when he climbed into the driver's seat.

Nevada looked out the windshield at a sky layered with gunmetal-gray clouds. When she'd walked from the plane to the waiting car, the air had felt humid and almost cool, so different from the desert heat she was used to. Even Reno had been dryer and warmer than this.

"Nevada?"

She shook herself and smiled at him. "The hospital, I think."

He was smiling his almost-smile and his eyes were so velvety looking, olive green. "All right. The hospital."

But then he didn't move. He just looked at her.

"What is it, Chase?"

She was wearing her favorite earrings, the thin gold hoops. He reached out and touched one, cleverly slipping his fingertips under the tangled fall of her hair. She felt the hoop tap the side of her neck. Then his hand slid behind her head to cup her nape.

"Chase?"

His fingers felt cool and knowing as he began a slow, tender massage. "You look so damn soft. Vulnerable. I like you best like this."

"It's those motion-sickness pills," she explained solemnly.

His fingers had picked up the warmth of her skin; now her body heat seemed to be something they shared between them. "So. Maybe I should keep you drugged."

"Naw." She leaned her head back into his touch. "I'd get boring after a while."

He cupped her head, his grasp firm and warm. "Probably so." And he pulled her a little closer to him, across the console. She forced her eyes, which kept wanting to droop, to open and look at him. *His* eyes seemed to be glittering. "But for a while, anyway, it would be a...nice novelty."

If she hadn't felt so languorous and lovely, she just might have been insulted that he would even pretend to consider drugging her. But right then, her mind was like a soft-focus lens, all fuzzy at the edges.

Vaguely, she wondered who she was, anyway. The past few days had been so beautiful. But totally out of her control. On "Honeymoon Hotline," she used to tell her listeners that an obsession with being in control was as much of a trap as allowing someone else to run one's life.

So maybe she needed to be out of control for a while. To let Chase handle everything.

After all, he did it so very well.

He pulled her closer. She went. And his mouth went right on past her lips to nuzzle her hair away from her ear.

"You drive me nuts," he whispered, so tenderly. And then she felt his teeth, light as a breath, grazing her earlobe. A shiver traveled out from the point of contact, like ripples in a waiting pond. She heard a tiny little click as his teeth met the post of her earring. And once again, the hoop grazed her throat.

And then he retreated to his side of the car. "We should get going."

She blinked and breathed deeply and sat forward herself. "Yes. Yes, we should...."

"There's a map in the—"

She waved a hand. "I know, I know." She opened the glove box and ordered her foggy mind to clear so she could tell him how to get to the hospital.

When they reached Oregon State Hospital on Center Street, they had to leave Babette in the car—with two of the windows cracked, of course, so she would be comfortable. She looked at them longingly as they left her behind.

They followed the signs to check in at the communications center, where they were given red clip-on passes and directed to Building 34, the medical ward where Gideon had been moved when he became too ill to function out of bed. At that hour, the door to the building was unlocked. They let themselves in and walked down a long hall, at the end of which they turned right. When they reached the door at the end of that second hall, they had to ring and wait to be admitted.

Inside, they found themselves on the main ward, where low music played and old, very ill men lay in rows of beds, many hooked up to IV drips, some watching television, a few reading books. After the ward came another door. Through it, they entered the acute wing, which held only a few beds, separated by white privacy screens.

A tall man with a kind face stood by the door that led to one of the two private rooms. His name tag said he was Barney Tilden. The ward clerk who had shown them the way introduced Barney and explained that he was the mental-health therapist assigned to watch over Gideon at all times.

Nevada understood that Barney Tilden was her father's guard. Gideon was dying. But those who cared for him now would never lose sight of the fact that, had he not been severely disturbed, he would be in a penitentiary, serving hard time.

Nevada glanced beyond the door and saw her Uncle Oggie standing in the narrow space on the far side of the one bed in the room. Oggie leaned close to the sick man, as if listening to some last, whispered secret from the lips of the dying man.

When Oggie glanced up and saw Nevada and Chase in the doorway, he straightened. "Nevada." He had a low, hoarse voice, the voice of a man who likes his cigars and takes his whiskey straight. "You made it."

He came around the end of the bed toward her, limping, favoring his right foot, which he'd injured a few years before in an accident with a hunting rifle. His face was wrinkled, his hair thin white wisps on the sides of his head. His eyes seemed to know all the secrets of life—and of death. He wore what he always wore: a frayed white shirt, red suspenders and wrinkled tan slacks.

"Gal. It's good you're here." He reached out and enveloped her in a hug.

Nevada allowed the hug, but gave little to it. She was fond of her uncle, but wary of him. In many ways, he resembled her father: crafty and manipulative, willing to go further than he should to get his way. But unlike Gideon, Oggie was a good man. There was no evil in his cleverness. Her sisters, more trusting souls than Nevada, adored Oggie unreservedly.

Oggie held her by the shoulders when she pulled back from the hug. "Who's this?" He wiggled his bushy brows in Chase's direction.

Nevada introduced them, then asked where her sisters were.

"They went to grab a quick bite," her uncle said. "They'll be back, though. And soon." He glanced over his shoulder at the man on the bed, then looked back at Nevada and shook his grizzled head. "Giddy ain't likely to last the night, I'm afraid."

From the still figure on the bed came the sound of labored breathing. The usual equipment loomed over the bed: an IV stand and what looked like a heart monitor, which beeped in a slow, faint rhythm. There was also an oxygen tank, not in use; the mask hung on the tank.

Nevada stared at the mask and wondered if Gideon really had been whispering to Oggie a moment ago. And if he had been, what secrets could he be telling? Gideon, she knew, had a thousand secrets. He had lived his life running from being known, yet he was endlessly crafty, and loved to ferret out the things other people tried to hide.

"He hates the mask," Oggie said, on seeing the direction of Nevada's gaze. "Shoves it off every time someone puts it on him."

A woman in street clothes who wore an ID tag similar to Barney Tilden's bustled in, greeted everyone and approached the bed. She checked the IV and the heart monitor. Clucking her tongue, she put the oxygen mask on the patient. Then she bustled out again.

Nevada stared after her, thinking rather idiotically how no one in the place wore a white coat, the way people in hospitals—especially *mental* hospitals—always did in the movies.

"They come and go all the time around here," Oggie said. "You kinda get used to it." He turned to Chase. "Outside, facing Center Street, there're a couple of benches and some walnut trees." He glanced toward the high, narrow window, which had wire mesh between its double panes. "It's cloudy out there, but the air's good and fresh."

Chase nodded. "Let's go."

Nevada, her mind slowed by the lingering effects of the motion-sickness pills and a headache that had come on just moments before, realized that they intended to leave her here. Alone with the man on the bed.

"Chase..." She put her hand on his arm. Beneath the brown leather flight jacket he'd thrown over a sport shirt, she felt him tense. She leaned into him a little. "Don't go...."

His arm went around her and he looked down at her. She saw his response to her plea in his eyes. He wasn't used to her asking him for support—and he liked it. Protectiveness moved into his gaze. As well as heat ...

But then Uncle Oggie cleared his throat. Chase glanced at the old man. "Those benches are waitin', son."

There was a moment, a split second when some message passed between the two men. Nevada didn't like it at all. She had a very strong urge to tell her old uncle to mind his own business. But she said nothing. Her mind felt so slow, and her headache was growing worse.

Chase's comforting arm fell away. "We'll be back soon," he said in the kind of voice people use on invalids and children.

She pointedly stepped away from him. "Fine." Their gazes locked, hers defiant, his so patient that it grated. Then Chase turned and followed Oggie from the room.

Nevada longed to trot right after them. She even took a step in that direction, but then she met the eyes of Barney Tilden, at his post just beyond the door. The man knew panic when he saw it. "I'm right here, ma'am," he said softly.

She swallowed and made herself smile. "Of course. I know." Then she turned. She put one foot in front of the other and she approached the bed, around the far side, where Oggie had been standing before.

Her first thought, after she made herself look down at the man lying there, was that his bones and his flesh seemed to have melted down somehow, leaving his skin hanging on a smaller frame like a too-large suit of clothes. He had never been a really big man. But once, he had *seemed* big. Once, he had filled her whole world with his selfishness and his heedless cruelty. She, like her sisters, had lived at his whim.

Surely this husk of a man could never have had the power to make three lives a living hell.

Oh, but he had.

The memories were there. A thousand upon a thousand of them.

For years, she had thought herself immune to them.

But now, looking down at this shell that remained of the man who had been her father, the memories rose up, new and powerful all over again. As if she had never really gotten beyond them at all. As if they'd always waited there, trapped inside, for this moment to get free.

"No welfare people will ever get my girls," he used to say so proudly. So, after he'd killed their mother—yes, all right, it was an accident, but all his fault, nonetheless— he'd gotten rid of poor Lillie, sold their home and taken them into his vagabond life with him. They lived on the road, chasing one big moneymaking scheme after another.

At first, because of their mother's money, there were apartments. And then residence hotels. And then rooms at nightly rates. And then no rooms at all. Just his big, battered old Buick, and pillows and blankets.

And each other, in the dark.

Of course, things got better after he started exploiting Evie, but before then, there was an endless, awful time.

They went to twelve schools in five years. And then school became impossible; they moved around too much. So they taught each other as best they could. From library books, when they could get them. Or from books that she, Nevada, would make *him* get for them. By threatening him with how the welfare people might like to know how they lived...

He would hit her, then—one good, hard one, usually across the face. And then he would get her the books.

He was not a terribly violent man. Not physically, anyway. But he would always yell at his daughters, as he had at their mother, when they got in his way or stood up to him. Nevada was the one who stood up to him the most. So, what blows there were, fell on her.

She saw him, now, in a memory even stronger than the rest, his face contorted with rage, his hand raised high, commanding, "Don't talk back to me, girl...."

But she *had* talked back. And frequently. And she'd paid the price. For the sake of the books. And for something in their bellies when he forgot to feed them.

And to keep him from hitting Faith or Evie instead.

Yes, she had taken the blows to protect her sisters. And she was proud that she had.

But now, all these years later, her sisters were good and loving women, leading full, rich lives.

Whereas she was . . .

Enough, Nevada thought. *Enough of this self-pity. Enough of the past.*

She made herself look again at the shrunken figure on the bed. The oxygen mask still covered the lower half of his face. He breathed easier now, with the oxygen helping. But his closed eyes were black holes in their bony sockets and his cheeks were so sunken that the mask stuck out on the sides of his face. A smell rose from him, a too-sweet smell. Like bad apples.

He stirred, groaning a little, as she watched him. And his skeletal hand came up to shove the mask away.

In reflex, she tried to stop him from getting rid of the mask and the precious oxygen it provided. But she jerked back, repelled, when she touched his dry, hot skin. She gripped the bed rail as he moaned and went on batting fitfully at the mask, finally dislodging it, so it dropped to the pillow on the side opposite where she stood.

And then, very slowly, he opened his eyes. He looked right at Nevada.

"Mary?" he whispered.

Nevada said nothing.

He peered at her, squinting. "Mary, is that you, Mary?"

Nevada stared down at him, appalled.

"Oh, Mary." He spoke in his dry, pained half-whisper. "Did you come to say you forgive me, Mary?"

No! She felt that she screamed the word, although it was really only in her head. Her lips didn't even move. *You don't deserve forgiveness and I won't forgive you. Ever...*

His bony hand lifted, suddenly, and closed over hers, where it clutched the metal safety rail. "Mary..."

His grip was so hot. And brittle. She felt that if she'd turned her hand and squeezed back, she could easily have crushed the bones, could have heard them cracking, snapping like dry twigs.

"Mary..." He kept saying that name.

Nevada stood immobile, although she wanted to pull away; she wanted to strike out. She wanted to rail at him for each and every one of his numberless sins. For all he had stolen—from her mother's life to a little white terrier to the childhoods of three innocent girls. For what he had done to Evie, the cruel way he had used her. When she was just a girl. And then more recently, when he'd taken her from her home, locked her away, nearly caused her death.

And for more, even, than that. For what he'd done to *her,* to Nevada. For the...lack inside herself. The incomplete place that somehow seemed to have left her wise in so many ways—and yet not whole. Afraid. Not knowing how to love a strong man as a strong woman loves.

Why had she come here, except to have her say? For her moment of righteousness, when she could tell him exactly what she thought of him?

"Mary? Oh, Mary, please..."

Nevada moved, then. But not to jerk away. She turned her hand and grasped her father's hand lightly, tenderly, with infinite care for his fragile bones.

And she heard herself whisper, so softly, "Yes, Gideon. It's me. And of course, I forgive you. I love you. You know that...."

She heard him sigh, watched his eyes droop closed in their hollow, shadowed sockets. "Thank you, Mary," he whispered. "Thank you, my love..."

His hand went slack in hers. She held it for a moment more, then gently laid it on his chest.

A few minutes later, the woman came in again to cluck over the oxygen mask and check all the machines that monitored Gideon Jones's fading life signs. Nevada stepped back while the woman worked. And then she moved close again when the woman had left.

She looked down at the man on the bed, feeling far away from it all, as she had in her dream last night; like some disembodied spirit, floating near the ceiling, looking down.

Abstractly, she decided that her father looked more peaceful now than before.

And then the heart monitor flattened out. The sound became one long, piercing beep.

The woman rushed in again, followed by three others, calling out orders as she came.

Nevada moved out of the way as they surrounded the bed. But she knew they were wasting their time.

Gideon Jones was dead.

And she had forgiven him.

And where her hatred had once lived, keeping her strong, now there was nothing.

An emptiness.

A void.

Chapter Twelve

Though Gideon had never lived in North Magdalene, Oggie and Evie decided to have him buried there, in the Jones family plot. The funeral was to be held in the North Magdalene Community Church, with the Reverend Johnson presiding. The body was flown to Sacramento and then a Grass Valley funeral home took over, arranging for transportation the rest of the way. Evie chose the casket and ordered the flowers, although Oggie, a much more prosperous man than his appearance suggested, insisted that all the bills be sent to him.

After one night in the hotel in Salem, Chase and Nevada flew to Marysville in the Cessna. Chase then hired a pilot to fly it back to Reno and its owner. In Marysville, Chase rented another vehicle, a big black 4X4 identical to the one he'd used in Oregon.

They drove to North Magdalene, where they stayed with Evie, as they'd planned all along. Evie moved her younger stepdaughter in with the older one so that Nevada could have the younger girl's room. Chase found himself installed in the studio room where Erik painted his landscapes. He stifled a grim sigh when Evie pointed out the narrow couch that would be his bed, but he said nothing. It was pretty much what he'd expected, after all.

And it wasn't the narrowness of the couch that really bothered him; it wasn't even the fact that his feet hung over the end of the damn thing whenever he stretched out on it. What really bothered him was sleeping without Nevada.

Somehow, in the few nights they'd had together, Chase had gotten used to sleeping with Nevada. He missed having her there beside him in the night. And he wanted her with him, however cramped the bed. But he also realized that Evie and Erik had three children, a fourth on the way, and certain standards to maintain.

So, for the time being, Chase slept alone without complaining about it. Right now, he had more important things to think about than his own comfort during the night. There was the funeral to get through.

And there was something else to deal with, too: a certain change in Nevada herself.

Something had happened to her. For a day or two, Chase had tried to pretend she was fine. But she wasn't. Since Gideon had died, she'd become distant and withdrawn. And she had become passive. She let other people handle things, which had never been her style at all.

Of course, she *was* easier to get along with than she'd ever been. Chase couldn't help appreciating that just a little. Now, if a decision had to be made, he made it. They didn't have to endure a long, involved meeting of the minds over things like who would drive the car and whose turn it was to pay. He drove and he paid. It was simple and efficient.

Yet, even though he found her a pleasure to deal with, he couldn't lie to himself; something wasn't right. More than likely, it had to do with her father's death. The change in her represented some phase she had to go through that would pass eventually. She would be arguing with him over every little thing again in no time. He just had to be patient—as he'd been about everything else having to do with Nevada.

But even if the difference in her was only temporary, he couldn't shake a certain feeling of unease about it. Her family didn't like it, either. By Friday night, her sisters had each approached him individually and asked him if Nevada was all right. He'd reassured them both. But their expressions of concern made him realize that he probably ought to pursue the problem a little.

The funeral was scheduled for two o'clock on Saturday afternoon. That morning, after breakfast, Chase told Nevada that they were going for a walk.

Just a few days ago, he would have felt the sharp side of her tongue if he'd dared to *tell* her anything. But this morning she fell right in step with him.

He led her out the front gate and down the street with Babette, looking proud in her studded collar, prancing along beside them. At the end of the street, the road narrowed into an unpaved trail that wound through the shadowed trees. Since the trail wasn't wide enough for them to walk abreast, Chase took the lead. As he walked, he looked for a good place to stop and talk.

He was so busy scouting out the right spot that he didn't even notice when Nevada quit following him. But then he turned to toss off a word of encouragement—and found himself alone. With a muttered oath, he headed back the way he'd come.

A hundred yards and a couple of twists in the trail later, he found her. She was standing very still, with Babette at her feet, looking up at the branches of the trees over-head. The sun, still to the east in the sky, found its way through all the branches in little patches of brightness. A few of them caught in her rusty hair, turning it to auburn fire. And her face looked so pale and pure, tipped up like that, touched by light and shadow. A dreamy, faraway smile curved her lips.

Gently, he spoke her name.

She blinked and then looked at him. "Hmm?"

"What happened?"

She frowned, as if his question made no sense. "Nothing."

"Nevada, you just...stopped. In the middle of the trail. I was way ahead before I even noticed you were gone."

She smiled again, an abashed smile. She looked adorable. "I'm sorry. I was watching the light and the shadows, the changing patterns the branches of the trees make when the wind blows them. I forgot to keep up, that's all." She shrugged. "Really. Nothing happened at all."

Since she'd stopped here, he decided it was as good a place as any for that talk they needed to have. "Look, Nevada..."

"Hmm?"

"Is something ... wrong?"

She was frowning again. "Like what?"

"Lately, you're acting strangely."

"Strangely..."

"Yes. Distant and withdrawn. As if you're going through the motions, but you're not really all there."

"I see." And she nodded.

He thought that she looked almost as dazed and dreamy as she had when she'd taken those motion-sickness pills. And then he remembered, just the other day, how he'd told her that he liked her that way.

He felt a stab of guilt. Because it was just a little bit true...

He reached for her, pulled her close and then shoved his hands in her hair, lifting her face up to his. "Nevada. I didn't mean it, what I said the other day at McNary Field."

Her brows drew together in puzzlement, so he explained, "The motion-sickness pills hadn't worn off, remember? I said I liked it, the way you were acting so vague and agreeable, the way you looked so soft and sleepy and vulnerable."

"Oh, right. I remember."

"You said I'd be bored if you behaved that way all the time."

"So?"

"Well, I'm not bored. But I'm getting worried." He let his hands slide down to grip her shoulders. "What the hell happened, just before your father died?"

The dreamy look faded. Now she seemed just plain withdrawn. "Nothing happened." She tried to slip from his grasp.

He held her firm. "Come on. Did he say anything?"

A gnat flew between them. She batted it away, managing to shrug off his hands at the same time. But although he released her, he didn't give up. "Come on. Tell me."

At last, she admitted, "My father...thought I was my mother."

Babette whined a little. Nevada knelt and scratched her behind the ears.

Chase looked down at the woman and the dog. "How do you know he thought you were your mother?"

She went on petting the dog. For a moment, Chase thought she wouldn't answer. But then she told him, "He looked at me and said her name."

"And what else?"

"Chase." She gave the dog a final pat and rose to her feet once more. "It doesn't matter."

"What else?"

She looked down at the ground between them. "He wanted her to forgive him."

"For what?"

She dragged in a breath and met his eyes again. "When I was eight, my mother fell down the stairs and broke her neck while she was having an argument with my father. In a way, he killed her. I saw it happen."

He ached for the eight-year-old who'd had to witness such a thing. But he didn't allow the sympathy he felt to distract him, now that they were finally getting somewhere. "Did he go to prison for it?"

"No. It really was an accident. But it wouldn't have happened if she hadn't been so upset."

"What do you mean?"

"He was yelling at her and she was walking away from him. He grabbed her arm at the top of the stairs and she jerked away. She wasn't paying attention and she tripped on her own robe. She fell. All the way to the bottom. And she was dead when she got there."

"Was there some kind of police investigation?"

"No. When the police came, my father told them what had happened. Then they questioned me and I told them the same thing. It was the truth, and the police believed us. So they let us stay together."

"Let *who* stay together?"

"Me and my sisters. We stayed with our father."

"I'm not sure I follow."

"Since my father didn't go to jail, he could keep us with him. And we could stay together." She raked her fingers through her hair. Again, he thought that she wouldn't go on. But then, after leaning against a pine tree and crossing her arms over her chest, she told him more.

"It was like this—when my mother landed at the bottom of the stairs, my father ran to her. I'd been standing in the doorway of my room when I saw her fall. But after that, I went out to the landing, to look down. He looked up and saw me. I ran back to my room.

"After a few minutes, he came and found me. He said the ambulance would be there soon and that my sisters were still asleep in bed where they belonged. But not me. I had to stick my nose in where I had no business. He ordered me to tell him what I had seen. I said that I saw him kill her. And he explained to me that it had been an accident, we both *knew* it was an accident. I yelled at him, 'You killed my mother!' and he slapped my face and shook me hard and said if I didn't tell the truth, they'd put him in jail and then the welfare people would come and take me and Faith and Evie. They'd send us to separate foster homes. And we'd never see each other again."

Chase held back a rude oath. The more he heard about Gideon Jones, the happier he was that the man was dead.

She went on, looking into the middle distance. "My father hated foster homes. He spent most of his childhood in them, and I guess he had a tough time. He always swore none of his girls would ever be taken away by the welfare people. He'd keep us together at any price. It was the one thing he and I were in perfect agreement on. Sometimes, after he took us from our home, I'd threaten to tell the authorities about the awful way we lived. But that was only to make him treat us a little better. I never would have done it. I would have done anything to stay with Faith and Evie. They were my family, my people. After our mother died, they were everything to me. I swore in my heart to see them grown-up and happy. And I kept my promise...." She looked down at her shoes again as her voice faded off.

After a moment, she lifted her head. Chase waited for her to say more. But apparently, she'd said it all. She seemed to be off in her own world, staring at a ridge of serpentine rock that stuck up from the bed of pine needles across the trail from where she leaned against the tree.

"Nevada?"

"Hmm?"

"What did you do, three days ago, when your father thought you were your mother?"

She kept looking at the ridge of green rock. "I wanted to yell and scream at him and tell him what an awful man he was."

He knew she hadn't done any yelling. The hospital staff would have stopped that in a second. "But what *did* you do?"

She wasn't looking at the serpentine rock anymore; now she was back to studying the ground between her feet. "I gave him what he wanted from me. I pretended to be her. And while I was pretending I was her, I said that I forgave him. I don't know why. I just ... gave him what he was begging for. And then he died."

"Hell." In two steps Chase had reached her. He pulled her close.

She sighed and rested her head against his chest. He stroked her wild red hair, thinking that he liked nothing better than the feel of her in his arms.

"It was a generous thing you did," he whispered.

"I didn't do it for him. I don't know why I did it, really. It just ... slipped out."

"Well, maybe you should have done what you wanted to do and yelled at him."

"Maybe so." She wrapped her arms around his waist and settled more comfortably against him. "But I didn't." She looked up at him. "I guess I missed my chance, huh?"

What the hell could he say to that? Nothing that would mean anything.

He kissed her fragrant hair and held her tighter and told himself that eventually she would get over whatever had stolen her fire.

And until then, he would look after her. And he would do one damn fine job of it, too.

At the service that afternoon, the church was about half full. Except for Evie, Erik and Oggie, no one who lived in town had even met the deceased. The little bit most folks knew of him wasn't good: that he had kidnapped and nearly killed Evie, whom everyone adored; and that he'd spent the last nineteen months of his life locked up in Oregon in that place where they filmed *One Flew Over the Cuckoo's Nest.*

But the turnout was respectable—out of affection for the Jones family, Nevada felt sure. Regina Jones, who was married to one of Oggie's four sons, played the piano— haunting, well-loved hymns: "In the Garden" and "Faith of Our Fathers"; "A Mighty Fortress" and "Beyond the Sunset."

Nevada sat in the front row. Her sisters and their husbands sat to her right and Chase to her left. Somehow, everyone just seemed to assume that Chase belonged beside her, the way Price belonged with Faith and Erik with Evie.

And Chase *had* been good to her. He'd been right there next to her, ready whenever she needed him, through the past three grim days. She felt for his hand—and it was right there, enclosing hers in warmth and strength. She turned and looked at him. They shared a smile.

The reverend intoned, "Gideon Ezekiel Jones is no longer with us...."

Nevada faced front once more. Above the altar hung a large, framed print: Jesus, the Good Shepherd, surrounded by a flock of woolly sheep. Nevada stared at the print as the reverend launched into a sort of all-purpose talk concerning the comfort of the Savior and the better place to which Gideon had now passed. When the reverend had finished, Oggie got up and said a few words about the Gideon he remembered from all those years ago when they were children.

Even for Oggie, who loved nothing so much as delivering a speech, there wasn't a lot to say. By the time Gideon had turned five, both of his parents had died. All four Jones boys of that generation had been farmed out to foster homes. Over the years, they'd lost touch with each other. To this day, none of the North Magdalene Joneses knew what had happened to Oggie's second and third brothers, Isaiah and Nathaniel. They were shrouded in mystery, rarely mentioned. To Nevada, they hardly even seemed real.

Actually, Nevada and her sisters were themselves newcomers to the North Magdalene branch of the family. Three years ago, Oggie had tracked Evie down in Santa Fe and convinced her to try making a life for herself in the small Sierra foothills town. Until that time, the three sisters knew no more of him and his children than they did of the other two vanished uncles.

"I don't think Giddy knew a lot of contentment in his lifetime," Oggie intoned in conclusion. "And those of you that know me have most likely figured out by now that I'm not a churchgoing man as a rule. But I do believe that there are powers greater than we are. I was honored to be with Giddy near the end, and I'd like to think that maybe, now, my little brother has found real peace at last."

Following the service, they proceeded to the cemetery, where the rough grass needed trimming and myrtle and rambling roses grew between the graves. Nevada stood between Faith and Chase, her eyes focused on the distant hills, which were covered with tall, proud evergreen trees. The reverend said a prayer and Evie threw the first handful of dirt on the coffin.

And that was it. They went back to Evie and Erik's big old house, where neighbors and family had provided an unending array of gelatin-mold salads and reheatable casseroles. Just about everyone who'd attended the service came to the house afterward. The rooms filled quickly with people drinking coffee and tea and talking quietly of the beauty of the day, of how they'd never known Gideon, but they'd heard he was very ill and that his going had been for the best, after all.

After exchanging greetings with a few people she'd met through Evie, Nevada poured herself some iced tea and found a seat on the couch. Chase hovered close, while Babette snoozed at her feet. But then Faith's husband, Price, approached Chase. The two men wandered off together—talking of business, probably. Price managed a stock portfolio and made investments for a living, so he and Chase had discovered that they had a lot in common.

Nevada remained on the couch, sipping her tea and staring at the painting over the mantel—the one of the meadow in the mountains of which she'd dreamed on the night before Gideon died. Although Erik made his living painting houses, he truly was a talented artist. The painting had an almost-magical feel about it. As if a person could step right into it and dance among the wildflowers, just the way she and Chase had done in her dream.

Looking at the painting, Nevada shivered a little. She sipped her tea without really tasting it. And when she glanced up from her glass, her eyes met those of her Uncle Oggie.

He was standing by the big windows that looked out on the porch, a drink in his hand. He raised his glass to her. She nodded and forced a smile and then looked away. Her uncle did make her nervous sometimes. And it seemed to her as if, in the past couple of days, every time she went near him, she could feel his little dark eyes on her.

Right then, the younger of Evie's two stepdaughters, whose name was Becca, came and knelt on the floor to pet Babette. "Oh, you're so sweet," Becca told the dog. "She's so cute, Aunt Nevada."

Nevada realized that the child was talking to her, so she looked down and smiled.

"Can I take her out back?"

"Sure, go ahead."

Becca stood and brushed off the pretty blue dress she wore. "Come on, Babette, let's go outside." Babette stuck her poufy behind in the air as she stretched and yawned. Then she got up on her dainty white feet and trotted off to wherever Becca led her.

"Nevada?"

Nevada turned from watching the child and the dog to see Faith standing above her.

"We haven't had much of a chance to talk, have we?" Faith sat down beside her.

"No, I suppose we haven't." Nevada stared at her sister, thinking how lovely Faith looked. With her soft brown hair and porcelain skin, Faith had always been quietly pretty. But now, since she'd married Price, Faith had the same glow that Evie had—a glow that made her truly beautiful. It was a glow of happiness. Of a woman fulfilled.

Faith put her hand over Nevada's and leaned close. "Are you going to be all right, Vada?"

Nevada blinked. It seemed like, in the last couple of days, everybody kept asking her that. "Of course. I'm fine."

Faith looked around at the people sitting nearby, then she suggested, "Let's go outside for a moment, why don't we?"

Dutifully, Nevada set down her glass, got up and went with Faith through the chatting groups of guests out to the front porch. There were people there, too, sitting on the lawn furniture and the folding chairs Evie had set out, even perched on the steps.

Faith took Nevada by the hand. "Come on. Let's get off to ourselves a little. This way." She pulled Nevada out onto the lawn, toward the wrought-iron fence that fronted the sidewalk.

A locust tree grew right beyond the fence, between a narrow bit of cracked sidewalk and the street. Its branches hung over the yard a little, providing a cool, shady spot.

Once they stood beneath the shade of the tree, Faith admitted gingerly, "I spoke with Chase this morning, after he talked to you. He's worried about you. And so are the rest of us."

Nevada absorbed her sister's words and tried to look alert and interested. But it required an effort. Inside, she felt distant and aloof and just a little numb. She'd been feeling that way for a few days now, ever since Gideon had died. She understood that her family, and Chase, were becoming alarmed.

She thought back to what had passed between herself and Chase that morning. She had answered all his questions about Gideon. And twice, while they talked, he had pulled her into his arms. It had felt wonderful to have him hold her. And as always, the scent of him had been seductive—as well as reassuring. With a man like Chase beside her, a woman didn't have to worry about anything.

"Nevada?"

Nevada realized she'd been woolgathering again. She put on a smile for Faith.

Faith brushed the side of her face with a tender hand. "Oh, Nevada. You always protected Evie and me from Father. And we both knew it. And we have an idea of what he put you through. And that it was harder for you, when we were children, than it was for us. It wasn't really fair, what you put up with for our sakes—or that you were the one left alone with him Wednesday, at the end. I wish I had been there with you, when he died. Evie does, too. I'm so sorry we weren't."

There was guilt in Faith's eyes. Nevada could see it. She didn't want that; her sisters weren't to blame for anything. She caught Faith's hand and forced an approximation of her old familiar briskness. "Oh, come on. It's just... the way it happened. And I'll be all right. There's nothing wrong with me. I'm... having a rough time right now, on a lot of levels. But I'll work it out."

"Evie and I... We want to help."

"I know. And thanks. But there's really nothing you can do." She patted the back of Faith's hand. "Except not to worry. Because I'll be fine."

But over the days that followed, it became more and more evident that Nevada wasn't fine. The members of her family tried, one at a time, to talk with her about their concern for her. Gently, she told them not to worry.

Since no one seemed able, in the end, to get through the cocoon of vague dreaminess that seemed to enclose her, they all treated her carefully, tenderly. But they had no idea what to do to snap her out of her fog.

On Monday, two days after the funeral, Faith and Price returned to the Bay Area. They were a busy couple, dividing their time between overseeing repairs that were being made to their mansion in Sausalito and the supervision of major renovations to the Foothill Inn, which they owned and which was the only motel in North Magdalene. Also, five days a week, from six in the morning until one in the afternoon, Price sat at a desk behind a wall of computer screens, where he could closely monitor activity on the stock market.

Erik, Evie, Chase and Nevada all walked out to Price's Jaguar with them to say goodbye. Faith kissed Nevada. Then she patted Evie's stomach, which was softly rounded now, in her fifth month of pregnancy.

"Take care of that little one," Faith said.

Evie promised that she would. Faith told Evie that she and Price would be back in a week or two, to check on the progress over at the inn. And then she gave Erik a hug—and Chase, too.

When Faith let go of Chase, Price shook his hand. "We'll shoot for early September, then?" Price said.

"Sounds good to me," Chase replied. "Give me a call in a month or so. We'll firm it up."

Bemused, Nevada watched the two tall, handsome men, and wondered what in the world they were talking about. Later, Chase spoke of how much he looked forward to the visit from her sister and Price, come September.

"What visit?"

He sighed. "Nevada, we talked about it several times. They're coming to Phoenix to see us."

"They are?"

He looked, for a moment, as if he wanted to shake her. But he only said, "Yes. They are."

* * *

As one day became the next, Chase stayed close to her side. More and more, Nevada found herself leaning on him, counting on him to handle things, to make decisions on how they would spend their time.

He wanted to explore her family's town, so she went right along with him, her hand in his, as they strolled up and down Main Street, stopping in at each little shop, either to buy something that had caught Chase's eye in the window—or simply to browse. More than once, he took her to dinner at the Mercantile Grill, which was run by Eden Jones, who was the wife of another of Oggie's sons. They both agreed that the food and service there equalled any they'd enjoyed anywhere.

Whenever they wanted to go someplace that required wheels, Chase always drove. He still had the black 4X4 that he'd rented in Marysville. And Nevada's car remained in the airport lot in Reno. In the back of her mind, she kept thinking that she ought to ask Chase to take her there, so she could pick it up. But that seemed silly, when she really considered it. It would be a four-hour drive, round-trip, just to get a car they would probably never use. No, they could get it when they were ready to leave.

Which was bound to happen pretty soon. Even if *she* didn't have a job, Chase did. He couldn't put his empire-building on hold forever. He got calls nearly every day—not on his cellular phone, because that didn't work too well with all the interference from the mountains that surrounded North Magdalene. But he'd given Evie's number to his people in Phoenix, so contractors and business associates were forever calling the house, frantically demanding to talk to Chase. He always managed, somehow, to set out procedures for allaying disaster. But the day approached when he would have to be there to fix a problem. And then they would have to leave.

On Friday, four days after Faith and Price left, Chase took Nevada down to Nevada City, where he treated her to dinner at one of the best restaurants in town. Then they saw a show and after that they stayed the night in a quaint little bed-and-breakfast.

They didn't sleep much. Chase said he wanted to make up for all those nights he'd had to sleep on that couch in Erik's studio. Nevada didn't mind losing the sleep. She loved it when Chase touched her. And the dreamy world she lived in came vibrantly alive again when he was inside her, moving, forcing her to feel, to respond, to cry out in startled pleasure at the things he did to her.

They liked the charming bed-and-breakfast so much— not to mention the privacy it afforded—that they stayed an extra night, returning Sunday morning to North Magdalene.

Sunday afternoon, Evie caught Nevada sitting by herself in the backyard. As she had more than once before, she tried to talk to Nevada about how concerned she was.

"You're just...not yourself lately," Evie said.

Nevada sighed and said she was fine. But she couldn't help thinking that all of this family concern really wasn't working out for her. She was ready to return to Phoenix.

And as it happened, Chase got a call after lunch the next day about one of his projects. A few problems had arisen that he had to handle personally. He couldn't put off returning to Phoenix any longer. They would leave tomorrow.

That suited Nevada fine. She loved North Magdalene. It was like someone's fantasy of small-town America, tucked in such a picturesque fashion among the pine-covered hills, filled with friendly people who helped each other when times got tough. Still, it would be a relief to leave all this family love and concern behind.

And then she remembered that she had to do something about her car, which still waited in that Reno airport lot.

"Chase, I think I'll have to drive. My car's still in Reno, remember? I'll have to get someone to take me there and then—"

But he only waved his hand and said not to worry. They would fly together in comfort, first-class from Sacramento. And he would take care of the car.

"Just give me the keys and the parking stub," he instructed, "and I'll see to it that the car is driven home, right to your house in Mesa, within the next couple of days."

"But, Chase, you know I hate to fly."

He patted her shoulder. "Look. I promise this time that the plane will be a big one. And you'll have your Dramamine handy, right?"

"Well, yes, of course . . ."

"So what's the problem?"

She realized there wasn't one. Life was just so smooth and easy, with Chase running things.

"Gal, how are you?"

Startled by the rough sound of her uncle's voice, Nevada jumped a little. She was sitting on the front steps, having wandered outside when Chase started making all the calls that would set up their trip tomorrow. She'd been staring dreamily at her sneakered feet and thinking about nothing in particular—and somehow she hadn't heard the old man come through the gate and stump up the walk to stand in front of her.

For a few seconds, she felt something like shame. What had happened to her, not to notice that a lame old man had just clanged through a gate and hobbled right up to her on his gnarled manzanita cane?

She'd missed so many things lately. She just wasn't paying attention to her life....

But then she sighed. And the numbness flowed back over her, like warm, soothing water. There was nothing really wrong with her. So she hadn't heard Oggie hobbling up to her. It was just one of those things that happens sometimes.

Lifting her arm to shade her eyes from the bright afternoon sun, she looked up over the old man's threadbare trousers and grimy suspenders and frayed white shirt into those beady brown eyes that always saw way too much.

"I asked how you're doin', gal."

"I'm fine, Uncle Oggie."

"I heard a rumor you were leavin' us."

"Yes. We're leaving tomorrow."

"Then I think it's time you and me had us a little talk."

For the first time since her father's death, Nevada felt a slight stirring of defiance, although when she spoke, her voice was lazy and unconcerned. "Oh, really? What about?"

He just studied her for a moment, looking so much like her father. And yet not like him at all . . .

At last, he said, "You just get on up and walk down to the end of the street with me, into the woods a little ways."

"Why?"

"Your sister's house is always full. Someone could come bangin' through that front door any minute. And I ain't of a mind to be interrupted when I'm talkin' to you."

Nevada thought that she would like nothing better than to simply say no. But the old man's eyes allowed no argument. So she kept quiet.

She rose from the step, brushed off the back of her jeans and went with him. Babette, who'd been lying on the porch a few feet away, got up and followed along behind.

Oggie proceeded with care, placing his cane precisely as he went, so it was a slow walk to the woods at the end of the street. When they reached the trail that wound into the trees, he moved a little faster. The ground was relatively even, there, at least for the first few hundred yards.

Soon enough, Oggie said, "This way." They left the trail and moved into the trees. In no time at all they came to a pair of round, flat-topped boulders that faced each other on either side of a clear space.

"This looks good," Oggie declared. With a fair amount of grunting and groaning, he settled himself on one of the boulders, propping his cane at his side. Nevada dropped to the rock across from him, drew up her knees and wrapped her arms around them. Babette lay right down on the bed of pine needles between them.

For a moment, they just sat there, soaking up the silence of the woods that wasn't really silence at all. A faint breeze made the trees whisper to each other. And squirrels chattered somewhere in the underbrush. And not far away, some small bird twittered. Another bird trilled out in answer. Babette's ears perked as she took in the sounds.

Nevada realized there was something she wanted to ask the old man. And just as she realized it, without her having uttered a word, Oggie let out one of his low, cackling laughs. "Go ahead. Ask me."

She rested her chin on her knees. "What did my father whisper to you, when Chase and I came in the room, the day that he died?"

Oggie's beady eyes bored through her. "It was about Nathaniel John."

"One of your missing brothers?"

"Right."

She waited, but of course he volunteered nothing. Oggie was often like that, downright irritating in his mysteriousness.

"What did he say about Nathaniel?"

Oggie took a cigar from his shirt pocket, ran it under his nose, and then stuck it back where he'd found it. "You never knew Nathaniel, did you?"

"You know I didn't. And you didn't answer my question."

He cackled again. "That's right. I didn't. And I'm not going to. You leave Nathaniel to me. Someday I'll find him—and his children, if he was fortunate enough to father any. And I'll find Isaiah, too. Just see if I don't. But that's someday. Right now, we got more pressing problems than finding two old men who've already lived most of their lives."

Nevada laid her cheek on her knees and stared back in the direction of the trail.

Quietly, Oggie said, "You built a life around a hatred, girl. Now the bad old demon is dead. And in the end, you saw him for what he was: a sad, ruined man, dying in a hospital bed. You got to start again. It won't be no picnic. But you can do it."

Nevada closed her eyes. She didn't really want to hear this.

But that didn't stop Oggie. "First, you get yourself away from Chase."

Nevada stiffened. She raised her head and met the small dark eyes of her uncle. "What did you say?"

Although she was looking daggers at him, Oggie didn't flinch. "I know you love him. Even if you haven't admitted it to yourself yet, it's no secret to the rest of us. But a woman has to earn the right to stand beside a man like that. Otherwise, he's gonna run all over her. She won't have nothin' left to call her own."

Nevada's heart was beating too fast, with a frightened, panicked rhythm. She lowered her feet to the ground and leaned toward the old man, willing, *demanding* that he understand. "No. You're wrong. *I* was wrong, to ever have fought what I felt for him. He's so good to me. You just don't understand...."

Oggie was implacable. "Right now, he's a danger to you."

She thought of Chase's strong arms. Of his lovemaking, which pushed back the numbness. Of his smile and his laughter and the power and energy that radiated from him. He was vivid, brilliant color in a world that had turned gray. She *couldn't* give him up. And she wouldn't. That was all.

She slid from the rock and rose to her feet. "You know nothing about Chase and me. I ran from Chase once. It was pointless and wrong. I'll never do that again."

Oggie looked up at her with real urgency. "Gal, I ain't sayin' you can't have him. Someday. Hell, I *want* to see you have him. But you got work to do first."

Work to do. The words echoed in her head. Somewhere in the back of her mind an ironic voice whispered, *Do the work.* Her catchphrase, on "Honeymoon Hotline": *Get back to me. Once you've done the work...*

But "Honeymoon Hotline" was no more. And she was no longer that Nevada Jones, the one who knew just who she was and where she was going. The one who had all the solutions to other people's problems.

"Gal. You with me, here?"

Nevada just looked at him. She saw no point in saying any more.

Oggie sighed. "All right. I said my piece."

She smiled then, relieved. He'd said what he had to say. Now they could go back. At her feet, Babette stood and wagged her tail, ready to go.

Nevada held out her arm to Oggie. "Let's go, then. Chase will wonder where I went."

Shaking his head, Oggie grabbed for his cane.

Nevada walked patiently at his side, back to the trail and then to the street and finally to the front gate of Evie's house.

"I'll just toddle on home," he said when she asked if he was coming in. He lived with his only daughter, Delilah, and her husband, Sam, on a street across town. He pressed his wrinkled lips to her cheek and patted her hand. "You have a safe trip back to Phoenix, now."

"I will, Uncle Oggie."

He couldn't resist adding, "And you give a little thought to what I said."

Nevada smiled vaguely and told the old man goodbye.

Chapter Thirteen

"God, is this happening? And *why* aren't I deliriously happy for you?" Maud asked.

She stood right behind Nevada. They could see themselves reflected a hundred times in the gleaming floor-to-ceiling mirrors of one of Scottsdale's most exclusive bridal boutiques. A month had passed since Nevada and Chase had returned from North Magdalene.

The two friends were alone in the "viewing room" of the boutique. Moments before, *madame,* as the proprietress liked to be called, had finished hooking Nevada into her wedding dress. Then the small, plump woman had stood back to admire the effect. "There. *Incroyable, non?*"

Maud and Nevada nodded.

Madame clapped her pudgy hands. "Now. I shall leave you. A few moments alone. To *feel* the experience of the gown.'' And she'd promptly bustled out to the main part of the shop.

Maud had watched her go. ''You gotta know she's from Yonkers, right?'' But now she was sighing. ''You do look fabulous.''

Nevada turned away from the mirror and glanced over her shoulder at the deep V back of the dress, which was delicately embroidered with a thousand tiny, gleaming seed pearls. She faced the mirror again, lifted the white satin skirt and took a few steps, then let it fall. It poured back into place like a lover settling into a clinging embrace.

''Yes,'' Nevada said. ''It'll do.''

Maud flopped into an imitation Louis XV chair, which was upholstered in crimson velvet and ornamented with gilded rococo carvings of Cupids, hearts and doves. ''Don't get me wrong. I do believe that my overbearing brother is the right man for you.''

Nevada pretended to wipe her brow. ''What a relief.''

''But there's something . . . not right.''

''Oh, come on.''

''I mean it. You're…different. You're not *yourself*. If you were, I'd feel just great about the whole thing.''

In the mirror, Nevada cast her friend a patient look. Billy Mooney had vanished on another of his endless tours, so Nevada had been seeing more of Maud again, although not nearly as much as she once had.

After all, there was Chase now. He filled Nevada's life. She and Babette had moved right in with him when they returned from California. Three weeks ago, as Nevada and Chase lay in bed together after making love, he'd pulled a diamond ring from beneath her pillow and slipped it on her finger.

''Marry me.''

She'd looked at the large, beautiful stone, then back into his eyes. "Yes. When?"

"Immediately. Sooner. Yesterday." So they were getting married this Saturday, in an intimate ceremony of family and close friends. They'd only waited this long because Nevada wanted her sisters and their husbands to be there. Otherwise, Chase would have flown her to Las Vegas and married her the morning after he gave her the ring.

She smiled a little, thinking of him. He was impatient. He wanted the commitment sealed and a baby on the way. The days of the little foil packets in every room were over. Now, when they made love, they used no protection.

They needed no protection. In four days, they would be man and wife.

Maud wouldn't give up. "If you would just take your old job back, I'd quit bugging you. I know damn well that Ira has been on his *knees* to you." Maud chuckled, a wicked sound. "They made a *big* mistake, letting you go. And they know it now."

Since she no longer intended to return to radio, Nevada wasn't terribly interested in all the uproar. But as it turned out, ever since her last night on the air, her fans had been picketing the station, demanding her return. Apparently the ratings had fallen and the proposed new format had bombed totally when they tested it out. Ira kept calling, leaving messages at Nevada's house and at Chase's, as well—somehow, he'd managed to discover where she lived now. More than once, Nevada had taken Ira's calls and patiently explained to him that she wasn't interested anymore. But he just wouldn't take no.

Also, although Nevada hadn't told Maud this, there had been other offers. Excellent offers. It pleased Nevada to be so vindicated. But in the whole picture of her life as it was now, none of it really meant much.

"Nevada."

"Hmm?"

"Did you hear me? Won't you just *talk* to Ira?"

"I *have* talked to Ira."

"You know what I mean. Take him seriously. Negotiate."

"Oh, Maud. We've been over this. I want to concentrate on Chase and our relationship."

"What ever happened to *having it all?*"

"I'm thirty-seven years old. I don't have a lot of time to waste. I just want to get pregnant, get going on our family."

"So. Get pregnant. Having a big stomach isn't going to interfere with your mouth, is it? You can still give advice just like you used to."

"I'm out of the advice business."

"But—"

"Can we please talk about something else?"

Just then, madame bustled back in. Nevada had never been quite so grateful to see the plump, faux-French dynamo as she was at that moment.

"So, *voilà!*" madame exclaimed. "Are we *extatique? Oui or non?*"

"It's perfect," Nevada said, and showed *madame* her back so the woman could start undoing the hooks. Already, Nevada's mind was turning to what else she had to do today.

She wanted to visit her gym and her masseuse, to meet for the umpteenth time with the caterer and the wedding designer. Tonight Chase had one of his business evenings on the agenda: dinner at a good restaurant and a musical comedy afterward. And she must remember to remind Chase's head driver that Thursday, her relatives would be arriving on three separate flights. Cars should be waiting for them at the airport.

In the red velvet chair, Maud sighed.

Nevada cast her a glance. "What now?"

But Maud just shook her head.

"You looked beautiful tonight." Chase whispered the words against her throat.

Nevada smiled in pleasure; at the compliment and at the lovely feel of his lips brushing her skin. Lazily, she raised an arm and combed her fingers through his hair. "I'm glad you approved."

He sighed a little, and rested his head against her breasts. She stroked his shoulder and pulled the midnight-blue satin sheet higher, to cover their entwined bodies. It settled over them as lightly as a breath.

"I'm happy," he murmured.

"I'm glad."

Idly, he ran his finger down the side of her arm. She enjoyed the sensation, reveling in the way her skin seemed to simultaneously shiver and grow hotter in the wake of his caress.

"Are *you* happy?"

She made a low, throaty noise. "Of course."

He moved his head out of the way a little, and cupped her breast. Nevada bit her lip. Little prickles of need radiated out from the point of contact. He toyed with her nipple. She felt it harden instantly, that marvelous, gathering sensation. Nevada moaned low and lifted toward his hand.

But then he raised his head. He pulled himself higher in the bed, so they were eye-to-eye.

"What is it?" she asked, trying to read his look. But the recessed lights around the big bedroom were all set very low, so it was hard to gauge the expression on his face.

"Ira Bendicks called me at the office today."

Nevada took a long, slow breath. She was thoroughly displeased. Ira had no right bothering Chase at work. "What did he say?"

"He wanted to know what the hell was wrong with you."

She made an impatient sound.

Chase put a finger against her lips. "His words—'What the hell is wrong with Nevada?'"

She caught his hand and kissed it. "He shouldn't have done that. I'll speak with him."

"He said he's made you some big offers. He even quoted a figure. It wasn't bad at all. You know, you're in a terrific position, here. You could just about name your price."

Very slowly and precisely, Nevada entwined her fingers with Chase's. "Why are we talking about this?"

Instead of answering her question, he asked one of his own. "Did you look at those articles I clipped from the paper for you?"

Chase read three or four newspapers a day. He'd found the two articles: Fans Will Not Let Popular Radio Show Die and Whatever Happened to "Honeymoon Hotline"? in the *Phoenix Gazette*. And he had cut them both out for her. Nevada hadn't told him that she'd already known there would be articles; the reporters who'd written them had tried to contact her. She hadn't returned their calls.

"Nevada?"

She pulled her hand away from his. "I read them."

He took a curl of her hair and smoothed it against the satin pillowcase. His body was so warm and good, stretched alongside hers. She moved a little, rubbing herself against him, and lifted her arm, laying it back on the pillow so he could see the outer curve of her breast where it sloped into the pale hollow of her underarm. It was a clear invitation, one he would never ignore.

And he didn't. She felt him growing harder against her thigh.

But when he spoke, it was about her old job again. "It looks to me like you could write your own ticket, if you went back."

Her stomach knotted suddenly. "Do you want me to go back?"

"This isn't about what *I* want."

"Fine. But tell me. *Do* you want me to go back?"

"I want you to be happy. Period. Whatever you decide to do."

She relaxed a little; her returning to radio wasn't something he would demand. Actually, the idea of getting behind a mike again frightened her. Although she would never tell anyone, she'd had more than one bad dream about it since Ira had started pushing her to return to KLIV. In the dreams, she sat in the studio again. Tully and Ira were watching her from beyond the glass of the engineer's booth. The calls started coming in. She opened her mouth to speak—and absolutely nothing came out.

"Nevada, maybe you ought to—"

She had no intention of letting him go any further with this. "Chase. That part of my life is over. I have other priorities now."

"But there's no reason why you can't—"

She reached down between them and touched him.

He gasped.

"I mean it." Her voice was a purr. Knowingly, she stroked him. " 'Honeymoon Hotline' is in the past. Now I want to be your wife. And the mother of your children." Her hand moved, caressing, teasing. "Do you understand?"

He muttered a low, husky curse. "Yes, ma'am."

"Will you please kiss me now?"

He groaned. "My pleasure." Then he lowered his mouth to hers.

And after that, they didn't need to talk anymore.

Nevada called Ira the next day and made it very clear to him that he was *never* to bother Chase at work again.

And then she repeated what she'd already told him a hundred times already. "Please, Ira. Believe me. I am never going to return to KLIV, so stop trying to change my mind."

She could just see him shaking his head. "I wanted you to quit," he said. "I saw it as your best move at that point. I had it all figured out. Your fans would go nuts. And the new programming would bomb. And then we'd bring you back in, bigger and better—and *higher paid*— than ever. It all worked. Except for one thing. You've gone south on me, Nevada. And I am not amused."

She felt a little ashamed, then, of letting him down. But it didn't change her mind. She murmured softly, "Everything doesn't always work out the way we plan."

He snorted in disgust. "Just tell me that this is all some sick, brilliant game you're playing to get more money out of me. Name a figure. Stop this charade."

"Ira. It's no game. Let it go."

There was silence on the line, then Ira sighed. "I'm starting to think you're serious."

"I *am* serious."

"I hate this."

"I'm sorry."

He muttered something unrepeatable.

"Still coming to the wedding?"

"I wouldn't miss it." His voice had softened. "You know that."

She hung up, feeling that just maybe he'd finally gotten the message—until later that day, when he had a virtual mountain of fan letters dumped at the gate in front of Chase's house. She started to tell the head gardener to gather them all up and burn them. But then she pictured all of those loyal listeners, sitting down to tell her how much they missed her show. At least she could put together some sort of letter to send them. After all, it was only fair that she explain to them— Well, she wasn't sure exactly *what* she would explain to them.

But once the wedding was out of the way, when she had a little more time to think about it, she would come up with something. She had the gardener bag the letters instead of burning them, and told him to put them away in the storage rooms above the huge indoor parking lot that Chase called his "garage."

The next day, Thursday, Nevada's family members were due to arrive. Both of her sisters and their husbands were coming, of course. Evie and Erik planned to bring the children. And Faith and Price would bring Price's parents and his younger brother, Parker. And then there was Oggie, who'd come with his daughter, Delilah, and her husband, Sam.

Secretly, Nevada had hoped that the old man might just stay home. She hadn't forgotten the hard things he'd said to her a month before. But he'd called her when he'd heard about the wedding and virtually invited himself. He'd said he wouldn't miss it for all the gold in California—which made her doubly wary. Although she knew it was crazy, deep in her heart, she feared he might have some wild plan for stopping the wedding. According to some of the family stories she'd heard about him, he'd done worse. Ultimately, you could just never tell what Oggie Jones might do.

Yet, coming right out and asking him to stay away wasn't an option; that would probably break his scoun- drelly old heart. And while she didn't adore him un- abashedly the way her sisters did, Nevada *was* fond of the aged troublemaker. She wouldn't hurt him for the world.

So Oggie was coming.

At first, she considered giving him and Sam and De- lilah the keys to her house in Mesa. After all, *she* wasn't using it. And the old man would have less opportunity for making trouble if he spent most of his time miles away from where she and Chase lived. But there was plenty of room for everyone at Chase's house. And in Phoenix, as in a lot of big cities, there weren't enough freeways to handle all the cars. Traffic could be a bear if you didn't know how to get around. Nevada wouldn't wish all that driving on anyone.

So everyone stayed at Chase's house. Evie and her family arrived first, at eleven in the morning. Faith and her crew were there by early afternoon. And Oggie, Sam and Delilah arrived at Sky Harbor International at four. There was a car waiting for each group, ready to trans- port them to Chase's house.

Maud and Molly came to dinner that night, making it a true family affair. Nevada thought it went off quite well. Her sisters and Maud had always enjoyed getting to- gether. And Oggie said he'd heard that Molly and her husband had been ranchers. And then he actually lis- tened while Molly explained how her husband's father had started the ranch and she and Buck had run it to- gether, then gradually sold off most of the land as the days of the open range came to a close. Even Lorelai seemed in high spirits. Gone was her usual deadpan expression. She served the dinner with a smile on her wide face.

After the raspberry-cheesecake dessert, Jenny, Evie's older stepdaughter, said she'd sure like to go swimming some more. She and Becca and their big brother, Pete, had spent most of the afternoon in the pool.

"Great idea," Erik said. There was a chorus of agreement. Everyone who actually thought they might get wet retreated to their rooms to change.

Nevada and Chase went upstairs together. But the phone started ringing just as they entered the master suite. Chase answered it. Of course, it was some associate who just couldn't wait until tomorrow to talk to him. He put his hand over the receiver and told her to go ahead without him; he would be down in a few minutes. She grabbed her suit and blew him a kiss on her way back out the door.

Outside, although it was nearly eight at night by then, the mercury was still well into the nineties. Nevada changed in the cabana not far from the pool.

The water felt wonderful when she dived in. She swam a few laps and played keep-away, teaming up with Becca against Jenny and Pete. As they batted the ball around, Babette waited by the side of the pool to nudge it back in with her nose whenever it landed out of the water. Nevada played the game for a good half hour, and then said she'd had enough.

"Aw, Aunt Nevada," Becca whined. "If you go, we won't have even teams."

"Help!" Nevada called to the adults lazing around the pool. Parker Montgomery, Price's younger brother, came to take over for her. Nevada climbed from the pool to find herself a lounge chair, where she stretched out with a contented sigh.

Lorelai came by and offered liquid refreshment. Nevada asked for Stolichnaya over ice, then lay back again and closed her eyes, smiling, thinking of the night in Winslow. And the night at her house, nearly two months ago, when she and Chase had danced around her own tiny pool to the haunting melody of a certain Willie Nelson song.

Interesting things did happen when she and Chase drank vodka....

And that reminded her: where *was* Chase? He'd yet to come down from the bedroom. He'd said he'd only be a few minutes. But it had been much more than that now.

She lifted her head and looked around. Parker and the children were splashing in the pool. And everyone else sat around in lawn chairs, laughing and talking and sipping the drinks Lorelai had served them. But Chase wasn't among them. Maybe, she thought hopefully, he'd gone into the cabana to change.

She rose from the chair and went to look. But there was no one in the cabana. She scanned the groups around the pool once more; no sign of him.

And there was someone else missing, she realized with a cold creeping of dread along every nerve: Oggie.

Chapter Fourteen

"She ain't the same. You know she ain't," the old man said.

They were in Chase's study in the west wing of the house, a long way from the pool where everyone else was having a good time. But Oggie had materialized at the foot of the stairs when Chase had come down from the master suite. He'd asked for a few minutes alone with Chase. So Chase had brought him here where they wouldn't be disturbed—a decision he was beginning to regret.

"You got to set her free."

Chase had poured them each a drink when they first entered the study. Now, very carefully, he set his drink down on the mahogany mantel over the fireplace.

He faced Oggie. "What did you say?"

Although Chase's voice had been low, deliberate and

chillingly calm, the old man didn't flinch. "I said, you got to let her go. You can't marry her. Not now, anyway."

Chase reached for his glass again, drained it, and headed for the liquor cabinet to pour himself another. Oggie held out his own glass as Chase went past.

Chase took his time pouring the drinks. When the job was done and he handed Oggie a refill, he asked, very reasonably, "*Why* can't I marry her now?"

"Because you'll destroy her."

Chase resisted the urge to grab the old man by the suspenders and toss him across the room. "That's ridiculous." He spoke with studied care.

Oggie's eyes narrowed, but he held his ground. "It ain't ridiculous. You know it ain't. I can see in your face that you know what I'm tellin' you. You know there's something . . . not right about her now. She's learnin' to cover up the big hole in herself. But the hole is still there. And someday she's gonna fall into it and never get out. Unless you give her the chance to fill that hole on her own."

"You're talking in riddles." Chase drained his second drink.

The old man grunted. "You know exactly what I'm tellin' you. You know, in your heart, that you can't fill that hole for her, no matter how much you'd give if you could. Nobody can fill that hole but Nevada herself. But you can *keep* her from fillin' it. You can make it all so easy for her. You can *take care* of her."

"Why shouldn't I take care of her?" He met the small, wise eyes directly. "I love her."

For an extended moment, the two men stared at each other. Then Oggie sighed. "Sure, you do. And that's why you gotta see that sometimes the best way to take care of someone you love is to get out of the damn way and make them stand on their own."

Chase decided he'd heard more than enough. He turned and picked up the swim trunks he'd tossed across a chair when they entered the room. "It's time we joined the others, I think."

Oggie shook his head. "She's *hidin'* with you, son." The old man's voice was barely a whisper, and yet it managed to hold all the sadness of the ages. "I don't see how you can put up with that. Now me, personally, I chose a more tractable type of woman when I found my love. But you didn't. You chose Nevada. And by nature, she is far from tractable. And since you chose yourself a woman of fire, I can't rightly see how you can let yourself settle for what she is now."

Chase said nothing. He was thinking of Nevada, as she was now. Thinking that, for him, it wasn't a matter of settling at all. Right now, she was just about exactly his lifelong fantasy of what his perfect woman would be. Bright and beautiful, completely devoted to him and his needs. Trusting him to make all the major decisions. Longing to have his baby. And every bit as incredible in bed as she'd ever been.

Hell, yes. Sometimes he missed the sparring matches they used to get into. But all in all, he could manage just fine if she wanted to hang on his every word and wait on his slightest whim for the rest of their lives.

Oggie broke into his thoughts. "Okay. I said what I wanted to say. And I guess you're right. It's time we went on outside with the rest of the folks."

Just then, there was a light tap on the door.

Chase called out, "Yeah?"

"Chase?" It was Nevada's husky voice.

Chase leveled a cold, warning look at the old man. *Not a damn word,* the look said. Oggie dipped his grizzled head in a nod of agreement.

"Come on in," Chase called.

* * *

Nevada pushed the door open. Beyond the threshold, she saw what she'd been fearing she might: Oggie and Chase, alone together.

"I was wondering where the pair of you had gone off to." She made her voice light.

Chase gave her the smile she loved best: an intimate one. He looked at the skimpy beach wrap she'd thrown over her suit and then lower, at her bare legs. She saw the appreciation in his eyes. "Your uncle was just checking me out," he said. "Seeing if I'm good enough for you."

"And what was the verdict?" Her heart was in her throat.

But then Oggie let out one of his rusty cackles of laughter. "He'll do, I think. He'll do just fine."

Relief made her knees weak. Obviously, whatever they'd been talking about hadn't been serious, after all. Everything was fine. She stepped forward between the two men and hooked one arm with Chase, one with Oggie. "Come on. The action's out by the pool."

Obediently, the two men went where she took them.

Much later, after everyone else was in bed, she and Chase made love in the huge whirlpool bath of his bedroom suite. Then they climbed into his big bed and made love some more. Nevada dropped off to sleep smiling.

She woke some time later to find Chase bending over her.

He touched her face, and wiped a tear away. "You were crying in your sleep."

She'd been dreaming. The "Honeymoon Hotline" dream. This time, the moment when she couldn't speak had gone on for what seemed like a lifetime. She'd stared through the glass of the engineer's booth at Tully. And Tully had started to cry—big, fat drops coursing down the five o'clock shadow on his cheeks. And then she'd been crying, too. Hopeless, powerless tears...

"What is it?" Chase was asking.

She smiled at him through the dark. "Nothing. Really. Just a bad dream."

The next night, the night before the wedding, they all had dinner out at a restaurant Chase particularly liked in downtown Phoenix. The food was excellent and the service superb. When the wine steward brought out the champagne, Oggie stood and made a toast. Then, one by one, the other guests took a turn.

Nevada's personal favorite was the one Ariel Montgomery, Price's mother, came up with: "May you share everything: sadness and laughter. Joy and sorrow. Good times and bad. And may you never go to sleep angry—or if you do, may you wake in the night and make love...." Right then, Ariel looked down at her husband, Regis. The glance they shared raised the temperature in the room a degree or two. Watching them, anyone could see passion never had to die, even between two people who'd been married for years and years.

Back at the house, Nevada and Chase turned in early, so they would be fresh for the big day tomorrow. But Nevada was too excited to sleep. Chase gave her a massage to help her relax. As always, it turned into lovemaking. They were all wrapped up together when she finally fell asleep.

But when she awoke, she found herself alone in the bed.

She peered at the bedside clock: 3:00 a.m. In the corner, curled up in the blue satin bed Chase had bought her, Babette stirred briefly. The dog lifted her head, yawned, and then laid her head down on her paws once more.

Nevada sat up, pushing the hair from her eyes—and caught sight of Chase, sitting in one of the easy chairs by the big window that looked out over the pool.

"Chase? What's wrong?"

"You had another bad dream."

"I did?"

"Yeah. You were tossing and turning, moaning a little. I held you until you settled down."

She rubbed her eyes, trying to push away the last cobwebs of sleep. She didn't remember what she'd dreamed. "But... why are you up now?"

He was sprawled in the chair totally nude, his legs out in front of him, his elbows resting on the chair arms and his hands folded in front of his mouth. His muscular shoulders lifted in a shrug. "I couldn't get back to sleep myself, that's all."

She pushed back the satin sheets and rose from the bed. The air-conditioned room was just a little chilly, so she reached for her light robe, which she'd tossed over the wrought-iron footboard. Once she'd pulled it on and belted it, she went to him and knelt beside him. "I'm sorry I woke you."

He looked down at her. Behind his hands, she thought that she saw a hint of a smile on his lips. "No apology required."

She reached up, touched the hair at his temples, smoothing it. "Is everything... all right?"

He lowered his hands, rested them on his hard belly and looked at her searchingly through the shadows. "Are you sure about tomorrow?"

"About us, you mean? About marrying you?"

"Yeah. That's what I mean."

"Of course, I'm sure."

His eyes kept probing hers. "Nevada. Since your father died, there's been... a change in you."

Uneasiness made her stomach tighten. She drew in a long breath and ordered it to relax. "What do you mean?"

"We talked about it a little the day of the funeral, when we went for that walk on the trail at the end of your sister's street. Do you remember that day?"

"Of course."

You told me what happened when your father died."

"Yes, Chase. I said I remember."

"And I told myself that the...difference in you was just a phase, that it would pass."

She gave him a reassuring smile. "And it *has* passed. You were right."

He was silent. Then he asked softly, "Has it?"

"Yes." She made her voice very firm. "It has passed."

"You *loved* that job of yours. And now you won't go back."

She stood then, and turned away. "Haven't we been over this already?"

"You never argue with me anymore."

She faced him. "I'm arguing now."

"No, you're telling me you don't want to talk about your old job. That's a statement, not an argument."

"Whatever. I'm happy with you. Why would I argue with you?"

"For the fun of it. To assert your position. To make sure you get your way. To *win*. Nevada, you always loved to win an argument with me—not that you won very often."

She shook her head. "Oh, Chase."

"And you have bad dreams. You cry in your sleep."

"Everyone has bad dreams."

"Not every night." He stood. And she sighed. He *was* so magnificent to look at. He watched her expression change, saw the desire in her eyes. He held out his strong arms. "Hell. Come here."

Eagerly she went into his embrace. She clung to him and whispered against his strong neck, "I love you. I want nothing more than to be your wife."

She felt his lips brush her hair. And then he swung her up into his arms and carried her back to the bed.

The next day, their wedding day, Chase was already up and gone when Nevada awoke. She felt a vague uneasiness, that he wasn't there. But she told herself it was only wedding-day nerves. He often awoke before she did. He was a busy man and, as a general rule, he wasted as little time as possible sleeping.

She rose and took her shower and went down to preside over the wedding breakfast, which she had decided to have catered at home to simplify things, since most of the family was here already.

Downstairs, everyone seemed in good spirits. Maud and Molly had already arrived. Excitement seemed to vibrate in the air over the big event soon to come. Lorelai had been up early to oversee the efforts of the caterer and his staff, so the long table in the formal dining room was covered with a pristine white linen cloth and set with the best china, crystal and silver.

There were place cards at each seat and a gift beside each plate. Nevada had chosen the gifts with care. They included Havana cigars in a gold box for Oggie; a vivid scarf for Ariel Montgomery, who loved bright colors; a stuffed squirrel for Becca Riggins; a carnival-glass candy bowl for Evie; a bolo tie with a miniature gold pan for a clasp for Delilah's husband, Sam, who sold gold-mining supplies in his store in North Magdalene. Everyone opened their gifts and seemed delighted.

At her own place, Nevada found three small boxes, each wrapped in silver paper.

"What's this?"

Since both of her sisters blushed and grinned, Nevada knew the gifts were from them.

"Should I open them now?"

"Absolutely," said Evie.

The first box contained a small pearl pin that Nevada recognized as belonging to Evie. A card lay on top of the pin with one word on it: "Borrowed."

The second box contained a garter. Its card read: "Blue."

In the third box lay an old-fashioned gold filigree ring with a single red stone. The card read: "Old."

"It was mother's," Faith said.

"I had it appraised," Evie added. "It's a real ruby."

Faith asked, "Do you remember it? She used to wear it when she dressed up."

"I remember." Nevada looked at her sisters. "But I haven't seen it since—"

"Before she died," Evie finished for her. "We know. It was in Father's things. And Faith and I thought you should be the one to have it. There was a pearl ring, too. I kept that. And Faith already has Mother's garnet earrings."

The garnet earrings were a story in themselves. Faith had stolen them from their mother's jewel box, to comfort herself, the day after their mother had died. She'd hidden them in the stuffing of her teddy bear and when their father had discovered they were missing, all three girls had sworn that they didn't know where they had gone. All through their vagabond childhood, Faith had kept those earrings hidden. And now, when she wore them, it was always with pride.

Evie said, "So now we each have something from her."

Nevada brushed away a tear and put the ring on her right hand. "Thank you."

Her sisters murmured that she was welcome.

Then she smiled at them. "But what's *new?*"

Faith chuckled. "We assumed your dress. And your shoes. And everything right down to your unmentionables. Were we right?"

Nevada nodded, stepping over to Faith and then to Evie and sharing a hug with each.

Soon after that, the meal was served. Chase joined them from the study just as they began to eat.

"Everything all right?" Nevada asked him.

"Business as usual," he said. Then he took her hand and kissed it and she felt reassured. Everything was fine. She showed him her mother's ring. He said it was beautiful.

But when he looked up from admiring it, she saw the way his gaze locked with Oggie's, at the other end of the table. Something passed between the two men; some silent message Nevada didn't understand.

She put her hand on Chase's arm. "What is it?"

He looked at her. "Nothing. Nothing at all."

As soon as they finished the leisurely breakfast, Nevada, Faith, Evie and Maud proceeded to one of the finest salons in the city, where Nevada had become a regular client of late. Now that Chase paid for everything, money was never an object. He wanted her to look good. And she wanted to please him.

The four women indulged in the works: herbal facials, massages, manicures and pedicures. The final touch was hairstyling and makeup.

It was three in the afternoon when they left the salon. They went directly to the Scottsdale church where the wedding would take place.

There, the church secretary showed them to a small room where Nevada could get ready. Her sisters and her friend helped her, holding the delicate gown so that she could step into it, doing up the hooks in back, and then arranging the full-length veil so that it covered her from head to toe.

They all sighed in admiration when she stood before them, haloed in snowy tulle. Beneath the veil, the slinky tube of a dress flowed down over her curves like another skin, making her body seem a shimmering white flame. The pearls caught the light now and then, gleaming through the yards of veiling. And on her right hand, her mother's ruby ring glittered, a drop of purest crimson in all that pristine white.

"Oh, Nevada. You are absolutely breathtaking," Faith said.

"Beautiful," added Evie.

Maud laughed. *"Incroyable! Fantastique!"* She picked up Nevada's bouquet of calla lilies and orchids, which would be carried beneath the veil. Faith held the veil up, as Maud gave Nevada the flowers. Then, with great care, they smoothed the veil back into place.

And then it was time for the other women to go and find their seats. Once they were gone, Nevada waited in the room where they had dressed her. She had chosen to forgo attendants, as had Chase. He alone, beside the minister, would be waiting at the top of the aisle.

Out in the small chapel, the organist had begun playing the final song before the wedding march: Nevada's signal. She poked her head out into the narthex. It was deserted, except for a lone usher, standing to attention by the tall, carved double doors that led outside. He nodded at her; she tipped her head. The wedding march began.

Mindful of her dress and all those billowing yards of tulle, Nevada emerged from the dressing room and moved slowly to her place at the door to the chapel.

She saw Chase immediately, wearing a perfectly cut black tux, waiting to one side at the top of the aisle. His expression was somber. She smiled at him. But he didn't smile back. No doubt he couldn't see her face beneath the pale cloud of the veil.

She took one step and then another. The wedding march played on. She heard the rustle of the guests as they rose to their feet at her passing. She thought she heard a sigh or two. But she didn't look at any of them. She looked only at Chase, who watched her approach, his eyes only for her.

And then she stood beside him. There was more rustling, as the guests settled back into their seats. The minister began to speak.

And Chase put up a hand.

Nevada's heart bounced into her throat. What was it? Why was he stopping the ceremony?

But then he knelt before her and took her veil and lifted it.

"Oh," said someone in one of the rows.

"Yes," breathed another, so low it was nearly inaudible.

Very carefully, he raised the veil over her head, and smoothed it down her back. It was the kind of delicate maneuver of which a man shouldn't be capable. But Chase McQuaid did it. He did it as he did everything: with absolute command and a minimum of wasted motion.

"The bouquet," he said. She gave it to him and he passed it to Evie, who sat in the front row.

Then he turned to Nevada again. His eyes met hers. He took both of her hands.

"Go on," he told the minister, without glancing his way.

"Dearly beloved, we are gathered here today..."

Chase went on looking at her. And it seemed to her, as the minister continued saying all the familiar words, that the way Chase looked at her wasn't quite...right. His gaze probed hers. He looked at her as he had last night in the darkness of his bedroom, as if he sought something in her face. Or in her eyes.

Something that just wasn't there.

His expression remained impossible to read. He didn't smile.

She tried to look right back at him. But she found it so difficult. What could he be thinking? What was going on?

The minister got to the part about how if anyone saw any reason why she and Chase should not be married, that person should speak now, or forever hold his peace.

Nevada heard a loud, rough cough from the rows of seats behind her. She gritted her teeth. She had no need to turn around to know whose cough that had been: Oggie's. She waited, sweat pooling at the base of her spine, for the old man to dare to utter a single word.

But he said nothing.

The minister went on. And Chase went on looking at her—so hard and so deep. His hands still held hers; his grip was too tight.

But she didn't try to pull away. She felt that if she did that, he would simply let her go. And she didn't want that. Above all, Chase must never let her go....

Not now, when she had no idea who she was anymore, no part of herself that wasn't defined by her relationship with him....

Her knees started shaking.

The minister asked her if she took this man.

And somehow, in a wobbly voice, she heard herself say, "I do."

And the minister asked Chase, "Do you take this woman...?"

And Chase just went on looking at her.

Now it was the minister's turn to cough. He tried again. "Chase, do you take this woman, Nevada, to be your lawful, wedded wife, to love, honor and cherish, for richer or for poorer, in sickness and in health, as long as you both shall live?"

And then Chase smiled. The saddest smile. And his eyes were shining with what might have been tears.

He released her hands and cupped her face.

She heard herself whisper his name.

He pulled her close and his lips brushed her cheek. His voice came low, for her ears alone. "I'll be damned if I can do this to you."

She pulled back, searching his eyes, bewildered, lost.

He pulled her close again, this time hard and fast. And he savagely pressed his mouth to hers.

And then he released her. She stumbled back, tripping a little on her long veil.

As she struggled to stay on her feet, he turned on his heel and started down the aisle.

Somehow, she found her voice. "Chase! Chase, wait!"

His broad back stiffened, as if her words had struck him between the shoulder blades. But he didn't stop. He didn't turn. He kept right on walking.

When he got to the big doors that led out to the street, the usher there did his job and pushed them open so he could go through.

The silence, after the echo of the doors closing behind him, was worse than any scream.

And then the rustling started, and the whispering.

"My God," someone said.

"He's gone."

"He just left. . . ."

"What's going on?"

"What the hell's this all about?"

Only one face in the whole chapel wore a smile: the face of Oggie Jones.

"What a guy," Oggie muttered in frank admiration.

Nevada, left at the head of the aisle with the baffled minister by her side, was looking right at the old man when he said that. She hated him, then. With the kind of pure, cold hatred she'd once reserved only for Gideon Jones.

Oggie met her eyes, unflinching.

She wanted to march up to him then and wrap her hands around his wattled neck and squeeze the life right out of him. With jerky, halting steps, she started down the aisle toward him.

But by the time she reached him, he had lost his importance. She kept on going.

Behind her, she heard Faith call. And then Evie. But she ignored them.

She ripped off her veil and let it drop in her wake, then she picked up her clinging skirts and sprinted for the doors through which Chase had left her. The obliging usher had them open before she got there.

But outside, there were only the bare stone steps leading down to the street and the blistering heat of August in the desert. And no sign of Chase at all.

Chapter Fifteen

Nevada went home to her house in Mesa. She sent Maud to collect her clothing and her dog. Chase, who was nowhere to be found, left word at his house that members of Nevada's family were welcome to stay there indefinitely. But they didn't hang around. They were all packed and out of there by the day after the debacle at the church.

Faith and Evie urged Nevada to find Chase, to talk to him, to learn from the source why he'd left her at the altar. Nevada listened to what they said and thanked them for wanting to help. And she knew that they were right.

Of course, she would find him and talk to him.

In her own time. When she could look at him without screaming at him for having left her the way he had.

When she could be sure she wouldn't end up begging him on her knees to come back to her.

Both Evie and Faith said they would send their families on home and stay on for a while, to be with Nevada. But Nevada wouldn't hear of that.

"I'll be fine," she lied in a no-nonsense voice. "Go home with your husbands. I'll call if I need you, I promise. And anyway, I have Maud's shoulder to cry on if I absolutely have to." Her sisters tried to argue, but she remained firm. So the day after Chase left her at the church, Nevada saw her sisters and their families off at the airport.

Oggie, though, refused to get on a plane and go back to North Magdalene until he'd spoken with Nevada alone.

"If I'm alone with you, I might have to kill you," she muttered when he came knocking at her door.

"I'll take my chances," the old man replied.

"Where are Sam and Delilah?"

"Waiting in the car."

"You'd better invite them in."

"Naw, the driver's keepin' the motor runnin'. This won't take long."

Cheered by that news, at least, she allowed him into her living room. She gestured at a chair. "Talk," she said. "And then go."

He didn't sit. "You know why he left you."

She flopped onto the sofa. "Was that supposed to be a question?"

"You know."

"Uncle Oggie, I am not in the mood for your vague, mystical questions that aren't really questions at all. Talk. And then go."

"He did it for *you*."

"Gee. That was big of him."

"You know he did it for you."

She glared at her uncle. Babette came over and nuzzled her hand with her wet nose. Nevada gave her a pat on the head.

"You know," Oggie intoned again.

"All right. Fine. I know."

"You go get your job back. That's the next step."

Just the suggestion made her stomach turn over. She tried not to let the old man know how she felt.

"You listenin'?"

"I heard you. What else?"

"That's all." He was looming over her, leaning on his cane. "You get your job back, the rest will follow."

She regarded him steadily. "You said that was all."

"Yep. I did." He managed to bend down and plant a kiss on her cheek. She let him do it. Then, grunting, he rose to his height again. "I'll be on my way now." He started for the door.

"Have a safe trip home," she said in a sour tone, and tried not to wish that the plane might crash. After all, Sam and Delilah and a whole bunch of innocent people would be on it with him.

"I'll do that." He gave her one last devilish grin, pulled open the door and went through it, closing it softly behind him.

When he was gone, Nevada stretched out on the sofa and closed her eyes. She lay there for a long time: hours. Until Mr. Alphonse came by to see how she'd been doing.

The phone rang a lot in the next four days. Nevada never answered it unless it was one of her sisters or Maud. Maud always wanted to come over.

"Thanks, Maud," Nevada would say. "But I'm fine. Honestly. I just need a little time alone."

Reporters called; word of her disgrace at the church had gotten out. They left messages wanting to know how an expert on romance felt about being left at the altar.

And Ira called. "Are you okay?" he would ask. Then, when she didn't pick up, he would command, "Call me." And then he would hang up.

Chase never called. Or if he did, he never left a message. Nevada longed, hungered, *ached* for word from him.

And yet, somehow, she couldn't bring herself to pick up the phone and dial his number. She knew in her heart that it would do no good. He would only turn away from her again.

And she knew why.

Oh, God help her, she understood perfectly.

She had seen his sad smile and the glitter of unshed tears in his eyes. She knew that what her scoundrelly uncle had told her was true: Chase had left her for her own sake.

She had work to do before he would even consider coming back to her.

Work to do.

As the woman she used to be always said, *Do the work, then get back to me . . .*

But Nevada did no work at all. She lacked the heart for it. She lay on the sofa and watched daytime TV. And at night, she hardly slept.

But when she did sleep, it seemed she always dreamed the "Honeymoon Hotline" dream, where she sat in the studio. And the calls started coming in. And she had absolutely nothing to say. Sometimes, in the dream, Chase would be sitting in Tully's chair on the other side of the soundproof glass. He would look at her so sadly. And as she stared at him, longing for him, he would slowly become transparent, and then fade from the chair as if he had never been.

On Friday, six days after the wedding that didn't happen, Maud called for what seemed like the hundredth time. As always, she said she would come over. Nevada said, "Please, don't."

Half an hour later, there was a knock at the door. Nevada peeked out the front window and saw Maud's car.

She let Maud knock, and didn't answer.

But when Maud started shouting that she wouldn't go away until Nevada talked to her, she rose wearily from the sofa and went to let her in.

Maud looked at the wrinkled pajamas Nevada had been wearing for the past couple of days and at Nevada's hair, which she hadn't bothered to wash for a while. "God. You look like hell."

"Gee, thanks."

Maud stepped over the threshold and into the living room. She went to the sofa, shoved aside the blanket and pillows Nevada had brought out from her bedroom, and sat down. Nevada dropped into a chair not far away.

For a long moment, her friend stared at her. Then Maud shook her head. "This has got to stop. You've gone beyond pitiful. Now you're within the range of absolutely hopeless. I don't know why Chase left you. And believe me, I've made every effort to track him down and have a few words with him."

Nevada groaned. "Please. Don't do that. Let it be."

Maud was shaking her head. "No. I won't let it be. I can't. I'm your friend. You held my hand for years while I cried over Billy and the mess I'd made of my life with him. You were *there* for me. In the most important way. And now, whether you like it or not, *I'm* here for *you.*"

"Maud—"

Maud stood. "Not another word. Go take a shower."

"But, Maud—"

"I said, not another word."

Nevada lifted both hands in a gesture of complete despair.

Maud marched over to her, grabbed her arm and towed her out of the chair, down the hall and into the bathroom, where she unbuttoned the pajamas, ordered Nevada to step out of them, and then pushed her into the shower.

An hour later Maud had fixed Nevada's hair and carefully applied her makeup for her. She'd hooked the gold hoops into Nevada's ears. She'd plowed through Nevada's closet and brought out a short, tight red skirt and jacket to match, which she'd made Nevada put on. Then she'd pulled Nevada into the kitchen and handed her the phone.

"Call Ira."

Nevada shook her head. Maud made the call herself. Nevada stared at her as she dialed, sure that Maud would give in and hang up any second now. But Maud didn't hang up. She put her hand over the receiver. "It's ringing," she informed Nevada. Then, "Ah." She spoke into the phone. "Hello. Ira Bendicks, please. This is Nevada Jones's friend, Maud McQuaid Mooney." Maud waited some more. Then she grinned. "Hello, Ira. Listen. I'm here with Nevada at her house. She would really like to talk with you. Could you come over here, please? Now."

"No..." Nevada croaked. She grabbed for Maud's arm.

Maud shook her off. "Good. We'll see you as soon as you can get here, then." And she hung up the phone.

"She will be there at four," Maud said.

Nevada just sat in the chair, looking at the trim red

pumps that matched the red suit Maud had made her put on.

"I don't know, Maud." Even though she was looking at her shoes, Nevada could tell by Ira's tone that he was scratching his chin. "She doesn't look like she's ready."

"She'll be ready. And I told you this would be a freebie, just so she can get her feet wet again. What do you have to lose?"

"My job," Ira said dryly. "I can't just slip her in."

"Yes, you can. All you're running in her old slot now are golden oldies and Dr. Laura Schlessinger on tape. You cut the oldies a little short, and you fit Nevada in. She'll do the rest."

Nevada felt their eyes on her, although she was still staring at her shoes.

"I don't know," Ira said.

Nevada made herself look up at him. "I can't do it."

"Don't listen to her," Maud said.

Ira frowned. "She says she can't do it."

"Trust me. You get her in front of a mike. Instinct will take over."

"I can't do it," Nevada said again.

Ira studied her face. "I like to think I've been your friend, as well as your boss."

"And you have." Nevada waited for him to tell her he understood that she just couldn't do it.

Instead, he ran his hand over the bald crown of his head and said, "Be there at three-thirty."

Her mouth was still hanging open in shock when he walked out the door.

"I will not go. I cannot do it," she told Maud a hundred times.

"You will go. You *can* do it," Maud would reply. "Now, tell me more about what you're going to say."

Haltingly, Nevada would tell her.

And Maud would say, "Great. You're going to do just great."

Maud drove her to the station. There were people milling around the back door, some of them carrying signs that read, Bring Back the Hotline, and Why Did the Honeymoon Have to End? and Welcome Home, Nevada.

"Ira must have put the word out," Nevada muttered grimly when she saw the milling crowd.

"The man believes in you."

Nevada sighed. "The man believes in publicity, wherever he can get it."

"Whatever. You're going to do fine."

"Keep telling me that."

"I will, don't you worry. You're going to do fine."

When Nevada emerged from the car, a reporter stuck a microphone in her face. "Is this it, Ms. Jones? Are you returning at last to KLIV?"

Nevada just stared; she watched the woman's lips move.

"No comment," Maud said, and hustled her out of there.

Maud elbowed through the crowd, pulling Nevada toward the back door.

People reached out and touched her as she went by, calling, "Nevada, we love you!"

And, "Nevada, welcome back!"

The real affection in their voices warmed her. She managed a smile and a wave or two.

And then the back door was pushed open, and Maud and Nevada slipped through.

Half an hour later, Nevada was sitting in the studio, the remote mike she always used anchored on her head. Next to her, at the stationary mike, sat Russell Anderson, who hosted an interview show on arts and leisure that aired earlier in the afternoon. Ira had explained to her that Russell had prepared a nice introduction for her.

Nevada understood that Russell would also take over if she bombed, although Ira had been careful not to say that in so many words.

On the other side of the glass wall, in the engineer's booth, sat Tully, with Ira beside him. Maud had volunteered to cram herself in there with them as well, for moral support, but Nevada had vetoed that. Even Maud couldn't help her now. Either she pulled this off...

Or she was finished.

If all went well, her segment would be an hour long. She'd given Tully a list of the tunes she wanted played. And outlined to Ira how she planned to proceed.

There was nothing more to do but do it.

The intro music played.

Beside her, Russell mouthed, "Good luck."

Her heart bounced into her throat, but somehow she managed to give him the high sign.

And then Tully counted down with his fingers. Five, four, three, two. And he pointed at Russell.

"This is Russell Anderson, here on KLIV, AM 850, your station in the sun."

Nevada stared at Russell, while her heart went on beating too hard and too fast. Her throat was like sandpaper, her palms dripping wet.

Russell continued, "And this afternoon, we have something very special for all of you. A visitor who once made her home here..."

Oh, she couldn't do it. She couldn't. She could not...

"A woman who has changed the lives of many of you, challenging you, always, to look into your own hearts. To examine your minds..."

This was impossible. Her nightmare. Not real...

"And to reach out for love when you find it. I think you know who she is. So, without further ado, may I give you..."

Nevada stared at Russell's mouth, watched his lips move. There was a rushing in her ears: her own blood, pounding fiercely, flooding her veins with pure, wild fear.

"Nevada Jones."

A deadly silence. Seconds that were years.

Russell coughed. "How are you, Nevada?"

She couldn't look at him. She looked past the glass. Where Ira looked terrified. And Tully just gaped.

"A-hem. It's been a while since we've seen you around here."

Nevada swallowed, convulsively. She glanced at Tully again, half expecting to see the tears coursing down his face, as they had in her dream. But there were no tears. Just that blank expression that said he couldn't believe she was messing up like this.

Ira nudged Tully. Tully punched a button. Soft music swelled.

Russell baldly lied, "Folks, we're experiencing a few...technical difficulties. Hang in there. We'll be back."

And that was it. She saw it in their faces. It was over. She had blown it.

Her nightmare had actually come true.

And at the moment that she knew she had lost all hope of pulling herself out of this, a thousand images crowded into her mind at once.

She saw herself and Chase, dancing.

Her father, falling into the hydrangea in front of her mother's porch.

An old man in a bed, begging her for forgiveness—forgiveness she had given, in spite of herself.

Her mother's ring, red as blood against her skin.

Chase, with tears in his eyes, whispering, *"I'll be damned if I can do this to you."*

And last of all, her uncle, leaning on his cane, looking down at her with that piercing, all-knowing black gaze: *"You get your job back. The rest will follow..."*

"Wait..."

It was her own voice. It sounded awful—ragged and breathy. But she had done it. She had moved beyond the paralyzed, endless silent horror of her nightmare.

"Wait."

Beside her, Russell's eyes were wide as pie plates. Beyond the glass, Ira whispered to Tully. The soft music faded out.

Nevada swallowed and her voice was there, a little huskier even than usual, maybe. But there.

She said, "Thank you, Russell."

Russell gulped. "My pleasure."

"It *has* been a long time. And I have...missed being here. You will never know how much." She had a little speech prepared, the one she'd gone over and over so agonizingly with Maud. But suddenly she didn't want to make a speech; she wanted to talk to her listeners. It really had been too long. She looked at the call monitor. "I see the lines are looking lively. So let's jump right in and take a few calls...."

The show lasted three hours. The phones kept ringing and Ira just let Nevada go where she and her listeners wanted to go. Everyone wanted to know where she'd been.

She told them that her father had died, that she had been estranged from him and that she hadn't been prepared for how hard his death had hit her.

"Frankly," she said. "I've had a little work of my own to do. And now—" she chuckled "—I'm getting back to you."

More than one caller said they'd heard a rumor that a certain local wheeler-dealer had left her at the altar.

"No comment on that one for now," she said.

"What about later?"

"If I knew, I'd tell you. But I don't."

Linda Lacklove checked in. "I've been working with one of the counselors you recommended."

"And?"

"She's helping. But I gotta tell you—it *is* good to hear your voice." And she launched into reports on the last three dates she'd had, all with the same guy. A very nice guy. She said she couldn't believe it, but this guy was actually fun, even if he was the kind of guy her mother had always hoped she would bring home.

Rantin' Raymond called. "It's been a nightmare for me, Nevada. No one to turn to. No way to vent. Are you coming back full-time? God. Tell me it's so."

"We'll see, Ray."

That got Raymond ranting. "We'll see? My God. That's just like every woman I've ever known. What is it with all of you? You're never straight with a man...."

Hildegard called. She'd met a good man. A gentle man. A man who listened when she spoke.

And Sunflower: "I've been on retreat. My body is cleansed. My soul is whole. I see the aura of the all..."

At seven o'clock, they wrapped it up. Nevada thanked everyone and reminded them, whatever happened, to keep on doing the work.

The station jingle came on. And Russell Anderson reached out to shake her hand.

Out in the hall, she hugged Tully and Ira.

Ira said, "Let's go over to Slim's."

So, after she made it through the crowds outside the station doors, Ira bought dinner for her and Maud.

* * *

Over the next week, she and Ira hammered out a contract. Ira groaned when she told him how much money he would have to pay her. But she got what she asked for.

She started work again on Monday, the eighteenth of August. The show went well. The ratings soared. Nevada did guests spots on local television shows, and found herself once again first on everyone's list when they needed an emcee for a charity event. Syndication seemed just a matter of time now. Everyone was happy.

And Nevada slowly came to accept that she was herself again. Strong and capable. Fully in charge of her life and affairs. She'd lost her job and her self-confidence and her very idea of who she was. And then, when all hope had fled, she had reached out and laid claim to her life all over again.

Everything was as it should be.

Well, just about everything.

Something *was* missing.

Some*one*.

Chase.

Sometimes, in the street, she would catch sight of broad shoulders and sun-shot hair. And her heart would skip a beat. But when she would run to catch up to him, it was always a stranger.

Every hour of every day now, some part of her was waiting. For him to come to her. Because he must know that she had done it. That she'd reclaimed her own life. All he had to do was tune in to KLIV on any weekday afternoon and he would hear the proof.

But if he did tune in, he never came to find her. She never found him waiting at her door when she got home. Or hanging around at Ocotillo Slim's when she dropped by there after work.

When she got up the nerve to ask Maud about him, Maud only suggested, "Why don't you call him and find out?"

And Nevada said, "I will. Of course, I will."

But somehow, she could just never quite bring herself to dial his number. She spent five afternoons a week advising women and men to go out and get what they wanted. But when it came to Chase, she didn't seem to be able to take her own advice.

Maybe, secretly, she wondered if he'd changed his mind about her. If he'd decided that he didn't want her after all.

In a way, the time they'd spent together seemed like a dream to her now. As if it hadn't really happened. As if it had been something she'd fantasized in her secret heart during a long and lonely night. Maybe he felt that way about it, too.

Or maybe he simply felt that it was over. Done. Maybe he had nothing more to say.

Of course, she would never know for sure what he felt until she saw him again. Until she heard from his own lips if there was a chance he might want her back.

And, as the weeks passed, it became more and more apparent that she wouldn't find out anything from him unless she went out and tracked him down.

In all the time they'd spent together, she realized now, he had been the one who pursued. And she had slowly, reluctantly, allowed him to catch her.

Now, if she wanted any hope of having him, she would have to do a little chasing. And here she was, an independent, self-assured woman who ran her own life—and she was absolutely terrified to go out and get her man.

But as August became September and September faded into October, Nevada knew that something simply had to be done. Especially when it began to look as if all that lovemaking they'd enjoyed without using any protection had produced the intended result.

Then, on Thursday, October second, Nevada got a call from Faith. Evie had just had her baby.

"A boy," Faith said. "Eight pounds, three ounces."

"What's his name?"

"Stephen. Stephen Ezekiel—and guess what?"

"Tell," Nevada demanded.

"Come spring, there'll be another one."

"Oh, Faith. Really? You, too?"

"Um-hmm. Price and I are the two happiest people in the world." Faith actually giggled. "I guess Evie and Erik are running a close second, though."

"I'll bet." Nevada almost told Faith her own secret, but held back. Really, Chase should be the first to know. She congratulated Faith profusely, thinking that the Jones sisters certainly were making up for lost time when it came to having babies. "Tell Evie I'll be there this weekend."

"You'll fly?" Faith sounded suitably impressed.

"It's the only way I can manage it. I have my show, you know. But a new nephew is something that doesn't come along every day."

Nevada arrived at Evie's bedside by noon that Saturday.

"Where's Chase?" Evie asked accusingly the minute all three sisters were alone.

"I'm working on it," Nevada mumbled.

"I suggest you work harder," Evie advised.

"I'll second that," Faith said.

And Nevada knew that her sisters had a point.

Each day it became more obvious that if Chase really expected her to make the next move, she had better get on it. He was clearly a man who was ready to be married. He'd been engaged to Virginia. And he'd come as close to marrying Nevada as it was possible to get without actually saying "I do." If she didn't make a move soon, she just might end up reading in the paper of how he had found someone else.

And this new fiancée might not be so willing to give him up as sweet little Virginia had been.

The thought that some other smarter, savvier, *gutsier* woman might snap him up mobilized her.

She decided she would call him.

And then the very day she made that decision, she read in the *New Times* that Club Paloverde would have its grand opening on Halloween night. It would be a costume gala; invitation only, of course. And everyone who was anyone would be there.

Club Paloverde. How many times had Nevada heard Chase mention that place? It was one of his pet projects.

She needed an invitation.

She called Maud. As it turned out, Billy and his band were part of the entertainment, so Maud would attend. She promised she could handle getting Nevada an invitation without telling Chase who she wanted it for. The next day, Maud showed up at her door.

"Here." Maud held out a black card embossed in gold.

"Did you tell him?"

"No. But I don't understand why you wouldn't let me."

"I want to surprise him." Nevada tried to sound totally self-confident, although that was far from the way she felt.

"Surprise him how?" Maud was looking at her doubtfully.

"Trust me."

"When people say 'Trust me,' I always get worried. You should call him. Just pick up the phone and call him."

"Maud. I want to do it my way."

Maud put up both hands, palms up. "Okay, okay. It's your life."

Nevada grinned. "Exactly. Now, come on in. Tell me what you're going to wear...."

"It's fabulous, Chase," a woman in toe shoes and a pink tutu whispered in his ear.

"A beautiful job," said a man dressed all in black leather with an ax tucked under his arm.

"Incredible." This from a gorilla.

"A hit," said the Lion King.

Chase moved through the rooms of the club, which were decked in party lights and gold and black streamers and a million helium-filled gold and black balloons. He wore evening dress instead of a costume, as did all the major investors. In a crowd the size of this one, with everyone pretending to be someone else, he was easily recognizable as himself. Which was the point.

"Chase. This is wonderful." A reporter from the Phoenix *Gazette* kissed his cheek as the photographer she'd brought with her snapped their picture.

"Yes, I'm pleased with the way it's turned out. Have you been upstairs yet?" Upstairs the reporter would find the theater, where a full-scale Vegas-style stage show was in progress.

"No, I was just on my way up there."

"Tell me what you think when you come back down."

"I will." She squeezed his shoulder. "You know I will." She signaled to her photographer and they moved away.

Chase leaned against one of the three bars on the second floor as Billy Mooney and his band swung into their first number up on the stage.

"What can I get you, Mr. McQuaid?" asked an eager bartender.

''Nothing, right now.'' Chase moved on, skirting the big dance floor and heading for the escalator down.

The ground floor housed the restaurant, which was as packed as the other two levels. He'd ordered the party designer to keep the Mylar and balloons to a minimum down here. On the walls, between the windows, a local artist had painted a series of paloverde trees in various stages of bloom, from the dormant phases of summer and winter, when they were all stark, bare branches, to the glory of spring bloom, when the leaves came out verdant green and the clouds of yellow blossoms rivaled the brightness of the sun.

He looked into the kitchen. He saw chaos in there, but carefully controlled, *organized* chaos. Not wanting to be in the way, he backed out quickly.

Then he took the escalator up to the second floor again. Just as he reached the top, out of the corner of his eye, he saw a flash of wild auburn hair, the glitter of a gold earring, and the silken sleeve of a red dancing dress, going the other way. Although his heart kicked against his breastbone, he did not turn to get a closer look. Over the past couple of months, he often caught a glimpse of women he thought were Nevada.

They never were.

Chase took the escalator up to the third floor, where he looked in on the stage show. He watched through two numbers. The applause after each rolled out loud and enthusiastic. In the middle of the second number, he could have sworn he caught a familiar scent. Musk and an echo of cinnamon. A sweet, tempting tartness...

Nevada.

But when he turned his head, there was no one there.

He wandered down to the middle floor again, and took a seat at a table with Grant Frasier and a few of the other investors. They were drinking champagne and toasting each other. They introduced him to a heartthrob from some daytime drama, and two players from the Suns basketball team. Chase raised his glass with the others and thought about red hair and the smell of cinnamon.

Billy's group, he thought idly, sounded damn good tonight. All those years on the road had payed off. They'd just cut an album that the critics couldn't stop raving about. Billy liked to joke now that he was "just another twenty-year overnight success story."

Right then, they finished one number. And started the next.

Chase knew the song the moment Billy opened his mouth and started singing the first line, a cappella.

"'If you had not fallen, I would not have found you....'"

He thought of the woman glimpsed so briefly on the escalator. The familiar scent that had teased him as he watched the big production number upstairs.

He told himself not to be a damn fool. If she had meant to come for him, she would have done it by now. And he'd already decided, that grim day in August when he'd left her at the altar, that the next move would have to be hers.

He knew she was doing well. That her show was bigger than it had ever been. That she had her life back now, on her own terms. And he also knew that if she'd wanted him to be a part of that life, she would have called. Dropped him a line. Showed up at his house and stuck her foot in his door and refused to go away until she'd said what she had to say to him.

But she hadn't.

And he was coming to accept that.

Coming to realize that...

His thoughts turned to mush.

Because either he had lost it completely. Or she was walking toward him across the dance floor.

Wearing a red dancing dress and red high-heeled shoes and a red half-mask with sequins scattered over it. Around him at the table, all the talking stopped. Even Grant Frasier had nothing to say.

Nevada stood before him, a teasing smile on her red lips. And then she pulled off the mask and threw it over her shoulder. She held out her hand.

"Dance with me," she said.

Chapter Sixteen

"Where the hell have you been?" Chase whispered in her ear.

Nevada snuggled closer to him as the music played, thinking that she'd never felt so wonderful in her entire life. "Getting up the nerve to find you."

"Okay, so you've found me. Now what?"

She sighed. "We finish what we started."

He pulled back so that he could look down into her face. "Get married?"

She nodded.

"When?"

"Oh, Chase . . ."

"Come on." He kissed the tip of her nose. "When?"

"It shouldn't be too difficult to make it to Vegas by morning."

He pulled her close again and spoke in her ear as they swayed across the floor. "You're talking about driving there, right?" His voice was grim.

Oh, was there anything so wonderful as dancing in his arms? "Uh-hmm."

"Listen. If we flew, we could be there in no time."

"We're not flying." She pulled back and pinned him with a look of pure determination. "We drive." She laid her head on his shoulder once more, and murmured tenderly, "I hate flying. You know that."

"But it's so much more efficient."

"We drive."

He made an exasperated noise in his throat, then grumbled, "Hell. All right. We drive."

"We take my car."

"Why did I know you would say that?"

"And I'll have to be back by Monday. I have my show to do."

"Great. That leaves us, what? About twenty-four hours in Las Vegas. And the rest of the time on the road."

"I just want to marry you. ASAP."

"All right. I want us married, too. And ASAP isn't soon enough. But what about the family?"

"What about them?"

"Don't you want them at the wedding?"

She considered. "It would be nice. But it would take too long to get them all here. You might change your mind again."

He put his lips against her neck. "Never."

She shivered in delight. Actually, all she wanted was to get him alone. "Chase. Come on. Let's go right now...."

He pulled her closer. "Wait. Until the song is through..."

"Chase?"

"Hmm?"

"Babette goes with us."

He swore, then grunted, "Fine."

"And Chase. I . . ."

"Yeah?"

"I'm really glad you want to marry me, because . . ."

"What? Say it."

"You know how we stopped using protection when we—"

"My God. You're pregnant."

"Uh-hmm. Is that all right?"

He only pulled her closer.

"And Chase . . ."

"Yeah?" His voice was gruff.

"I love you."

The last bars of the song faded away.

He pulled back for the last time and tipped up her chin. "And I love you." He kissed her then—a long, sweet kiss.

"Chase, Nevada . . ." It was the woman from the Phoenix *Gazette*. Flashbulbs went off in their faces. "Is this what it appears to be—a reconciliation?"

They looked at each other, then back at the reporter. "No comment," they said in unison.

And then, their arms around each other, they headed for the parking lot and Nevada's waiting car.

* * * * *

MILLION DOLLAR SWEEPSTAKES

Add a double dash of romance to your
festivities this holiday season
with two great stories in

Christmas
Celebration

Featuring full-length stories by bestselling authors

Kasey Michaels
Anne McAllister

These heartwarming stories of love triumphing
against the odds are sure to add some extra
Christmas cheer to your holiday season. And this
distinctive collection features **two full-length novels,**
making it the perfect gift at great value—for
yourself or a friend!

Available this December at your favorite retail outlet.

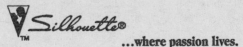

Silhouette®

...where passion lives.

The collection of the year!
NEW YORK TIMES BESTSELLING AUTHORS

Linda Lael Miller
Wild About Harry

Janet Dailey
Sweet Promise

Elizabeth Lowell
Reckless Love

Penny Jordan
Love's Choices

and featuring
Nora Roberts
The Calhoun Women

This special trade-size edition features four of the wildly
popular titles in the Calhoun miniseries together in
one volume—a true collector's item!

Pick up these great authors and a chance to win
a weekend for two in New York City at the
Marriott Marquis Hotel on Broadway! We'll pay
for your flight, your hotel—even a Broadway show!

Available in December at your favorite retail outlet.

NEW YORK
Marriott.®
MARQUIS

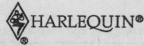 

As seen on TV!
Free Gift Offer

With a Free Gift proof-of-purchase from any Silhouette® book,
you can receive a beautiful cubic zirconia pendant.

This gorgeous marquise-shaped stone is a genuine cubic
zirconia—accented by an 18" gold tone necklace.
(Approximate retail value $19.95)

Send for yours today...
compliments of ▼ *Silhouette*®

To receive your free gift, a cubic zirconia pendant, send us one original proof-of-purchase, photocopies not accepted, from the back of any Silhouette Romance™, Silhouette Desire®, Silhouette Special Edition®, Silhouette Intimate Moments® or Silhouette Yours Truly™ title available in August, September, October, November and December at your favorite retail outlet, together with the Free Gift Certificate, plus a check or money order for $1.65 U.S./$2.15 CAN. (do not send cash) to cover postage and handling, payable to Silhouette Free Gift Offer. We will send you the specified gift. Allow 6 to 8 weeks for delivery. Offer good until December 31, 1996 or while quantities last. Offer valid in the U.S. and Canada only.

Free Gift Certificate

Name: _____

Address: _____

City: _____ State/Province: _____ Zip/Postal Code: _____

Mail this certificate, one proof-of-purchase and a check or money order for postage and handling to: SILHOUETTE FREE GIFT OFFER 1996. In the U.S.: 3010 Walden Avenue, P.O. Box 9077, Buffalo NY 14269-9077. In Canada: P.O. Box 613, Fort Erie, Ontario L2Z 5X3.

FREE GIFT OFFER   084-KMD
ONE PROOF-OF-PURCHASE
To collect your fabulous FREE GIFT, a cubic zirconia pendant, you must include this
original proof-of-purchase for each gift with the properly completed Free Gift Certificate.

084-KMD-R

Silhouette

SPECIAL EDITION ™

Three Brides and a Baby

by Trisha Alexander

Not just anyone can tame the Taylors! Watch for
more wooing—and weddings!—in these books:

Best man Luke Taylor meets his match in
A BRIDE FOR LUKE: April 1996
Special Edition #1024

Single dad John Taylor gets a little help from
some pint-size Cupids in
A BRIDE FOR JOHN: August 1996
Special Edition #1047

Still single Rebecca Taylor marries Mr. Right at
last—the father of her child!—in
A BABY FOR REBECCA: December 1996
Special Edition #1070

Three Brides and a Baby
Don't miss this newest miniseries from Trisha Alexander—
and Silhouette Special Edition!

Look us up on-line at: http://www.romance.net